# MARTIN & HANNAH

Nicholas Clemente

Cover photo and design by Patrick Hildebrand
Book design by D.F.L.

www.dfllit.com
contact@dfllit.com

D.F.L.
LIT

# I.
## The Survival Of The Organism

# II.
## Martin & Hannah

# III.
## Coda: The Survival Of The Organism (Reprise):
## Isaac & Cordelia

But then we were children: That was a moment ago,
Before an outrageous novelty had been introduced
Into our lives. Why were we never warned? Perhaps we were.
Perhaps that mysterious noise at the back of the brain
We noticed on certain occasions – sitting alone
In the waiting room of the country junction, looking
Up at the toilet window – was not indigestion
But this Horror starting already to scratch Its way in?
Just how, just when It succeeded we shall never know:
We can only say that now It is there and that nothing
We learnt before It was there is now of the slightest use,
For nothing like It has happened before. It's as if
We had left our house for five minutes to mail a letter,
And during that time the living room had changed places
With the room behind the mirror over the fireplace;
It's as if, waking up with a start, we discovered
Ourselves stretched out flat on the floor, watching our shadow
Sleepily stretching itself at the window. I mean
That the world of space where events re-occur is still there,
Only now it's no longer real; the real one is nowhere
Where time never moves and nothing can ever happen:
I mean that although there's a person we know all about
Still bearing our name and loving himself as before,
That person has become a fiction; our true existence
Is decided by no one and has no importance to love.
That is why we despair; that is why we would welcome
The nursery bogey or the winecellar ghost, why even
The violent howling of winter and war has become
Like a juke-box tune that we dare not stop. We are afraid
Of pain but more afraid of silence; for no nightmare
Of hostile objects could be as terrible as this Void.

– W.H. Auden, "For The Time Being"

# I.

# The Survival Of The Organism

"TELL ME WHAT YOU WANT. Then maybe we could work on getting it."

Never any light in the apartment – permanent dusk, light flickering, diminishing, failing. The wiring faulty, the bulbs always bursting. Topher and his friends, coming in blind drunk in the middle of the night, find ways to shatter those which have not yet died natural deaths. No light but the blinking of the VCR display: 00:00. It could have been midday outside, the world shining in the clarity of midwest winter, but all eyes had lost the power of sight. No one had left the apartment for days. No scenery, no stimuli: Topher somewhere in the dark, awaiting an answer.

"I don't want anything."

"Nothing?"

"Nothing."

Tip of Topher's cigarette waxing from red to orange and then waning away again; pulsing like an organ completely apart from him, and appendage of the indoor darkness trying to push itself into the world. Tree branches rustling outside, blinds banging against the windows in the gusting wind. Objects in motion, time standing still. Years pass, and yet time has stood still. Topher listening, thinking, shifting his weight on the couch: leaning forward, planting his feet, ready to sink his teeth in.

"You're lying."

A light that belongs to neither twilight or dawn pressing against the drawn blinds – light that is neither natural or manmade, light that is not really light. Eclipsed now and then by the pacing of Topher, his hands clasped behind his back, chin dropped thoughtfully to his chest.

"Have you ever said a prayer, Isaac?"

"No."

"Never? Not even when you were a kid?"

"No."

Topher laughing through his nose: without sound, without levity, just a venting of inner bitterness. Hands held out in front of him as if molding the air around him, conjuring a concept from the spell of language and introducing it to the realm of the concrete and contingent.

"Most people don't know how to pray. Most people don't know what prayer is. And when they keep praying and never get what they're praying for they wonder what it is they're doing wrong. For a long time I didn't know either. But I'm going to tell you about the only type of prayer that's effective; a prayer that most people don't even know that they're doing. But everyone already does it, whether they want to or not. These are constant prayers, silent prayers – silent and yet very powerful prayers. I'm talking about prayers to Satan. Prayers to the devil."

The orange point of light disappearing as the cigarette hisses out against an ashtray. Nothing anymore in anyone's hands. Beer in the fridge, but to open the door would invite eye-destroying brightness. Seconds simultaneously passing and not passing – the ticking of a clock in the kitchen that's never been right and never will be.

"I'm only telling you this because you might need to know it one day. Because it is an essential component in the process of wanting something and then getting it. I'm telling you this because prayers to the devil always come true."

Topher's phone lighting up, psychedelic blue flashing through the room. Doors opening, closing – light from the landing coming in the opening and drawing a crooked square upon the floor. Voices not lowered but somehow hushed; voices as if from elsewhere, filtering down to the here and now. Parcels swapped, payment changing hands – the whole transaction ending quickly and almost wordlessly. Topher entering again, loudly sheafing stacks of bills, pretending to recount the money, pretending to head into his room. Voice blocked in the throat, jaw locked against itself. Impelled by necessity, making haste to speak before he has a chance to disappear:

"Something I wanted to talk to you about."

One band of golden light reaching out from the half-open door. Topher's hands and nothing else sitting in the light, working the new bills into the existing fold, shuttling through like a weaver at his loom. Loud like prop money, amplified by hidden microphones, too shiny, too new, too much to be real.

"Okay. Talk."

"I don't have rent for this month either. I was wondering if you could spot me."

"No. I can't spot you. That's not how this works." Hands coming to a halt, suddenly, arbitrarily, several large bills fanned out clearly from the others. "But tonight there's something you can help us with."

Chicago in lamplight: forest shadows falling dark on crooked sidewalks. Trees bare but thick in the sidestreets, branches reaching up like inverse roots drawing strength from the blank haze of the sky. Quiet blocks, sleeping houses. Former neighborhoods, future neighborhoods, sites dense with possibility, with things living unseen in every window and doorway, every open alley and every warm dark room in every two-family wooden house, every three-family brick, all emptied now of families and given over to the independent and near-alcoholic.

An apartment covered with skulls and bones: on bookshelves and end tables, hanging from fishing wire on the ceiling: tiny rodent skulls with their small square teeth grinning, cattle skulls with empty eye sockets staring balefully, mysterious human-sized femurs and forearms scattered here and there. Runic symbols painted on the walls next to religious images salvaged from the gutter and then defaced and deformed: grinning saints, naked Virgins, decomposing Christs. Calendars marking the phase of the moon: Xs struck through the days which have passed, tomorrow's square ringed about with thick red ink. Julia lounging on the couch, Michael Reality burning Topher's message over the stove. Lighting a cigarette off the burning scrap and holding it until the flames kiss his fingers and holding it a second longer still and then dropping it to smolder in the sink. Again walking out to the interface between the two rooms:

"You busy tonight?"

"No."

"Nowhere else to be?"

"No."

"So you wouldn't mind making another stop?"

"No."

Julia watching it happen, holding back laughter. Ageless, emotionless, almost genderless, gazing upon the world like a visitor from someplace far away and more important.

Julia's eyes unblinking, her long dark hair unmoving. Julia's eyes glistening with a hideous sort of life, dark and gelatinous like underwater eggs. Julia with potions and powders lined up on the coffee table in front of her, measuring doses with pipettes and electronic scales. Beakers and burners, tubes and coils behind her in the living room laboratory. Michael Reality very close now, watching carefully the act of watching Julia.

"I need you to run this over to Dan. You remember where he lives?"

"Sort of."

"Good. Figure it out." Handing it over – a normal paper envelope, licked shut. "Make sure it doesn't break open. If it does, make sure you don't get any on your skin. We're still not sure what it does." And as an afterthought: "You want anything before you go?"

"No."

"We got coke, we got molly, we got uppers, we got downers. We got weed, we got hash, we got edibles. We got caps, we got stems, we got blotters. We got some synthetic shit Julia made yesterday. We need someone to be the first to try it."

"No."

And Julia smiling her beguiling smile – lips dark red, almost black, against the pallor of her skin: "Leave him alone. Isaac doesn't want anything."

Then scooping reagents off a scale and pressing down on the surface like a wave goodbye. The display blinking off and then resetting: 0000.

Bus ride down the thoroughfare to the latter end of the city. No neighborhoods, no homes, no landmarks, no loci, no nodes: the city existing in conceptual whiteout, without distinguishing characteristics: a matrix sprawling north and east and south and west without purpose, without aim, without end. The grid pervading space beyond all natural and arbitrary borders, shooting through the lake and the countryside, up into the atmosphere and the world of the spirit, an invisible indomitable grid strangling all creation beneath its chickenwire persistence.

Off the bus and a walk into the after-hours world of light industry, auto body shops and trucking depots and humming tortilla factories. Dan Drugs's building the only one with lights or windows, the only one not pouring out smoke, the only one whose sidewalks are not ringed with dumpsters and scrap and sludge. On the west side of the structure a tall fence containing nothing: no rubble, no job site, just tall stalks of grass clumped together and swaying soundlessly back and forth in the wind. Chicago like a state of longing that has crystallized into matter, a flat expanse of piled bricks and poured concrete that point only to something far outside of themselves, that bring to mind not cosmopolitan culture and refinement but the lonely whistle of wind in some forsaken prairie a hundred miles hence.

Dan Drugs's eye blown up to three times its size, first in the magnifying glass and then through his own smudged lenses, every vein visible, every crack in the cornea, every twitch of the dancing pupil.

"You sure this is all he gave you?"

"That's all."

"No note? Nothing?"

"There was a piece of paper, but Michael Reality burned it."

Dan Drugs letting his long hair fall forward and using both hands to push it back again. "It would be nice if I could call him like a normal fuckin' person, but Reality still thinks the feds are onto us. Guess it keeps you in a job at least."

Dan Drugs looking at the blotter paper between the

tweezers, studying the watermark, putting the magnifying glass down and squinting as if to see better.

"You know what this is, right?"

"No."

"Well, *this* is nothing But if it was what it was supposed to be – that would be something."

"What's it supposed to be?"

Tongue stuck out, purple and twitching, tweezers moving closer, paper dropping neatly onto the flesh and instantly dissolving to transparency.

"Michael Reality said not to–"

Tab taken, tasted, swallowed. "Michael Reality should know better than to waste my time on dorm room synthetics. He's the type of guy who bought dime bags of oregano in middle school."

Dan Drugs picking a jacket up off the floor, tossing it aside, taking another one, dusting it off, putting it on. Checking pockets for contraband, kicking over furniture in search of his keys.

"Now I gotta go find him and straighten this shit out. Waste of my whole fuckin' night. Like I don't have anything better to do than play secret agent."

"Does that mean I can leave?"

Dan Drugs jingling his keys in front of him. To his credit, at least thinking about it. "No. We might need you later."

Heat blasting in the gray interior of the car. Cheap fabric lining smoke-stained and drooping in tents from the ceiling. CD player skipping, check engine light on. Floor shaking as the car guns its way west, broken dials lying inertly on the dash. Dan Drugs lighting a cigarette, rolling down the window to ash out the side. Leaning forward into the accelerator, urging the car past fast food joints and chain hotels, out of industry and then back again, ethnic enclaves and bullet-pocked storefronts, clean suburban blocks scattered here and there, through a multitude of worlds existing on top of one another, dissociated and disconnected, as if several puzzles had been dropped together and the pieces cut to squares to better fit the patchwork: facets of every culture and every era failing to fit entirely in their slots of being and instead hovering uncomfortably half in and half out of reality. Dan Drugs pushing the car faster, onward, streaking over the road as if trying to draw a seam in the city and skin it alive.

Out of the car's interior and into the gusting wind. Only one intact building on the block: a lone warehouse standing atop its lot like a sorcerer's castle, its walls of broken blacked-out windows rising high over the surrounding neighborhood and casting long invisible shadows over the scrapyards and foreclosed houses. Blank clock faces staring down at the street from intermittent cupolas, their brass hands stripped by thieves and never replaced. Up three flights of sticky stairs to a black door marked by spray-painted pentagrams. No heat in the stairwell but warmth radiating out from behind the door: a mass of people within, all clothed in black denim, their pants shiny with wear and their jackets crusted over with a pinkish layer of dried sweat. Clouds of smoke overhead, the smell of substances sundered, broken down to their component parts and joined alchemically to the greedy molecules of the body. Beyond the crowd Topher and Andy Valentine standing behind tables of audio equipment conjuring waveforms, Michael Reality screaming incantations into the microphone. Julia standing motionless at the very back of the stage, the two batteries of speaker cabinets rising up between her shoulders like huge black wings. Wash of white noise pouring forth, distorted and modulated to greater and greater peaks of intensity: thousands of plateaus mounting one after the other, a high-decibel death march of buzzsaw whining and digitized nightmare noises seeking to displace every cell in every surrounding body, shake them free of the constraints of the organism and merge them into the mortar of sound filling up all the emptiness in the room and in the denuded and strip-mined world beyond the walls of the warehouse: a sound propulsed from some seat of emptiness far beyond or before the known world, clawing at the skin of this one, working its way slowly in.

Unfamiliar faces in a familiar place. And yet the danger present of encountering a familiar one. Fraught pathways of past lives, intersecting misalliances, tangle of politics both party and personal. Pushing forward, head down, onward towards nothing. Hand on the shoulder, voice in the ear:

"Isaac."

Ravi standing there, expressionless, his eyes cut off from whatever source they once borrowed their light. Staring for a moment and then mouthing words silently, his voice snatched up in the hurricane of sound. Gesturing up at the roof and saying what he's been saying one last time before moving on: out the emergency exit and up the stairs without once looking back.

Desert of pebbles and crushed glass, all surrounding lights walled off by a gathering of fog stained reddish in the haze. Ravi walking to the end of the roof and leaning over the parapet, intent on staring, intent on not talking.

"Didn't expect to see you here. I heard you went crazy."

Ravi turning around as if only now discovering the presence of another on the roof: "That's funny. I heard the same thing about you."

"No. Not crazy. I've been spending time with crazy people. That's all."

"You've been spending time with neo-fascist noise band Absolute Manhood. You live with one of them."

"How do you know that?"

"You'd be surprised at some of the things I know." Strolling forward with loping steps, gravel crunching underfoot. "Maybe they didn't find you by accident. Maybe it's not a coincidence. Have you ever thought about that?"

"I needed a roommate. I don't know too many people." And gesturing at the roof encased in smog: "This is not exactly the life I always pictured for myself."

"Are you sure about that, Isaac?"

Ravi loping closer now, as if to make bodily contact, but brushing past and proceeding to the opposite end of the roof, leaning over the second parapet in the same morose way he had leaned over the first.

"You know what they're looking for, right?"

"No."

"No idea whatsoever?"

"No. I don't care. I was never into any of this stuff."

"That's good. Because they're not just looking for drugs this time. They're looking for something a little more powerful."

"Are you going to make me guess?"

"I'm surprised you haven't figured it out already. They're looking for Hannah."

Ravi calmly contemplating the night as if nothing out of the ordinary had been said. Drumming his hands on the masonry, waiting for the bait to be taken.

"She doesn't have anything to do with this."

"She has everything to do with this. She has everything to do with everything."

"But they don't even know her."

"Are you sure about that, Isaac?"

Raising himself up on his toes to get a better angle,

studying with disinterest a disruption in the fog: lights flash-ing below, white red and blue, flaring up in the clouds like heat lightning. Ravi settling back down, getting ready to go:

"Looks like the cops. If I were you I'd go and tell your friends before they get locked up for the night."

"What about Hannah?"

"I guess we'll have to save that for another night, won't we."

"No. Tell me now."

Ravi continuing on his way: "I can't. It's a long story."

"Then give me the short version. Give me *something*."

Halting on the stairs, turning around, face twisted and snarled with anger: "There's never a short version with her. I'd expect you to know that by now." Continuing down to the fourth floor, pointing out a doorway near the defunct freight elevator: "Fire escape's out that way. If I were you I'd take it. And make sure to find your friends unless you want to start paying your own rent again."

"How do you know about that?"

"If I were you I'd get used to me knowing things I'm not supposed to know. Otherwise this is going to be a very confusing weekend for you."

"Wait." Hand reaching forth, picking out Ravi's shoulder from the many. "How can I get in touch with you."

Speaking over his shoulder, walking away: "Don't find me. I'll find you." And disappearing then into the still-seething crowd.

Michael and Julia nowhere in sight. Topher and Dan talking to Andy Valentine in the corner: earnest, seri-ous, sober or at least seeming so.

"You were *in* the band with him. And you're telling us you have no idea?"

Andy Valentine, bored and unafraid to show it, scanning the crowd for boys suitably ephebic: "He was both very secretive and fond of lying. That's a bad combination. I suppose you could ask him now, but of course he's just going to say no regardless of the truth."

Topher stepping forward, ready to get angry: "Then why did you send us to get ripped off by that other guy."

"I owed him a favor. I thought maybe he wasn't entirely full of shit. I was bored. Take your pick."

"Hey." A sound eliciting no response. Dan Drugs, sweating, his eyes consumed by pupils, gazing down sightlessly, searching for the place where the voice came from. "Hey guys."

Topher waving his hand dismissively: "Not now, Isaac."

"Cops. Cops."

"What cops?"

"Outside. There's cops."

Harsh knock on the door, room falling silent. Bolt sliding into place, everyone stuffing pockets and donning coats. Drugs stashed, flushed, taken, dozens of black boots pounding their way towards the emergency exit, the metal door banging at intervals like a broken metronome. Rusted fire escape swaying out from the brick structure, sagging from the weight, the staircase crashing against the sidewalk, feet scuffing against asphalt in the general dispersion. Topher running ahead, Dan lagging in the back. Sirens and lights behind, spiraling and circulating, without apparent center, enclosing the pursued. Through alleys, over fences, across the street into a dark line of trees. Pausing a moment, panting, leaning forward on knees. Dan Drugs lost somewhere in the whirlwind of lights. Helicopter passing overhead, searchlight blazing white. Bare branches casting a web of moving shadows on the ground as the searchlight moves on to probably more serious business. Topher looking up, breath collected, taking stock of the situation.

"Keep moving. Still too close to the road."

"What about Dan?"

"What about him."

Frozen earth crunching underfoot, crystallized grass squeaking. No sound, only breath. Dark lanes of trees, rolling hills, bluish moon-washed fields. Scanning shadows, seeing things, faltering in step and then trying to play it off cool. Wet creeping in through the shoes, hands numbing in pockets, cheekbones and earlobes starting to sting. Trees circling around and no sign of the city anywhere on the dark horizon.

"Topher."

"Yeah."

"Where are we?"

"I dunno. Some park."

"And how long have we been here?"

Checking over his shoulder, incredulous: "Five minutes. What are you talking about."

"No. It's been longer than that. How long have I been awake? How long has it been dark out?"

Topher walking on, pretending not to hear.

"You guys dosed me. You gave me one of your experiments." Trying to catch up, trying to sound angrier. "I'm not going to take your money anymore. I'm not going to be your guinea pig anymore."

Topher fending off attacking hands without much difficulty, grabbing both wrists and holding them at arm's length.

"You're not dosed, Isaac. Life is a dose. Get used to it."

"What are you looking for?"

"The same thing everyone else is looking for."

"No. Not just you. You and Dan and Michael and Julia. What are you looking for."

"If you knew any more it would compromise your

role as messenger. And I don't think that would be good for either of us."

"What about Hannah?"

Topher undoing his grip, looking down in genuine puzzlement. "What Hannah. I don't know any Hannahs."

"Oh."

"You have to keep it together, Isaac. Don't become a liability to me or else I'll have to replace you." Still studying the sight, features softening to something like pity. "When was the last time you slept?"

"I told you. I don't remember."

"When we get home try to get some sleep. I don't want you bugging out on us."

"I don't want to go home."

Topher pressing on without responding, breaching bushes and low fences on the other end of the park. Beyond the road an empty gas station and a shuttered car wash with sheets of ribbed ice running down the sidewalk. Shadowed dudes huddled outside, smoking cigarettes, talking low. Wanted posters, warped by moisture, plastering a street sign up and down: muggings, break-ins, attempted sexual assault. Roadside memorials of candles and prayer cards and rosaries and black flowers liquefying.

"I know where we are now."

"Good for you." Topher craning his neck to look up and down the thoroughfare. "I'm gonna hop in the next cab I see."

"There's never any cabs around here."

Topher raising his hand, whistling through his fingers, stepping to the curb as a cab pulls up. "You coming or not?"

"No. I'm gonna stop by Guy's place. See if he's home."

"Forget about Guy. He's just another sap with a job

and a girlfriend."

"That's not the worst thing in the world."

"Are you sure about that, Isaac?" Topher grinning, cabbie honking impatiently. "Tell him I still think he's a tool. And keep your fucking phone charged – we might need you tomorrow."

Cab speeding away, and with it all the rest of the traffic, all buses and all pedestrians – the world rolling up like scenery, the stars and streetlights dimming with the passing of Topher from the scene.

Cracked sidewalks, blown trash, mailbox doors open and banging to and fro on house porches. Two-family wooden, three-family brick. Maybe some families left, but who knows for how long. Lights on at Guy's place but no response from the buzzer. Reaching through the bars, tapping at the window. Guy behind the curtains with a baseball bat, setting it down, moving to open the door.

"Isaac? What are you doing here?"

"I don't know."

Guy staring, hesitating, unsure if he's allowed to have visitors at this hour. Then stepping aside, eager to conceal his hesitation: "Come on. Come in. It's freezing out there."

Apartment all new inside: shining floors, track lighting, granite countertops. Neighborhood crumbling outside, world crumbling beyond, but the apartment renovated to prevent with caryatid fury the total collapse of all. Heather on the couch in front of a TV, the latest in high definition, the on-screen figures glass-eyed and uncanny, puppeted stiffly from without: technology designed to depict new conditions of monstrosity which it itself had helped to bring about.

Greeting Heather briefly, wordlessly, following Guy to the refrigerator: "Topher told me to tell you he thinks you're a shill and a narc."

"Anything else?"

"A stooge and a fed."

Guy producing two beers, wrestling them free of their plastic webbing: "You can tell Topher I don't give a shit what he thinks. Tell him I don't take life advice from drug dealers and acid casualties."

Cat jumping to the counter, hand height for petting, sniffing fingers for scents of strange cats or familiar cats. Ears perking up at the hiss of air escaping aluminum. Liquid cold and yellow-gold hidden in the damp freshness of the canister: cold beer on cold lips, flat and tasteless. Walking back to the living room, taking a seat on the couch. Heather pausing the program, saying nothing. Guy speaking up:

"Cordelia's been looking for you. She's been texting me all night."

Phone tossed on the coffee table like a folded hand of cards: "Battery's dead."

"I think she's worried about you. Especially with your new shall-we-say line of work."

"I'm sure she has better things to worry about than me right now."

Heather finally coming to life: flipping fragrant brown hair, looking sidelong up and down:

"Do you always get jealous of Cordelia's boyfriends?"

"I don't know. Cordelia's never had a boyfriend before. And I'm not jealous."

"And of course you never get lonely."

"No."

"You're too smart for that. You're too manly."

"No. It's not that."

"You don't need love, or attention, or any human

affection whatsoever. That's too bourgeois for you."

"No. I'm not acting from a perspective of class warfare. It's just not necessary for the survival of the organism."

Heather scoffing, exasperated already: "So dramatic."

Empty can raised in mock salute: "Scatter my ashes on Ashland Avenue."

"So you don't love her except you've already slept with her before."

"Not as far as you know. I guess Guy's been filling you in on the details."

Guy quick to speak up: "She didn't mean anything by it, Isaac."

"No. Of course not."

Guy smiling broadly, acting natural, soundlessly rattling his empty can: "Get you another?"

Mouth dry, eyes burning, heart throbbing, head pounding. Dawn somewhere very far ahead or very far behind; a warm bed all the way at the other end of the city.

"Sure."

Moving again to the neutral territory of the kitchen. Pressing palms into eye sockets, fighting empty-stomach nausea. Not talking, hardly even drinking. Guy leaning in with concern or curiosity on his face.

"What's up with you, man? You look like shit. Heather didn't even want to let you in."

"She wouldn't want to let me in anyway." Pressing into the eyes again, not to relieve pressure but to obscure the vision. "What time is it?"

Guy stepping aside to check the clock on the stove. Green light blinking: 00:00.

"It's late. Let me give you a ride home."

"I can't crash here?"

"No. We're not in college anymore, Isaac."

"I don't want to go home."

"You should've thought about that before you moved in with Topher."

"I've told you before. I don't know anyone else."

"Then get a girlfriend. What do you want me to tell you."

"It's not that easy."

"Yes it is." Stepping forward, snatching the beer away.

"I'm not done with that."

"Yes you are. Let's go."

Doors auto-locking as the car pulls out, high tech headlights painting the street an icy blue. Vents blowing cold air onto hard leather. No use asking for a cigarette because Guy doesn't even smoke anymore.

"You can't keep living like this, Isaac. I'm not sure if I like it when you show up at my place strung out and incoherent in the middle of the night."

"You mean Heather doesn't."

"You know what I mean."

"I'm not even on anything. I'm clean. I've always been."

"That doesn't mean you're not strung out and incoherent. You look like shit."

"I know. You said that already."

Conversation ceasing at a red light. Gang of young men stalking through the crosswalk, a few of them peering into the windshield. Light turning green, held breath expelled, conversation unfolding once again.

"I just don't see how you do it."

Guy staring straight ahead, unengaged: "Do what."

"I don't know." Gesturing vaguely at the dash. "This."

"Driving you home?"

"No. Just going to work. Living with Heather. Living like nothing's wrong."

"*Is* anything wrong?"

"Lots of things."

"Like what."

"I don't know."

Engine humming silently, white lines vanishing beneath and white globes passing overhead. Watching the numbers on the street signs count down to zero and then count up again as the car travels further north.

"Maybe you don't have it all figured out. That's all I'm trying to say."

Guy taking his eyes off the road to show disgust and incredulity: "And you do?"

"Maybe you haven't actually chosen the best life. Maybe you haven't actually chosen anything. Maybe you chose nothing. You ever think of that?"

"Maybe you can walk the rest of the way. Isaac, what the fuck difference does it make?"

"Because I chose nothing too. But I *chose* this. Do you understand? You chose nothing, but I *chose* nothing. Not because it's what I want. Because it's less like what I don't want than whatever it is you're doing."

"Whatever it is I'm doing. You mean working. Doing friends favors. Bourgeois stuff like that."

"I don't mean bourgeois in the sense of class warfare."

"Go fuck yourself, Isaac. I don't care what you mean."

Pulling up to the curb, clicking the car into park. Engine ticking, no goodbyes. Not at the apartment yet, but close enough for walking.

Chicago is a city for sleeping. Chicago is a city for secondhand mattresses and yellowed pillowcases and ashtrays on bedspreads miraculously unoverturned. Dry mouths, eye-pressure headaches, time spent searching spotty memory for gaffes or conspicuous gaps. Empty tall cans near the bed, opened and drained after the bars had closed. Cord wrapped tight around the face of the phone to give it charge through the shoddy port. Messages from last night, from this morning: Cordelia, but she can wait. Voices on the other side of the door: Topher and clients, Topher and friends, Topher plotting further schemes and missions. It may be hours until they're gone. But Chicago is a city for waiting.

Expired Tylenol washed down with cloudy tapwater. Cigarettes smoked without relish, the fumes irritating a sore spot on the inside of the lower lip. Jacket slipped over a T-shirt and feet shoved sockless into old Adidas. Down a flight and into the cold: red brick Chicago, overcast and trafficless, sleeping still. Cleansing cold, scouring cold, whistling down the avenues and grating against the skin. Through the pores and into the blood, pushing into the person the sunbright clarity of sky above clouds. Gas station coffee, stale donuts individually wrapped. Broken caution tape fluttering forth from a streetlight: a car had gone airborne in the night, uprooting a mailbox and crashing through the wall of a Polish import/export office. No emergency services present, not even anyone looking on. It's almost noon but the city is sleeping still.

No cable hook up in the apartment, no fancy media console: only a clumsy plastic Toshiba with a tape player built in and a catalog of thrift store VHSes strewn caseless on the floor. Long dark Chicago afternoons of second childhood, colored only by flickering blue electricity, half in and half out of sleep. No prospects, neither any responsibilities: heavy bodily peace, pleasant like an illness: peaceful waking sleep in the somnambulant city. The twilight outside joining the twilight inside and the colors matching perfectly for a fraction of an hour before the window turns solid black behind the glass.

Wet womb warmth of the laundromat, empty fluorescent and humming. Occasional cars outside, cold slipping in through the plate glass window. Sitting nodding in front of a novel, giving up and tucking it into the pocket of an unzipped parka. Spare quarters sorted out on a pizzeria counter across the street. Wanted posters taped next to the register showing blurry stills from an armed robbery in progress. Then the walk home, laundry bag slung over the shoulder, bare hands numbing as they fight to retain their grip.

Empty apartment, dark apartment, messy apartment. Weary already from the invisible labors of the day. The gods challenged Hercules and said do what thou wilt. Figuring out what the work is: that is the shape of the work on Saturday afternoons in Chicago.

Parka wrapped once more around the body, scarf stuffed in place, phone shoved in pocket. Still not much of a charge but it will have to do. Short walk on Chicago Avenue under yellow sulfur light and tree shadow. Pot of drip coffee behind the bar; Cordelia waiting with a cup in front of her. Plain white mugs with chipped lips and long vertical cracks stained permanently brown. Coffee turned gray with milk and set down with the spoon still spinning, scraping along the side until it comes to a halt, a tiny nebula of froth spiraling apart atop the milk.

Other girls there besides Cordelia: out with their friends, reading by themselves. One older couple doing a crossword, everyone else dateless. All the men they know drink too much and do too little, work part time and without benefits at warehouses and mail rooms and coffee shops. All the other men know other girls or go to other bars or live on other planets. Chicago women aging gently out of young adulthood: Cordelias all, growing wiser and kinder with time, given up on romance and given now to doting upon animals and other people's children.

"Where were you yesterday?"

"Around. My phone was dead."

"I'd prefer it if you didn't disappear on me like that."

"Don't take it so personally. I'm not trying to disappear from you specifically."

"Just disappear in general."

Reaching over, chummily patting her thigh. "You know me so well, Cordelia."

Fingers drummed against the bar, lukewarm coffee gulped down before it gets too cold. Wind coming in the door, icy air mixing with the smell of spilled beer and chemical cleanliness. Mugs taken, cans opened. Cordelia sipping with prim catlike prudence from her Special Export.

"Paolo's coming over later. I want you to meet him."

"I'm busy later."

"No you're not."

"I might be. And I don't want to meet Paolo anyway."

Cordelia exasperated in a calm and practiced way, having had plenty of practice: "But *why*, Isaac. Why."

"Because what does it have to do with me."

"It makes me happy. Don't you want me to be happy, Isaac?"

"No."

"You lie." Cordelia singing softly to herself, smiling softly to herself: "You lie, you lie, you lie, you lie."

"I saw Ravi last night. He hangs out with Topher's crowd now."

Cordelia spinning her damp napkin with one finger. "Does he."

"You want to know who he was talking about?"

"Hannah."

"How did you know?"

"Because I know everything, Isaac." Taking a satisfied sip of her beer, pinkie up. "And because it's the only thing he ever talked about."

Head thrown back to empty the can, picking up

Cordelia's beer to gauge its weight, signaling the bartender for one more.

"I still think about her sometimes."

"Do you."

"Yeah."

Cordelia feigning boredom, using two fingers to stretch the fibers of her napkin. "I don't think you ever loved Hannah. And I certainly don't think you love her now."

"How do you know?"

Cordelia exasperated and preparing to explain: calm, practiced, setting her drink down and wiping her hands of condensation and smoothing her cardigan in her lap.

"Because love is not something you do all by yourself. Love is not about thinking about someone else and getting even deeper inside your own head. I may not be an expert, but I know that much. Love is about going outside of yourself."

"But I don't know how to do that."

"Yes. I am aware, Isaac."

Can finished, crushed, left standing on the table. Cordelia still sipping delicately and formally from hers.

"Have I told you about Julia."

"No. Guy did."

"I guess you and Guy are good buddies again."

"He told me one time when *you* invited me to hang out with you two. Don't start." Running her thumbnail along her napkin, tearing the first layer of tissue open where she hits a patch of moisture. "So why don't you tell me about Julia."

"She reminds me of Hannah."

"How so? Because she's also an abstraction you've invented for yourself?"

"Because there's something about her. Because she means something more than what she just is. I don't know how to say it."

"Well, I can't help you. Because I don't know what you're saying either." Propping her cheek in her hand and with the other razoring the napkin up, down, sideways. "Maybe you can discuss it with Julia if she's so pretty."

"Nobody's prettier than you, Cordelia."

Cordelia studiously failing to react to this: mouth flat and closed, blinking pattern regular, face betraying nothing. Brushing her palms clean, shedding a flurry of paper snowflakes over the bar: "I should go. I have to get dinner started."

"Don't go. I don't want to have to go to work."

"I'm still not sure exactly what you do, but I'm pretty sure it doesn't count as work."

"I'm sick of it. I want to quit."

"Then quit."

"But what else is there?"

"There's a whole world out there, Isaac. Believe it or not."

Cordelia pulling on hat, scarf, jacket, in the same motion leaving money on the bar.

"Let me pay for mine."

"No. Forget it."

A hug that lasts longer than it should. Breaths held and with tenderness expelled. In Chicago girls smell like the cold when you get close to them; refrigerated city air layered thick in their clothes and hair, and only under this a hint of perfume and everything else.

"You're not taking care of yourself."

"I know. I don't need you to tell me that."

"Call me later tonight. Just to let me know you're okay."

"Okay. How late is later?"

"I guess we'll see."

"You're sure you won't be busy?"

Cordelia squeezing harder, from anger and from affection. "I guess we'll see, Isaac."

Walk home on Chicago Avenue, shoulders hunched forward, fighting to pierce the headwind. Building mental lists of women to call, women to bother, women to hope for, women to think fondly about. But the list only lasts as long as Cordelia and then falls away into nothing.

Noise in the apartment: feds or cops or friends or thieves or strangers. Waves of static washing across the TV screen and casting ghostly pallor over the faces in the room. Topher and Michael Reality, their eyes in shadow, speaking quietly and ceasing altogether when they hear the door.

"You can keep talking. I live here."

"No. Nowhere is safe. Not yet." Michael Reality standing, approaching, huge and unsmiling. "Where have you been? We have a job for you."

"I don't want to work for you anymore."

"I don't care."

Topher standing unsteadily, wandering clumsily over, too fucked up to be threatening. "Just this last night."

"No." Both of them looking down, squinting through the gloom. "Tell me what I'm looking for. Tell me now or I'm not going."

"Just this once, Isaac. Just once, and then never again."

"But why can't I know?"

"Because you wouldn't understand. So there's no use telling you."

Michael Reality stepping forward, authoritative: "Because it's not safe. You think it's a coincidence that warehouse just happened to get raided the night we show up there?"

Topher raising his hand again: "Because we don't want to confuse the boy."

Things moving too fast to stop, Michael Reality scribbling on a piece of paper and holding the address up: "Tonight you're going to meet Andy Valentine at his apartment. He's going to have you meet a guide. Then just go wherever he goes, and do whatever he tells you."

"And how long will it take?"

"We don't know. It could take fifteen minutes. It could take all night."

"And how long is the night?"

Topher stepping forth with a bottle and a glass, pouring a small measure of whiskey. "Don't lose your head, Isaac. We know you can do it."

Seizing the glass, gulping down half, waiting for the taste to go away. Topher exerting a gentle pressure on the bottom of the glass, guiding it back up towards the lips:

"Just one thing: Andy's our friend, but he has a reputation. If he offers you a drink, don't take it."

Bus kneeling with a hiss to the curb and exhaling passengers and hot air. Light pooled to a glow in the splendor of the intersection, each lamp throwing volumes of haze from its crystal core of illumination. Dim stars, still trees, lit windows hanging in squares atop blank building faces. One bus departing and another swerving into place with bricklike grace. Signs of life: muffled people moving through the wind, doors opening into bars and restaurants and laughter issuing out like the calling of distant birds, high flying and lonely.

Andy Valentine's apartment: a one-bedroom in a big brick building near the lake. Photos taped and tacked everywhere, faded posters, amateur glossies, computer printouts blown up and badly pixelated. Flesh tones and black leather: men chained and bound, men big and small, fat and muscular, men evidently willing or evidently reluctant: mouths gagged with balls or rags, faces fixed with fear or ecstasy, all eyes wide and helpless. Andy bound only in a thin silk robe, waiting on his couch with fat and spiderly patience.

"I thought they were going to send someone bigger."

"Sorry."

"I'm not asking for anything unreasonable. But you'd think a pair of supposed artists would be willing to make concessions for the sake of aesthetics."

"I wish they had someone else to send. But as far as I know it's just me."

Andy gesturing vaguely at a sideboard and a closed cabinet: "Anything to drink? Smoke? Take?"

"No."

Andy heaving himself up, drinking and taking something, carrying something back to the couch to smoke. "Last chance."

"No."

"Your loss. I hope they're paying you."

"They are."

"Not enough."

"No. Not enough."

"Well, you might as well make yourself comfortable. The other guy hasn't shown up yet."

Overstuffed loveseats, clawfoot chairs, shiny leather beanbags: walls painted black, all doors closed. Andy watching the process of indecision with a mouth smiling widely.

"Or you can come sit over here if you like."

Sliding down the wall at the farthest possible point, coming to rest on the thick black carpeting. "No. I'm fine where I am."

"Come on, Isaac – you *are* Isaac, right?"

"Right."

"Come on, Isaac. I don't know how long it's going

to be until the other kid shows up. Of course I can't have you poking by yourself around my apartment. But I don't intend to wait in silence either. So it would be nice if we could find something to chat about."

"Okay. Are you allowed to tell me why I'm here."

"Maybe because you live with Topher and you two have finally figured out that dropping out of college does not pay the bills."

"No. I mean what I'm supposed to be looking for. They still haven't told me."

Andy thinking about it or pretending to think about it. "Sure. I don't see why it has to be such a big secret."

"I think Michael Reality is afraid of the feds."

"Michael Reality doesn't have a clue. He's never had one, and the only reason people can't see this is because he put some muscle on a couple years ago. So please, I beg you, do not worry yourself about Michael Reality. Or the feds, for that matter."

Andy hesitating still, smoothing his robe, eyes roaming about: second-guessing himself, waiting for a further prompt.

"So tell me."

Opening his mouth, closing it again with a clicking sound: "I was in a band years ago. This band broke up under rather unfortunate circumstances. My current bandmates are trying to track down extant masters of the unreleased last album. Unfortunately, due to the unfortunate circumstances alluded to above, the members of my prior band are no longer on speaking terms. They don't want anything to do with us anymore, and frankly I can't blame them. I wouldn't speak to us anymore either if I had anything better to do. This other fellow you're meeting up with is supposed to be on better terms with one of my old bandmates than I am. You two are going to find him, and then you're going to do whatever it is you're going to do. I don't know why at this point, nor do I care."

"But it seems like they're looking for something a lot more important than an album."

"They're looking for something important to be looking for. They've already tried everything else, and they're looking for the next last thing to try. That's my expert opinion. Expert as in I used to do it too, and still do it. Any other questions?"

"Why."

Andy taking a moment to process the question and then giggling with exaggerated abandon, growing red in the face and kicking his legs out in front of him. Finally gaining composure enough to speak: "How cute. He wants to know why. He thinks there's a why behind all of this." Another short fit of laughter, the rolls beneath his neck shaking from the violence of it. "There is no reason. At least not that they know of. But even if they had a reason – though I can tell you right now that they don't – they would surely have the wrong one."

Less manic now, almost serious, but still grasping and un-grasping his hands to release latent agitation: "They think they want more life. That's what they all think. That's what all this–" gesturing vaguely at the world outside the window, "–is all about. But they don't understand. We're not in love with life, with noise, with action. We're in love with sterility. We're in love with silence. Whenever we make noise – and we make plenty of noise, all of us – we're not trying to enter more deeply into the world. No. We're trying to tear the world to shreds. Because behind it there's a silence that lasts forever. Can't you feel it, Isaac? Glassine and perfect. But we can't enter into it. We're not perfect enough to reach it. All we can do is yell, and scream, and cry – and *beg*, Isaac, to be silenced."

Buzzer shrilling through the apartment, Andy starting as if waking from a dream. Pointing a fat finger at the intercom: "Get that, would you?"

Waiting in silence for the guest to arrive. Trying to find a surface for the eye to land on that does not have a bound man looking back. Andy standing again and taking something and drinking something. Knock at the door, the knob turning by itself. Ravi standing there, smirking knowingly.

"Isaac. Didn't expect to find you here."

Andy spinning to look, his robe swishing around his ankles: "Well. If you two have already been introduced that saves me a little trouble." Jingling a glass already filled with ice: "Ravi, can I interest you in something to drink? I understand it's going to be very cold out there tonight."

Wet wind in the streets: small shards of ice rolling in clouds under the low grey sky. Permanent gloom of city illumination, colors false and harsh within the enclosing darkness. Ravi charging down the sidewalk with long strides and easy confidence, like he has somewhere to be, like he actually knows where he's going. Still moving forward, looking over his shoulder:

"You didn't take any drinks from Andy, did you?"

"No."

"Good. I need you thinking clearly tonight."

"Why? What's tonight?"

"You'll see when we get there."

Forced marches to cover the gaps in the public transit system. Long rectilinear streets that stretch out to the horizon, jeweled with distant light like the rings and coronets of huge and invisible gods; gods without shape and without substance, gods who lie dormant at day but wake up in the night, who lie silent and perfectly still beneath the traffic and chaos and crime, who could at any time lift themselves up and grow arms and legs and assume control over the city, but who prefer to wait in silence, in stillness, closed-mouth smiles drawn over shining fangs – ruling the city still, but ruling in secret, accepting without a murmur of gratitude all sacrifices dressed and cut and immolated upon the city's many altars. Particles popping atop hoods and shoulders, jackets growing shiny and slick with ice.

"We can't take a cab? That's not in tonight's budget?"

Ravi hatless, fearless, his coat half unzipped, his face unprotected, glowing with cold and enthusiasm: "Don't worry, Isaac. We're almost there."

Diagonal avenue lined with bars: six on each block, three on each side, the only viable business in the new urban economy, the only acceptable pastime. Bars cycling owners and décor every six to twelve months, bars built to recall eras or regions or subcultures long past or never to come – the world reduced to a mock-up of a real place where real people might live, a training ground where the training takes forever and is the only real thing. Patrons standing out front, sheltering under windows and awnings, pluming cigarette smoke out with their clouded breath, forming miniature pillars that float in the air between them and take the place of speech. Ravi turning off the main strip and plunging into a neighborhood crowded with trees and simple frame houses. A bar lodged in a low brick building, leafless vines creeping across the walls, neon beer signs throwing red and purple illumination onto the sidewalk.

Spiderweb of gold Christmas lights drooping in clumsy arcs from the ceiling inside. Dim red lamps filling the air with blood-colored darkness. Bartender's hair changing color as she moves from shadow to shadow, ombre to black to streaked yellow. Smooth skin above a low tanktop, deft small hands filling orders. Ravi checking his watch with a quick annoyed motion.

"He's not here yet. We must be early."

Leaning forward, trying to see: "Early? What time is it?"

Ravi jerking his arm away: "Forget about the time for now. We'll have to wait."

Ravi sliding into a booth upholstered with cracked and peeling vinyl. Only one other patron inside: a monstrously tall girl wearing too much makeup and nursing a plastic cup of wine at the end of the bar. Ravi gesturing at her with his eyes:

"You know who that is?"

"No."

"Look closer. Look longer. Think about it for just one second, if you would."

"No idea."

"I'll give you a hint. College."

Shock of recognition like a sudden bolt of panic: "Kim."

Kim's eyes rolling slowly over the booth, as if she had heard. But no expression on her face, no indication of curiosity or consciousness: her earphones firmly inserted, her eyes rolling slowly onward after failing to match the sight with any of her memories.

"Did you know she was going to be here too?"

Ravi leaning back against green vinyl, grinning to himself, supremely satisfied: "You'd be surprised at some of the things I know."

"It's time to tell me some of the things you know, Ravi. Otherwise I might not stick it out until the end of the night."

"And what else are you going to do?"

"I'm not an idiot. I could do whatever I wanted."

Ravi unfazed, unafraid: "You sure about that, Isaac?" Licking his lips, glancing again at his watch. "Well, it must be your lucky night. We have time to talk."

"I want to know why they need this album. I want to know what's so important about it."

Ravi smiling gently, almost warmly: "Oh, Isaac. It's

not the album they want."

"Then what is it?"

"I already told you. But you didn't want to listen."

Ravi standing and ordering two drinks from the bar. Keeping his shoulders hunched and his face turned away so Kim won't notice him. Returning with the drinks and sliding one across the table. Sipping somewhat ludicrously from his cocktail straw, the thin plastic stuck in the corner of his mouth like the hose of an ornate pipe.

"This is not just an ordinary album. There's something inside the album. We're not entirely sure what, we're not entirely sure where. Right now the smart money is saying it's the formula to a synthetic hallucinogen, totally new, totally untested. Some say it's hidden in the liner notes. Some say it's coded somehow into the audio files themselves. Unfortunately, no one knows where to find either of these things. But that's what we're going to do. And we're going to do it tonight."

"Why tonight? Tonight's gone on long enough."

"Tonight's only begun, Isaac."

"And why me? Why don't they just send you?"

"They don't trust me. No one trusts anyone. Can't say I blame them."

Ice melting in two empty glasses. Ice sifting down from the sky and filming the frozen city. Layers of ice encasing all things and all people inside and out – icy hands gripping icy glasses.

"And what." Clearing the throat, gathering courage. Trembling internally – shivering in inner cold. "What does this have to do with Hannah."

"Everything has to do with Hannah. But I think I already said that."

"Don't play games with me. Just tell me."

Ravi taking his time to think out an answer, satisfied

like a chess player at the puzzle presented to him:

"Well. If we want to explain Hannah we have to explain a lot of other things, don't we. Who is Hannah really. Maybe she doesn't even know herself."

"I told you. I'm not in the mood for riddles."

"There are no riddles here. It's all very simple, actually." Ravi resetting his footing, hunching shoulders forward. "Do you have any idea why your buddies Topher and Michael Reality keep Julia around?"

"Because she's Michael Reality's girlfriend."

"But why do you think he's dating her? Do you think it's because she has some sort of special arcane knowledge that the others lack? No. It's because she knows nothing. That's why she's useful." Checking over his shoulder, leaning in closer, almost whispering now: "Why do you think you use a woman's body for the altar at a black mass. Forget about the capes and robes and just think about that for a minute. Why do you think the Romans had temple prostitutes. Why do you think serial killers are always cutting up the women they capture. Because they want to see what's inside, Isaac." Ravi staring off, lips trembling wetly, trying to compose himself.

"And you're in on this too."

"Don't be so dense, Isaac. Don't be such a romantic. Everyone's in on it, whether they know it or not. Whether they want to be or not."

"Hannah is not in on it, as far as I can tell. Nobody's heard from her in years."

Ravi slamming his palms on the table, raising his voice, almost rising from his seat: "Hannah's at the *center* of this. Hannah *started* all this! What do you think you were looking for when you were looking for Hannah? What? Do you think you were going to build a life together? Do you think you were going to make her life better?"

Voice small and strangled, lingering at the back of the throat. It doesn't want to come out, but Ravi's not going to proceed until it does: "No."

"Of course not. Isaac, faithful husband. Isaac, devoted life partner. Don't make me laugh. Don't make me sick." Calming down, fixing steady sober eyes on his target. "Hannah isn't who you think she is. She used to sleep with Martin Hightower."

"So what. I already knew that. Everyone knows that."

"You know *nothing*. Hightower is not just another idiot college professor. He's the one who made that album. He's the one who encrypted those formulas. Do you have any idea what that means?"

"No."

"It means *Hannah* is in those sound waves. It means Hannah is in those formulas. It means Hannah is in those compounds. Everything you were looking for in her – everything you thought you were looking for – it's all there."

Ravi settling back down, wiping the spit from his mouth, glancing around to make sure nobody else – the bartender or the girl at the bar – had taken notice of his outburst.

"And you think you're so much different from us. You think you're so much better. That's what makes me sick. You think you're not looking for the same thing we're all looking for. You are, but less successfully, less clearly, less consciously. That's the only difference. I bet you think you meant a whole lot to her. I bet you think you know her better than anyone else."

"I do."

"Oh yeah? Prove it."

Ravi attempting to gesture with his empty can, raise it to his lips in such a way that will signify anger, but there isn't enough weight in the thing to give the motion any meaning. No more satisfaction in his actions, no more levity, only an expression of mounting suffering, an invisible splinter driven further by the constant pressure of all constant forces, all gravity and appetition and lust and circulation. Invisible goad inside every person and animal and plant and molecule, yet felt and known only by a few. Ravi, eager to communicate the awareness, not finished yet:

"I bet Hightower thought he knew her better than anyone else. I bet everyone she ever slept with thinks he knows her better than anyone else. I bet those fifty fucking guys in Germany–"

All in a blur: hand flying out, seizing him by the collar. Trying to stand all the way up, trying to shake him like a dog with its prey, but the table too long and low to allow the motion. Ravi coaxing the grip gradually apart, removing the fingers one by one and placing the hand back on the table.

"Isaac. I know you don't believe me, but I'm saying this as a friend. Forget about Hannah. If we do this job right we won't have to worry about it anymore. We won't have to feel that way ever again."

"I don't want Julia. I don't want anyone else. I want Hannah."

Shaking his head: "There is no seeing Hannah again. I'm not sure that there ever was. Even if you met with Hannah you wouldn't be meeting with Hannah. You wouldn't be talking to Hannah. There is no Hannah. Hannah is a symbol for Hannah. That's all. That's all that any of us are. The only thing to do is to let it go."

"You mean like you?"

"Yeah. Like me. This is my letting go. Maybe you can do something more constructive if you're so fucking smart."

Ravi nervously wiping the sweat from his forehead, glancing around in suspicion. Eyes fixing on a position and remaining there, either awed or fearful. "He's here."

Turning shoulders, neck to look: skinny guy standing rigidly behind the bar, scribbling with furious concentration in a small notebook. Kim gazing upon him with her big green bored eyes, neither of them taking notice of anything else. The world frozen in time, making exception only for the motion of the man's hand: no music in the place, no TV, no hum of refrigeration, no ambient street noises. The world beyond the front door disappearing, the moving molecules of the universe replaced with sluggish reddish-blackish light. Ravi swallowing hard, hesitating:

"I'll go talk to him." Ravi remaining where he is, doing nothing about it. "You come with me."

Approaching the bar under the gently swaying net of golden lights. Time slowing, motion slowing. Keeping an eye on the front door as if hoping for a rescue. Kim noticing first but failing to react – only gradually, but too late, her big bored eyes focusing with sudden recollection. The man looking up, letting his notebook fall open on the bar. The page inked near to black, covered with spirals, crosses, sigils, drawings or words or some eldritch combination of the two. And the same manic activity in his eyes: endless restless motion, no clear process of empathy or signification.

Ravi with a faltering step forward: "We came here to ask about Martin."

"I don't know any Martins."

"Martin Hightower."

The man leaning menacingly on the bar: "I *said* I don't know any Martins."

"We'll cut you in on the product once it's manufactured."

"What product?"

"Martin's product. Once we track down the formula."

The man backing off somewhat, glancing off to the side, making sure his coworker was really gone. Not making much of an effort to sound convincing: "I don't know any-thing about that either."

"Well I do. In fact you might be surprised at some of the things I know, Paul Demian."

Silence in the room. Metronome click of metal pen against the bar. Kim studying the scene, putting it all together:

"Oh my God. Ravi."

Demian pausing, smiling slowly, revealing teeth long and fanglike: "That's right. I remember you. My, my, my. How things have changed."

Ravi feigning bravery, feigning indifference: "That's not important. We don't have a lot of time."

"Actually, Ravi, I think it is important. I think you don't really know what you're dealing with here."

Ravi straining to speak confidently, the words coming too fast and too shaky: "No. We do."

"This is a *warning.* For your own good. You don't want to find the synthesis. Because if you did it wouldn't help you put things together. It would pull you apart. It would tear you to shreds."

"No it wouldn't. You don't know me."

Demian leaning forward again, leering with a sort of hunger drawn on his face. The ambient light fading in and out, waxing and waning as if an immense presence stood behind it, trying to push its way through. Demian dis-torted: proportions all wrong, his body too tall and his limbs too long and his fingers when he spreads them stretching out like talons. Kim intervening with one stern word:

"Paul."

"No."

Demian waiting to see that the word had taken effect – instantaneously, like a spell. Reaching over the bar, grabbing hold of Ravi's arm. Ravi flinching back, going limp when he's pulled in closer.

"Tell me. What do you believe in."

Ravi trying not to look at him. "Nothing."

"I already know that. But have you ever thought what that might mean. It could mean that you believe in doing evil. But it could also mean that you don't believe that evil exists. Do you believe in evil, Ravi?"

"No."

"Do you believe in me?"

Demian holding Ravi's forearm for a long moment after – staring hard at him for a long moment – and then releasing his grip.

"I can give you Martin's address. But I don't imagine he'll be very happy to see you." Picking up the sleek metal pen, flipping to a blank page in his notebook, scratching something in it and tearing the page out. "If you manage to find him, make sure to tell him Paul Demian sent you. Now get out of my bar."

Houses dark, trees stripped and towering above. Wind at rest – absolute stillness, absolute silence. The clocks not moving, the seconds not passing. Streetlights smearing like a time lapse photo of a world in motion, first flakes of snow floating down from purple clouds rapidly veiling and unveiling the moon. Turning to face Ravi, watching him stare out into the street:

"I guess that's that then."

"What's that."

"That's it for tonight."

Ravi unmoving, unbreathing, voice slow and quiet: "No. We're just getting started."

"I'm not going to Martin's house. That's not what I signed up for."

"I don't care. I didn't 'sign up' for this either. And yet here we are."

"You can go by yourself. Or we can go together in

the morning. I'm not going now."

Ravi rotating around – slowly, as if mounted on casters – and reaching his hands out: "No. You are."

"I'm going home."

Ravi grabbing hold of the parka where it comes apart at the zipper, dragging it down with his weight: "Isaac. You're coming with me. Believe me when I tell you that you don't want to go home. Not right now."

Bar door banging open, Kim stepping out in an ankle-length coat of fake pink fur. Lifting her long legs down the sidewalk, calling out:

"Ravi!"

"There's still time to find Martin. There's got to be a way." Ravi pulling himself closer, growling his words out: "He'll know how to help us. He's the only one who can."

Kim arriving to intervene, her big green eyes now dotted and jeweled by the white and gold reflections of the streetlights burning above: "Isaac, you don't have to go with him. You don't have to do any of this."

Ravi sneering, baring teeth, ready to pounce: "Don't listen to her. There's no other way."

"You don't have to go either, Ravi."

"No. You're wrong. You don't know anything about me."

"I know more than I'd like to." Studying him for a moment, arms folded low at her waist, searching for the lines of his past self within the twisted form of his present. "I'd like to talk to Isaac for a moment."

"He's coming with me."

"That's for *him* to decide. I want to speak to him alone."

Ravi opening his mouth, curling his lips, stopping himself just short of speech. Eyes full of hate, body postured for surrender, shuffling off a short distance and then sitting down to mope on the curb. Kim watching carefully until he's swallowed in shadow and then slowly, as if taxing her will and strength, rolling her big green eyes towards their new destination.

"So. You too."

Shrugging, deflecting eye contact, conscious of being physically trapped within her gaze: "Is it really so surprising?"

Kim's face assuming an expression of pain: skin tightening, lines deepening, yet these contractions performed with habitual grace, as if the muscles were falling into long-accustomed place: "But why her? Her of all people. I never understood it."

"I don't know. I'm still trying to figure out what it is. I'd think I was crazy too. Except I'm not the only one."

"No. You're not." Kim extending herself subtly, stretching in a motionless sort of way, craning her swan neck this way and that, the synthetic fibers of her coat quivering in the wind. "But if I were you I'd work a little bit harder. That's all I'm trying to say."

Kim drawing out a long, thin cigarette and cradling it in a complex configuration of her long, thin fingers. Sparking it with a lighter held at a great distance, a long, thin flame reaching up to touch the paper. Inhaling as if to preface a speech but saying nothing and instead trapping the smoke behind her lips.

"Other women don't understand her because she never got close to other women. If you knew her the way we did you'd be saying the same thing."

Kim exhaling finally: "You knew her better than anyone else."

Searching her tone, her face for signs of contempt, signs of mockery. Finding none: instead rose-colored tears brimming in her big green eyes.

"Yes. I did. I do."

"Ravi thinks he knows her too. I'm not sure what

good it's doing him. Or you."

"Maybe I could try to tell you. But you probably don't want to hear it."

"No." Kim taking her cigarette from her mouth, moving her hand down behind her hip, as if to hide it. "Tell me."

Deep breaths, bit lip. How many times already – how many times rehearsed, how many times botched in the telling. It never comes out right, it hardly comes out at all.

"No. I can't."

"Why not?"

"Because I don't know the words. Not yet."

"Then maybe you should work on finding them. I wish one of you would at least try."

Kim breathing out smoke and keeping her mouth parted slightly, long teeth shining in the lamplight, eyes roaming the small cityscape. The huge proportions of her body throwing off the scale of everything else, as if she were walking around in a diorama.

"You and him. Paul Demian. Are you dating?"

Shrugging theatrically, wrapping her arms protectively around her waist: "We're together. There was never any dating to speak of."

"And it's working out alright?"

"No." Laughing to herself, quietly, mostly without malice. "No. That's not the point, Isaac. It never is. Though it's very sweet of you to think that sometimes, somehow, somewhere, with some magical people, that's how it works."

"Is it really that bad?"

"No. But that's how it is."

Another gust of wind coming down the street, gentle at first but mounting in intensity, slow and mournful like a violin bow drawn across a string.

"I should go."

"Back to your boyfriend."

"Yes."

"He needs you."

"Yes." Taking hold of a hand and pressing her warm soft lips into it. "Maybe we'll see each other again."

"Maybe."

Backing slowly away: "I hope you're not going with him tonight."

"I am. If only to keep an eye on him."

"I guess someone has to. And I did my time, Isaac. I did my time."

Blowing a kiss, slipping back inside the bar, closing the door upon the snow now falling with gentle regularity and dusting the unswept streets and sidewalks. Snow spiraling in the wind: pushing vortices down the street, howling through long invisible tunnels. Ravi sitting hunched on the curb, clutching a small piece of paper in his bare red hands, the snow piling in small drifts atop his shoulders and shoes. Motionless even after a second shadow appears beside his upon the untouched snow: white canvas washed in golden light, broken only by two figures, one sitting, one standing, and the flecks of snow flurrying about, and the tree shadows veining the street.

"I'm coming with you."

Ravi's shadow unmoving: "I know."

"How are we getting there?"

"I have a ride coming."

"The streets don't look too good."

"We don't have a choice. The trains will be shutting down soon."

"Already? What time is it?"

Finally moving: craning his head over his shoulder and up, squinting to shield his eyes from descending flakes of snow: "Let me worry about what time it is, Isaac."

Single light approaching from the road: moving so

slowly it can hardly be differentiated from the stationary lights surrounding. Ravi watching its approach with eerie calm, the paper in his hand growing wet and ragged under the weather. Beneath the streetlights Dan Drugs's crippled car taking shape: one headlight smashed out and the other flickering its light feebly through the Chicago darkness. Grinding through the snow, halting finally at the curb.

Ravi at the passenger side already, opening the front door and motioning with his head at the back seat: "Get in."

Merging onto the main avenues, crawling through lanes of darkness, Dan Drugs silent and morose at the wheel. One lens of his glasses glinting under the strobing sequence of lamplight, the other an empty space within the bent frames. Skidding to a halt at a red light, banging the wheel and swearing: "I don't know how I let them talk me into this. Running around the city with a bunch of kids. Like I don't have anything fucking better to do."

Ravi shaking his head beside him, calm and confident: "Just wait. It'll be worth it."

"Bullshit. Nothing is worth a hassle like this."

"But you haven't tried it yet. No one has."

"Then call me when it's done. I'm a little too old to sit around casting spells in my friend's apartment."

Ravi silent a moment, reflective. "There's also the other thing."

"The other thing. Tell you the truth, kid, I'm a little too old to give much of a shit about the other thing either." Turning the wheel, leaning on the gas, calmly fishtailing around a corner. "And even if we do get the formula out of Martin it's already too late. Tonight's not the night."

"No. Tonight is the night."

"I don't care what phase the moon is in. I don't give a shit if Mercury is in Capricorn. What if something goes wrong. What if we don't have the right equipment. It'll take forever to make the stuff. The sun will be up already."

"Then we'll close the blinds. Drive faster."

City dissolving as the car pushes southward: into ghetto and out again, into suburban parkland and the wilderness of campus quadrangles. Trees too big to be city trees arching their branches over the street, projecting shadow over the snow below. Snow falling faster now, in thick wet flakes that frost along the lines of mailboxes and electrical wires. Pulling to the curb outside a row of newish duplexes adjacent to the university, snow crunching under tires as the car settles in. Dan Drugs spinning the wheels forward and back, nothing happening. Flinging his broken glasses onto the dashboard and covering his face a moment before he speaks:

"You guys go in. I'll start digging us out."

Stepping out into the whirl of snow and wind: "You sure we have the right place?"

Ravi pushing his shins through the snow banked on the curb: "It has to be."

Ravi forgoing the bell, knocking hard on the door. Three separate bursts of rapid knocking, and at the third one the door opens.

A tall man standing there with thinning hair slicked back and a gray mustache trimmed close to the lip. Severe angle in the nose and a severe glint in the eyes, as if he already knows exactly what he's looking at.

"Who are you."

Ravi wilting under Martin's gaze, squinting through the flurries of blown snow: "Friends of friends."

"I see." Martin thinking it over, running quick calculations in his mind. Thinking through the action of his eyes: methodically scanning the scene in front of him and deriving its inner workings through some complex but instant process of intuition. "I don't want to leave the door open. You can come in, but I need you to make it quick."

Shaking off snow in the narrow hallway, gestured into a dark kitchen. Woman peering from the open portal, hair dull and undone, thin middle-aged face scowling with suspicion. Martin waving her off:

"Don't worry, Ellie. This won't take long."

Real fear creeping into a quiet voice: "Students?"

"No. Not students. But I'm sure it won't take long." Sitting down, addressing his two guests: "Isn't that right."

Ravi waiting for the woman to recede, remaining standing: "Not if you give us what we want."

"What are you going to do if I don't." Martin smiling to himself for a moment, making a welcoming gesture with his hands: "Go on. Tell me what you came here for."

"The synthesis, Martin. We're looking for the synthesis."

"I'm guessing Paul Demian sent you. Do you know how I know that?"

"No."

"Because Paul Demian is one of the only people who knows me well enough to know for sure that there is no synthesis. And there never was."

"No."

"Yes. I'm afraid I know what I'm talking about in this case"

"You're lying."

Martin shaking his head, laughing softly, without hostility: "We never alluded to it. Never thought of such a thing. It was a rumor dreamed up by some confused kids after they found our records on the internet. Wishful thinking, if you want to call it that."

Ravi crumpling up, stricken, lowering his head slowly to the table and banging his fist against the wood, groaning out at each blow:

"No. No. No. No. No. No. No." Raising his head up, proceeding weakly: "You're just trying to get rid of us."

"If I wanted to get rid of you I wouldn't have let you in. But yes. I would like you to leave, in fact. I have a family. I have a life."

"There has to be a synthesis. There has to be."

"I can't give you what I don't have."

Ravi standing up shakily: "I'm going to get it. I'm going to find it. Even if it kills me."

Smiling again, almost grandfatherly: "You're certainly free to try. And you're absolutely right about one thing. The process just might kill you."

Ravi stumbling out of the room, tramping in dazed diagonals through the hall. Opening the door and stepping out, moaning high up in his throat, a low-volume howl: looking back once over his shoulder and loping with unsure steps towards Dan Drugs's idling car.

Martin watching him go, waiting to shut the door: "Well? Aren't you going with him?"

"No."

"No?"

"No." Swallowing hard, summoning courage: "I want to talk about Hannah."

Martin blinking as if hit by a blast of air. No surnames, no circumlocutions. Extending his arm and grimly checking his watch: "Alright. How much time do you have."

"All night."

Nodding: "We might need it."

Waiting for a cab outside Martin's apartment, the last of the snow flurrying down in bursts of sparkling spray. Body buzzing with warmth all over, witness to a greater intensity of life than could be found even within the bloom and insect-hum of midsummer. Mind brimming with impressions, outlines, inchoate forms teeming propulsively through every level of conceptualization, imaginary yet tangible, begging to be made real.

"That girl doesn't know her own strength," Martin had said around the third drink. "If she sees it at all, it appears to her only as weakness."

Cab shuttling soundlessly through the plowed streets. City peaceful beyond the window, its process of inner and outer decay arrested in the deep winter refrigeration. Dawn perhaps brimming in the sky – perhaps – but its light obscured by the ceiling of clouds. Moving quickly, discharging their final flourishes of snow as the cab pulls up at the apartment.

Hesitating outside the door, listening with an ear pressed close to the wood. Silence within: but a silence pregnant with activity, an atmosphere of held breath.

Candles lit in the apartment: landslides of wax pouring forth from makeshift holders, clear streaks of wax snaking over tables and floorboards. Weak orange light dancing through the room, reaching and subsiding without purpose or pattern, shifting like sunshine on the forest floor. Candles gurgling like empty stomachs, towers of wax sinking down beneath the constant pressure of flame.

Four figures sleeping in the living room: Michael Reality hanging off of the couch, Ravi curled childlike on the floor below, Dan Drugs slumped over in the easy chair, Topher propped against the wall near the door. And yet another presence in the apartment – the silent sibilance of additional breath, the unconscious weight of another person existing. A solid pane of darkness in the doorway to Topher's bedroom exerting a gentle gravitational pull. Only the alarm clock within shedding any light, red digits blinking: 00:00.

Eyes adjusting to the dark. Searching for human forms within the wild undergrowth of discarded books and dirty laundry. Foot making contact with a floorbound mattress. Halting, holding breath. Reaching over, searching the nearest surface for a switch. Desk lamp toppled over on its side, lying bulb-down, emitting only a faint white halo when it's turned on.

Julia sunk into the bedding like a jewel in its case, her skin pearlescent and corpselike against the dark sheets. Blackish veins twisting across her body, bones sagging under her flesh like the beams of an old house. Eyes coming slowly unglued, the orbs within sickly gray in contrast to the whiteness of her skin. Something unsettling about the angle at which they sit, the whites diminished to slivers by the crowding of the irises. Small smile taking shape upon her lips. Waiting, watching.

"You didn't have to do this. You don't have to be here."

"Yes I did. Yes I do." Closing her eyes, opening them. Whispering, dazed and dreaming, her tongue too big for her mouth: "Wherever we are, that's where we have to be. You have to be here too."

"No I don't."

"Are you sure about that, Isaac?"

Propping herself up on one elbow, letting the last of the sheets slither off. Silence in the room, hospital smells lingering in the air. Tubes of jellies and ointments on the floor, medical devices sealed and sterilized, the smell of death waiting within – death mass manufactured and publicly sanctioned, a death that had taken decades, generations, hundreds of years of research and development to reach its fullest potential. The death smell oozing out to fill the room, seeping out the window and into the street, breeding in the air and blooming out to fill the world: so that every molecule becomes touched by this death, and even when someone turns on the tap to wash their hands it's the same death that comes pouring out.

Reaching out, clicking the lamp off. Stepping gingerly through the room, shutting the door firmly but quietly behind. But the smell still lingering in the apartment and the world beyond.

Cigarette smoke detected first by the nose and then by the eyes: small cirrus clouds weaving gray threads through the darkness. One reddish point of light waxing and waning somewhere in the vicinity of Topher's body.

"You're just wasting your time. You can't save any of them." Topher's shadow lolling its head from on shoulder to the other. "This is what they want."

"No."

"This is what you want too. So you might as well take it."

"No."

"These women carry paradise around in their bodies. And if there's no hope for them what makes you think you stand a chance?"

"I guess the synthesis didn't really matter."

"No. It didn't."

"So what was the point. Did anything happen."

"No. Nothing happened."

"If everything came together as planned – the drugs and the girl and the spells and the phase of the moon – do you think anything would have happened?"

"No. I don't think anything would have happened."

"Do you say that only now that it's over or did you also think that before you started."

"No. I never thought anything would happen."

"So there was never any point."

"No. There was never any point."

Incense smells, smoke smells, chemical smells, sweat smells swarming and choking. Out to the landing for some fresh air, compelled further down the stairs. Out the door, expecting dawn or daylight, finding instead the same night. And getting darker somehow: the streetlights flickering and dimming, their spheres of illumination shrugging and drooping from the strain. The city close enough to touch but infinitely far away at the same time, as if viewed from the wrong end of a telescope: lights of the city distant like a skyline glimpsed from a plane spiraling up and away from everything there is to try and fail to care about. The world existing only as a consequence of outside events, a by-product of a more important process happening somewhere else and for more important people. The world drifting away from itself, pulling itself apart, canceled out like an equation. Towns and cities spreading slowly away from each other, and every day the official maps and units of measure adjusting themselves to cover it up. Buildings drifting too, and the streets and sidewalks easing ever so gently away from whatever used to be trapped beneath them. Molecules fleeing like galaxies – even faster, yet remaining always within proportion, rendering the change imperceptible to the less subtle senses. Distance no longer a relation between things but a state within things, and every day and every night the distance growing yet more distant.

Walking down dark avenues forsaken by all motor and foot traffic. Turning off the main road into a neighborhood of neat gardens stripped of their fruits by the winter, small houses beyond the fences unlit and sleeping silently. One more silent than the others – low-slung bungalow, a beach house in the urban desert, the type of place where a widow might have lived for the past thirty years.

Peering through dark and curtained windows, knocking where the bedroom might be. Cold fingers numbing against the window frame, trying to force it open. Whispering first: "Cordelia!" Banging on the glass, first with palm and then with knuckles, growing gradually louder, gradually more desperate: "Cordelia!"

Light flashing on in one of the windows. Dingy floral curtain pushed aside, Cordelia staring out. Motioning to wait and angrily pulling the curtain back into place.

Ten minutes of standing in the quiet Chicago streets. Residue of mottled snow streaking the plowed roads; inch or two of snow sitting untouched on roofs and lawns. Air cool and clean and calming, sweet to breathe but sharp when it hits the lungs. Ten minutes of waiting, ten minutes of wondering if the door will ever come open, wondering what has already gone wrong. Finally Cordelia shuffling out in untied boots and a hooded parka thrown over pajamas, a mug of tea steaming eagerly between her two hands. Her eyes blinking by themselves, irritated by the fur trim of her hood, her lower lip trembling already from the cold.

"You said you'd call."

"My phone died."

"Of course it did."

Shudders moving down Cordelia's entire body, teeth knocking soundlessly behind her parted lips.

"If you're cold we can talk inside."

"No." Teeth chattering audibly for a moment before she makes the effort to lock her jaw. "We can't."

"Why not? It's your house."

"Because I don't want to talk in there. Paolo and I just had a fight."

"About what?"

"About you waking us up in the middle of the night."

"So what? I don't care what Paolo thinks."

"He's inside. Probably listening."

"Okay. What did I just say."

"Maybe you should care about what I think then." Hunching over her mug, blowing ripples across the surface of the tea. "I've put up with a lot from you."

"Poor Cordelia. What else do you have to do?"

"I have a lot to do. I have a boyfriend. I'm taking night classes. I have a *job*, though it may not be the most glamorous one." Eyes reddening, face flushing in the darkness – a supernatural spring, an early thaw, her skin transparent and all the inside colors radiating warmly out. "I have a *heart* and *dreams* and *real feelings*, and I don't think you could ever understand because you don't have any of those things."

Cordelia sipping her tea, her giant hood again falling over her face. Silence accumulating, seconds into minutes, pressing down like the weight of the night.

"What do you want, Isaac. Just tell me and I'll do what I can to get it for you. But I can't read minds. You have to tell me first."

"I want Hannah."

"No. Maybe two or three years ago I would've bought that. But not anymore."

"I do."

"I'm sure you think you do. But that's not quite the same thing."

Insistently, petulantly, as if the saying of it might make it more true: "I know her better than anyone else."

"I'm not sure that you don't. I have my doubts, but I'll grant you that much."

"You just don't care."

"I do care. But I've already heard it all, and I'm sick of hearing it."

"No. Not everything."

Wind whipping up again, tearing fissures in the clouds above. Night sky on the other side, stars shining down with supernatural clarity – stars that had been hidden for so long it's like the first time they'd ever shone, undimmed by the passage of time. Final wisps of steam curling off the tea and dissipating into the night. Cordelia waiting patiently for a response and giving up without getting one.

"Isaac. I don't have all night. I still don't know why you came here. Tell me what you want."

Voice rising hysterically in pitch: "I just want to *talk* to you!"

"Okay. We can talk about anything except for Hannah."

"But everything is about Hannah."

Shaking her head: "Try again, Isaac."

Swallowing hard, scrambling for lies or answers, desperate to keep the conversation going: "Julia. I want Julia."

"No you don't. Try harder."

"I do."

"All you're doing is spinning a mythology around her the same way you've spun a mythology around Hannah. The only difference is you've spent a few more years on Hannah, and that's why she looms so large in your mind."

"No. It's true. We did it."

"Did what."

"We had relations."

"Excuse me?"

Nodding vigorously: "We all did. Me and Topher. And Ravi and Dan Drugs and Michael Reality – we all did it with her."

Cordelia lifting her head to get a better view from beneath her hood: "Why."

"Why not."

"Because that makes you the same as any of them."

"So what. I never said I was any different."

"You would be if you let yourself." And her voice shrinking somehow: not in volume but now deprived of air and weight, as if coming from a smaller and smaller person: "It's not going to happen again, is it?"

"What does it matter to you?"

"It just does."

"Who knows. We're two consenting adults. We're in love."

"No you're not."

"You're just jealous it's not you."

"Fuck you, Isaac."

Silence in the street, silence in the city, silence in the atmosphere all the way up to outer space. Cordelia waiting for an apology or a better explanation. But there's only so long a person will wait. Cordelia sipping cold tea, pouring the rest out onto the snow and taking a long breath before she speaks.

"I try to help you. I really do. Maybe I don't try as hard as I used to, but only because this is the way you treat me every time I've ever tried to help. So I'm not sure why I bother anymore, except that maybe I'm stupid enough to care about you."

Taking one more pained look from beneath her hood and then retreating again behind the fur trim. "But I know I'm not the problem. I know Hannah's not the problem either. The problem, whatever it is, is something you're not telling me. And I think you know that too. And yet you always ask me to help you, and you always react badly when I try. And I really try really hard, and I've always tried, and you still don't care."

Turning around, reaching for the door to her apartment: slowly, though, still waiting for an answer, an excuse, anything at all. Pausing, finally, when she turns the knob, speaking stiltedly over her shoulder:

"So if you ever want to tell me what it is, now would be the time to do it."

"I'm not going to tell you." Throat dry, words expelled like foreign objects, inventions of someone else. Cordelia hesitating, half in the door and half out, cocking her head to listen. Voice rising, forced out and ringing and echoing in the stillness of the night: "I'm not going to tell you!"

Door clicking shut, Cordelia slipping instantly inside. Chicago, huge and silent, stretching away in every direction – miles and miles of sidewalks covered in crystallized salt glinting like broken glass in the streetlights. Bars closed, lights out, doors locked – nowhere to go, nowhere to be, nowhere to even keep warm. Chicago in lamplight: forest shadows falling dark on crooked sidewalks. Trees bare but thick in the sidestreets, branches reaching up like inverse roots drawing strength from the blank haze of the sky. Quiet blocks, sleeping houses. Former neighborhoods, future neighborhoods, sites dense with possibility, with things living unseen in every window and doorway, every open alley and every warm dark room in every two-family wooden house, every three-family brick, all emptied now of families and given over to the independent and near-alcoholic. The city awaiting the sun and its warmth, the morning and its clarity of thought. Standing on streetcorners, leaning in doorways and alcoves, hands clenched in pockets, eyes stinging from cold and exhaustion, nodding off standing up, trying to stay awake, trying to think things through: the past and what it might mean for the future if the future ever comes.

# II.
# Martin & Hannah

A JOLT, A SHORT MOMENT OF TRANSPORT, a disappointment. Mostly just disappointment: engines humming aseptically, sunlight sparkling cold and uniform above the clouds, queasy pressurized boredom drilling the skull until it was impossible to read or even think straight. It was like a nightmare of the afterlife: neither joy or perdition, just an eternity of time with nothing to do. Flight was everything that had gone wrong with the twentieth century. Here was all the audacity of the past and all its squandered and commodified potential. Flying didn't feel like anything except whatever the opposite of flying was. Living, thought Martin. It felt like living.

They were descending. Past the clouds the city came into view: a gray silhouette of skyline suspended between the gray of the sky and the gray of the water. Beyond it a network of sprawl clung like bacteria to the central growth, smudged in ambient light the color of old dishwater. Martin didn't like cities to begin with. But this one was worse than most: plunked down at hazard on a swamp, whipped up from nothing by itinerant traders. Like a computer model willed to life, marooned in an uncanny valley between its physical and ideal state. Your feet met solid matter, yes; but there was no way for the eye to absorb the lines of the city. As if it were intentional, an obstacle to comprehension. Designed to baffle, to incohere. Like the plane was standing still and the city lunging forward to meet it; the city running away with itself, metastasizing out of control. Junk cells ate away all interiors. The skin was still intact, puffed up bigger than before. But inside: nothing.

They were descending. Below them a joyless hive of concrete and slush puddles, numb toes and blank stares. Millions of men milling around, half frozen by the winter weather and the winter-of-culture, spurred to motion only by the contagious insect-consciousness of the crowd at their heels. Clockwork men, forgotten men; half-men, imaginary men, unconscious men. All nursing with care their petty crimes of the heart: connivers, dissemblers, corrupters, seducers, sycophants, hypocrites, traitors. Not because they were driven by willpower but only because they had no better ideas; because within this desolation they had nothing with which to define themselves besides their clung-to pathologies.

They were descending. The city vanished, churned to mush by the empty vector of speed. However many hundreds of miles an hour. Still it felt like stasis, suspended animation. Martin was empty, leaking, decompressing. A puff of air swelled in his inner ear, expanded out until it swallowed his head and the space beyond. He was being colonized: his blood forced out and empty space forced in. He was as hollow now as the city and its inhabitants. This was not what man had been built for. The body was hurtled forth at hundreds of miles an hour but lacked any animating principle of its own. Death was instant here, without the dignity of pain. Just a flaring of fuel, a disunion of particles. And then?

There was a heartbeat of contact as the wheels kissed the ground. A fat woman gasped. A baby cried. The engines wound down, and he was back in Chicago. The air sickness remained.

Ellie was already waiting behind the door by the time he got it open. He let go of her first; she kept her arms around his neck. And when he saw she wasn't letting go he placed one hand on her back and with the other shut the door and ushered them out of the cold. She didn't resent him for going away. He had made it understood before they married that he needed his space. Space to "think" – that was the stated intention. It often went unfulfilled; but Ellie never knew, and probably wouldn't have cared. She wasn't much of a thinker herself.

It was always a shock seeing her after a period of separation. Almost like seeing her for the first time: shin-length skirts, earth tone stockings,  rugged winter sandals. Always older, always grayer, always drier and thinner. Always smiling. She loved him very much. This he was sure of.

She took him by the hand and showed him the improvements she'd made to the apartment: new drapes, new throw covers, all matching, homemade. Ellie was not a city person either. Sometimes he wasn't sure what century she had fallen out of. Her father had told him as much: they don't make them like this anymore. Martin himself was old-fashioned enough to have taken the trouble to court her. And a church wedding and all the rest. They were very young at the time. He told himself he was lucky to have her.

He scanned the living room. "And George? Sleeping?"

She shook her head no. Her eyes sparkled behind wireframe glasses. She put a finger to her lips and led Martin with motherly pride into the interior of the apartment.

George was on his hands and knees in the central hallway of their narrow duplex, where the white walls had been smudged grey by his handprints. His own room was somehow too big for him, though he was growing – physically at least. He made a rumbling in his throat as he pushed his toy car. He'd never done this before, with or without sound effects. It implied a certain advance, however belated, in cognitive ability. This was what had cheered Ellie so much.

"He's been doing this all week," she said.

Martin nodded. George pushed his car forward and back again. Forward and back again; and Martin once more could think of nothing to say. Coming home, for him, sometimes made him feel like the guest of honor at a party thrown by strangers. His son had been doing nothing but pushing that car forward and back for a whole week.

"George," said Ellie. She bent low over their son. "Georgie. Look. Daddy's home."

George did not look. Nor was he going to, no matter how long they waited. Ellie scooped him up off the carpet before she had a chance to be disappointed. Bouncing him in her arms, she brought him close to Martin, taking certain subtle cares to make sure he was eventually facing his father.

Ellie always told him all her dreams. There was a backlog since he'd been away. Lying in the dark, her voice took on properties outside of sound. He could see it flow silken on the darkness; felt it ringing down his spine. She dreamed in sensations, singularities, free of the nightmare logic that bothered the sleep of men with heavy consciences. She could dream a flower, a sunset, the feeling of dew on her feet. She dreamed of flying.

"But you don't understand," she said. "Not like normal flying."

"Not in a plane."

"Of course. But not just that. Not just like normal flying through the air."

"Normally people don't fly through the air."

"You know what I mean."

He didn't though. He rarely dreamed. Life, to him, was like troubled sleep, an unease that stalked him without ever expressing itself allegorically. His air sickness still hadn't gone away. It pounded in his head, lumped in his throat. His blood struggled in its veins, thin, sticking, slow. He still hadn't landed. Was still whipping through space at hundreds of miles an hour. Ellie knew it; could feel it, through him. She listened to the silence and understood. She explained:

It didn't feel like fantasy when she dreamed. There was nothing magical about it. It was aggressively real: a wheeling flight, exposed to the elements, pummeling and vertiginous, so violent it was hard to keep her eyes open. The force of the air pulled at the roots of her hair. Her skin, afterwards, felt tender and beaten by the wind. Maybe she didn't have the right words for it, she said.

"It probably just sounds crazy to you," she said.

"No it doesn't," he said. He was at least humble enough to know that he was the crazy one for not dreaming.

Her hair was thin and brittle, her skin cracked and scaly at the extremities. It was smooth only at the core: below the neck, above the knees. In the places shown to no one but him. Martin knew it all by memory; could find his way in the dark, by touch. Yet something was different now. All he could hope was that Ellie wouldn't notice. But of course she would. He closed his eyes and shut himself inside an exponential darkness. He didn't belong to this world any more than he belonged to the world outside. He was somewhere else, and he didn't know where yet.

THEY WERE BENT FORWARD, lurching into the wind, half lost in the dark sprawl of the world beyond campus, the porous border separating the city from the surrounding prairie. The houses were crumbling, caved-in, syphilitic: missing windows, missing doors, missing porches. Young trees grew up through the floorboards and leaned out of torn-open walls; old trees dropped branches big enough to cave in ceilings. Any farther south and the city ended. Not like in Jersey, Connecticut, Long Island, where the city segued gradually to suburbs and farms and nature. Here it just ended. Died completely like a conjuring trick: all along it was just fooling. All the crime, all the cold, all the struggling millions and all their sweat, every brick and every second of the city's history: it was all for nothing, make believe. Maybe, out there, beyond the frozen tundra, under the light of the stars, hamlets of civilization continued their existence. But it was hard to tell from their current vantage point. All they could see through the trees was one road and a drive-up ATM, a close-up view of the lonely dots they saw from high above as they jetted between metropolises.

The wind blew tiles from a roof and spun them into the road. Guy had to duck to keep from being guillotined.

"This better be worth it," he said.

"It's not going to be," said Isaac.

Somewhere in this cracked network of streets, amid the squats and foreclosures and untended lots, all the would-be saviors of the world, all the poets and activists and all their unemployed hangers-on, lived in a drafty Victorian house named Neverworld. Packed past capacity, crooked on its foundation, it managed to hold between its walls a fluid mass of cats, roommates, and found furniture. There was some sort of meeting taking place tonight. But that wasn't why they were going.

"You said she's your ex-girlfriend?" said Guy.

"No."

"So you're trying to date her."

"No."

"So who is she."

"Long story."

They reached the house. It was the only one on the block that was lit up; the only sound for a square mile. It was the only house that wasn't bolted or boarded, the only one whose screen door, front door, and vestibule door had all been blown open by the wind. Because of this it was no warmer inside than it was outside. Guy put his shoulder against the door and shoved it closed, throwing the bolt as if fending off an invader. He looked around.

Tea candles were set out in séance profusion on every surface capable of supporting one. A skinny kid in rimless glasses sat in a chair in the corner, reading from a notebook to a group of freshman girls on the floor in front of him. Someone dressed in casual business attire was handing out activist leaflets. In the kitchen kids in hoodies exchanged sheafs of bills for bags of pills. Several people were separately occupying themselves with various disinterested cats. Many girls were crying or bore mascara streaks from having cried.

"What the fuck kind of a party is this," he said.

Cordelia emerged from the chaos wearing an off-white sweater splotched with red wine and was subsumed again a moment later, harried and grasped-at – exasperated in a calm sort of way, as if she had already become accustomed to it. She shuttled through the house like a paramedic, guiding girls down the stairs, helping them find their phones, talking them out of calling ex-boyfriends, feeding them bread and water to calm their troubled stomachs. To calm their troubled souls: she took the crust off each slice and kneaded the dough into balls like a mother feeding a teething child. When she next reappeared, serving as a crutch for a taller and drunker girl, Isaac raised a finger to catch her attention. Cordelia saw this and ignored him, stumbling with her patient to the first floor bathroom. The door was still half open, so Isaac poked his head inside.

"Can it wait?" said Cordelia, kneeling behind the girl and holding her hair behind her ears. The girl glanced up at Isaac and retched.

"Have you seen Hannah?"

Cordelia shook her head; but at the world, not at Isaac. "Unbelievable. Everyone's looking for Hannah. You'd think this was her party or something. You'd think she lived here."

"Is she here?"

"No. And if she's not here by now I doubt she's coming. I'm sure she has better things to do."

It was the first vibration of a string wound tight and waiting to be plucked. Isaac missed, if not the feeling, the music it produced. Better things to do: Cordelia was too smart not to know how Isaac would interpret this.

"Like what? Do you know where she is?"

The girl in Cordelia's arms twitched and heaved; made gasps and small noises when the fit was over. Cordelia rubbed her back and called her sweetie and shot a look at Isaac. As he nudged the door shut he heard her voice echo, cooing, off the tiles:

"You believe this? Dozens of eligible girls in the house, and the only one they want isn't here. Serves them right if you ask me."

Guy had already found a way to occupy himself: he had conned a drink off someone and was leaning against the wall, perfectly at ease, chatting up a girl with choppy blue hair.

"Isaac," he said, "meet my new friend Blue."

"My name's Heather," she said.

Guy joined their hands together. "Isaac, Blue. Blue, Isaac."

"Pleased," said Isaac.

Someone grabbed his other hand. Someone raised it to his or her lips and placed a wet kiss on the back of it. Someone wouldn't let go, and Isaac was too polite to be the first one to withdraw.

Kim looked down from a great height: six, maybe seven, eight inches above him. She watched his growing discomfort with growing amusement and parted her lips to smile. Even her teeth were tall: long and straight but with odd gaps between them; white enough in real life probably but deep yellow in contrast to her caked-on lipstick. For reasons he couldn't explain, Isaac had a certain appeal to awkwardly tall women. He told himself it was because they responded in a maternal way to his helplessness. Women were having babies later and later these days; until then, they had him. Kim snapped her fingers, bobbed her head, jogging her memory.

"Zach," she said.

"I-zach."

"Hi, Zach. Are you having a good time?"

"I don't know. I just got here."

"Some boys wouldn't know a good time if it came up and kissed them on the hand."

Isaac looked to Guy for help. Guy gave a shrug full of meaning, head cocked, eyebrows raised, lips protruding: You could do worse.

"What brings you here," said Isaac.

"I live here."

"Oh." Panicking slightly, he looked again to Guy,

but Guy had already busied himself again with Blue. "I didn't know that."

"Upstairs. Second room on the left."

The pallor of Kim's skin contrasted sharply with the electric blue of her eye shadow. Guy was right: he could do worse. Word might get back to Hannah and prove to her his virility. Guy wouldn't judge him for it. Cordelia might, but he had little esteem to lose in her eyes. Yet in the second or two it took to make these computations his window of opportunity had already closed. Counterfeit Cody approached and put his arm over her shoulder. She kissed his hand; smiling, stuck his index finger in her mouth and bit down. He dug around in his oversized pants and flashed some bills from the pocket. Real ones – per the terms of his probation, his counterfeiting days were over. This left him with plenty of time to sell pharmaceuticals to underclassmen on and off campus. Kim motioned for him to put the money away, unsmiling, all business now. She pointed at the ceiling. Isaac read her lips: "Second room on the left."

Cordelia tried to pass undetected; Isaac grabbed her arm before she could.

"You," she said, "are needier than all these drunk girls put together."

"I know. I don't care. Stay here and talk to me."

"Okay. What do you want to talk about."

Isaac ran through topics in his head without finding anything. Cordelia saw this, reading his expression, reading his mind. She rolled her eyes at him and left to lift up a girl who had just knocked over an end table.

Guy had his hands on Blue's hips and was leaning in close as he talked. Isaac turned his attention elsewhere; locked eyes with Ravi, who was standing marooned in the middle of the room, looking for someone to lock eyes with. He stepped over empty bottles and pushed a pamphlet into

Isaac's hands.

"Isaac," he said. "Glad you could make it. We're organizing. Too bad you missed the meeting. Lots of good ideas."

Isaac glanced at the half-sheet of photocopied paper: RESIST IMPERIALISM. Ravi was the de facto chairman of the Students For A Progressive Society. They weren't supposed to have a chairman, this being a somewhat imperialist concept, or were supposed to elect chairmen-and-women on a rotating and egalitarian basis, but since no one else ever wanted to do it Ravi was happy to fill the role in perpetuity. Isaac used to go to meetings because Hannah used to go to them. But though he sometimes claimed, to himself, that he was willing to do "anything" for her, the thought of sitting through an entire SFPS meeting was already enough to break his resolve.

Ravi tapped the paper in his hand, aware that he hadn't read it. "The university wants to expand again. They're going to tear down an entire neighborhood just to build another research facility. We can't let this happen. Who knows what would come next."

"What are they doing with all the people?"

"Shipping them out to the suburbs. A whole population uprooted. It's disgusting."

"Who knows. Maybe they'll be happier out there."

Isaac was baiting him. Not just for the fun of it; moreso because he knew it wasn't really what Ravi wanted to talk about. Here, in an odd way, he'd finally found a willing audience.

"Was Hannah here?" said Isaac, hiding his satisfaction, baiting him once again.  "No. No." Ravi shrank before his eyes; hunched his shoulders, withdrew into the folds of his oddly formal clothing. "She said she'd come. She *promised*. But she never comes to the meetings anymore."

Isaac shrugged. "Oh well. I'm sure she has better

things to do."

Isaac watched. He knew all the signs; had lived them himself. He could pinpoint the exact moment the shaft hit the heart, saw to the millimeter how deep it penetrated. Ravi winced, but he didn't think Isaac noticed. No one else would have.

Isaac knew that Ravi had slept, once, with Hannah. Around the same time he did. For probably the same reasons, or lack thereof. Like a queen curing lepers with a touch, she sometimes took pity on the awkward and friendless, and granted them favors usually reserved for the more mentally and physically fit members of society. Isaac hated to see his worst qualities reflected back at himself, and watched with pleasure as Ravi writhed in front of him, pierced through like a worm on a hook.

"What do you mean, better things?"

"Hannah's not really the stay in on a Friday type. I'm sure she's not starved for company."

Ravi shook his head and raised his mug to his lips. He was drinking coffee, not liquor; he would wait up all night if he had to. His eyes were focused somewhere else, looking in on imaginary bedroom scenes. He narrowed them as if to squeeze the unwanted pictures out.

"What makes you so sure of that."

"You hear things. You can ask anyone."

But Isaac could only play the torturer for so long. He plucked wings from butterflies and then, feeling pity, hastened to glue them back on. He squeezed Ravi's bony shoulder, trying to redirect his anger.

"Come on, man. That's just how she is. Everyone knows it. You can't change her. You can't save her."

"I don't care," said Ravi. "You're wrong. Hannah's different."

He stared back at Isaac. Unblinking and manic —

the inner violence of a man who'd carefully trained himself against its outward expression. He was going to keep staring until Isaac took his hand away.

Ravi, who was wrong about everything else, was right about Hannah. Isaac, who had never cared about anything before, floating through life on a cloud of apathy, had been thrown into chaos by this girl. This woman, whoever she was. Who didn't even seem to be trying, who created whole worlds on a whim and knocked them down by accident. Ravi and Isaac had wasted months and years of their lives trying to figure her out, and yet she only seemed to look with favor on the guys who didn't understand her at all. Isaac let go of Ravi, his brother in rejection.

Words meant for Ravi turned in on himself. Exploded internally: whole magazines of stored ammunition. *She has better things to do.* His hindbrain threw pictures up, drive-in gigantic: Hannah in bed, twisted and hot like a snake. No faces, only limbs and slippery organs. Hannah and someone. Hannah and anyone. Hannah and everyone. The girl conjured whole multitudes from nothing, and every imagined or would-be suitor became another tongue of flame in Isaac's inner inferno. But this was what he deserved.

The party was winding down – or meeting or group therapy session or whatever it was. The man in rimless spectacles had left his easy chair, and the girls sitting cross-legged around it had nothing to do anymore but stare dolefully down at the floor. Ravi was pacing the room, stoop-shouldered, bending to pick up soggy and stepped-on leaflets. The cats came downstairs to join him, sniffing at crumbs and lapping at puddles. Kim was upstairs with Cody in the second room to the left. Guy was necking with Blue in the corner. Cordelia fit the last of the drunk girls in a cab and walked back through the three open doors, scanning the room in search of someone else to rescue.

There was never any light in the apartment. Maybe it was only because she had made a habit of sleeping through the day and waking only at night. Lying motionless in the dark: no motion in the apartment except for the invisible passing of the seconds. Sometimes she wondered if the problem was that she was not diligent enough in waiting. If only she didn't stir, if only she didn't breathe, maybe time would never move again. But she was too impatient to ever try to make it happen.

Hannah lived alone. She had to; she'd lasted only one semester in the dorms, and hadn't made any friends during her time there. Maybe she'd forged some temporary alliances, but this was more a matter of survival than camaraderie, and she had no need of them since getting her own place. Girls had a way of not liking her. Or maybe she had a way of not liking girls. She could never tell whose fault it was. It didn't matter either way; she liked living by herself, away from everyone else she once knew.

Sometimes, though, she needed a pair of eyes on her – anyone's, for any reason. Just because she needed someone for whom to present herself. Otherwise, without anything to distract her, she risked falling down into the sinkhole of her ego. She forced it sometimes, sick of waiting for the inevitable – closing her eyes, willing herself deeper, deeper, deeper. She lost hours like this, bingeing so she'd reach the end and never have to do it again. She never did though. She wanted to see how far she had to go before she hit something solid. She never did.

She stood in front of the mirror, mind focused intently on not looking at herself. Not at herself but only at her clothes, the envelope into which she packed her lack of being. She tweaked her silhouette, played with her contours;

felt the fabric press taut against her skin and give shape to the upflowing fountain of her body. But at a certain point she lost it, the spark of suddenness, the dissociation that allowed her to see herself as others might see her. There she was again: there she wasn't. Just Hannah. But only her lines and colors: not even Hannah, not even that.

The cold stole through the windows and slithered like a hand across her skin. No snow had survived the first couple thaws; but somehow, when there was nothing to distract the eye, that only made it seem colder. The world was hardened and impenetrable, stripped to its skeleton and whipped by the wind. She pressed her forehead against the window and felt with pleasure the cold cutting in on her scalp. The night was calling out to her; she lusted for it as if after the warmth of a body. But she almost never went out anymore. Sometimes she still pretended: sometimes she made plans, got dressed. But she knew all along that this was only so that she would feel better when she finally gave up, finally changed her mind.

She wandered the apartment, tracing absently her fingers on the walls. Vacant, methodical, she opened every drawer and cabinet. Looking for what. Looking for food. But she never kept any in the apartment, and there was a reason she never kept any in the apartment. She turned off the lights and fell fully clothed onto the bed. Her phone buzzed and spun pirouettes on the nightstand. The blue light of the screen washed in a cloud over the wall. She turned the phone over without looking at it; consciously, studiously, just as she'd avoided looking in the mirror earlier. Lately she'd become an expert at this. The selective embrace of intolerable truths. She liked to think herself more stoic, more mentally hardened than the other students, and thus able to perceive reality with greater clarity. But when she was truly seeing clearly she saw that this too was a lie. She cheated the same as everyone else. She cheated, she cheated, she cheated.

She lay there, looking at the dark, a sterile Venus, without thoughts. When her eyes adjusted she saw light again: green blips from her laptop, yellow spears of streetlight lancing through the blinds. There was no escaping it. It was daylight in her mind all the time. That was why she could never sleep. That was why she could never get anything done. That was why she made such bad decisions. That was why she could never sleep. The cycle went on.

She could feel her cells growing. Spreading out, suppurating slowly, until she was one with the mattress, a stain of biology leaking onto the cotton sheets. Sleep was no escape. Sleep was like the rest of her life, only moreso, intensified, without any of reality's contingencies to dampen her prevailing preoccupations. She saw things in her sleep; not dreams, but she didn't know what else to call them. They weren't narrative; were hardly representational, hardly visual. It was more like a suffocating sensation that could be best described as an image. Like her brain was too numb to produce even the nonsense of dreams, and when she slept her body surged forth to fill the empty space where her spirit should have been.

It was like a seething and unbroken mass of organs stamped in unending pattern across her eyes; burrowing larvalike into the nerves which received light and produced image. That was how she could see in the total eye-shut darkness. And see so clearly: a sea of meat sweating and throbbing; churning amongst itself and zippered through with streaks of metal; each deformed liver and mutant heart fitted with mechanical claws and teeth to tear its way through to another moment of life. The organs swallowed and gave birth and left new organs in their wake, bleeding and new as they tore forth from their placentae. And kept tearing, and never stopped until stopped by something stronger. That was the world she lived in when she was trying to sleep, and it was this more than anything else that kept her always so skittish and awake. She sleepwalked through her days and looked for ways to further exhaust herself. Anything but wakefulness and anything but restless sleep; better to be spent and tempest-tossed, blacked out by passion or its nearest equivalent. All the essayists, all the editorialists, all the self-help frauds and sinecured psychologists, all said the same thing: moderation only, moderation always, moderation at all costs. But moderation numbed, moderation killed. Hannah could live only in the extremes. Yet no matter how hotly she pursued them she still had not found them. She still hadn't reached the end.

Her phone buzzed again; she turned it off this time. Still without looking. Whatever it was, whoever it was, she didn't need it or them. It could only mean more problems. Yet here she was and she had nothing to replace her problems with. If she took the problems out of her life there was no life left for her.

Her eyes were forced open. The light invading her room flooded in her skull and brightened the white night of her mind. Time passed – she didn't know how long. Refused to look at the clock. Another one of her tricks. Her eyes stung when she tried to close them. There was too much energy inside them. She pushed it through, pushed it out; concentrated until it simmered unseen in the air above her skull and focused only on it and not on the thoughts cluttering her consciousness. Focused only on one thing, on one non-thing with a disciplined non-focus until she became, briefly, a part of it.

She woke up. Something was knocked loose inside her, rattling. Blood dripping from her heart; falling a great distance into her body and echoing through the emptiness.

But the locus of the sound moved gradually away from her. It was coming from outside of her, not inside of her. Someone was in the apartment. No: someone was outside the apartment. Knocking.

She leaned her head out the living room window and felt the cold rushing her, drying instantly her eyes, pricking deep in her throat and sinuses. She saw, standing in a pool of streetlight like an ice floe, a small man dressed in the clothes of a middle-aged civil servant. She stared until her sight unfogged: she saw Ravi.

He wasn't knocking anymore by the time she opened the door. But he wasn't preparing to leave either. He was just standing there, blue-lipped, hunched with cold, looking like he would have rather been anywhere else. When he saw her he stepped aside as if trying to hide. Maybe he wasn't expecting her to actually come out. Hannah plucked at her hips to remind herself what she was wearing: jeans, badly stretched, and a hoodie too tattered to wear outside the house. Modest though she was, Ravi kept his eyes roaming so he wouldn't have to look at her. The interruption she could deal with. The loss of sleep she could deal with. But this hesitancy, when it came on top of everything else, was too much for her.

"Well," she said.

"Well what?"

"Are you coming in?"

She turned and climbed silently upstairs without waiting to see if he'd follow. She was sure that he would.

She flicked the lights on and fell, squinting, into a chair in her kitchenette. Cast a cursory glance into the living room to make sure she hadn't left anything too embarrassing laying around. But she didn't really care. This was Ravi's choice, not hers.

Everything she needed for coffee was within arm's

reach: filters, grounds, the machine; some water, if she lifted herself from the chair and stretched toward the tap. This was where she sat in the mornings, her head in her hands, bringing herself back to life after a night of waking death. Today the morning had come earlier than usual. That was all.

"Sit down," she said. "You're making me nervous."

Ravi placed himself, straight-backed and stiff-limbed, on top of the couch.

"I mean sit down in *here*."

Ravi did as he was told. And sat there waiting for her to start the conversation. She remained silent, but only for his own good. She gave a sly smile and prodded him with her eyes: Come on, Ravi. You can do this.

"How come you didn't answer your phone?" he said. "I was worried."

"When have you ever had to worry about me?"

He didn't answer. He'd never seen any of her worst behavior firsthand, and could only have heard of it through his roommates at Neverworld. But he didn't want to admit this. Hannah helped him out.

"My phone's off," she said. "I didn't feel like going out tonight."

"You said you would though."

"Did I miss anything important?"

She was expecting him to respond in kind, light-hearted, half-sarcastic. But this was something Ravi never joked about.

"Not too important. We didn't get a lot of discussion in. But there were some good talking points in there. I was typing minutes if you want me to email you–"

Hannah shook her head. But tried to be nice about the way she did it.

"And you were so excited you had to come tell me

about it?"

"I already told you. I was worried."

"You take a cab?"

"Biked."

"Oh my God. Ravi, it's below zero."

Instinctively she shot her hand out to feel the temperature of his. But regretted it immediately after, when his eyes glazed over with something honeyed and glowing. And also dull, like a drug haze, something synthetic and self-induced. This was what he was after, and she was giving it to him. It wasn't that she loved him in particular, or anyone else in particular either. But she loved, and couldn't help it, even if individual people kept getting in the way. She took her hand away and stood to pour the coffee.

"Coffee?" she asked.

He shrugged, and she set a mug in front of him. He waited for her to sit and fell into a sulk when he saw she wasn't going to. She leaned back against the counter and took a sip and felt with pleasure the caffeine strolling through her mind, lifting its torch and lighting her lamps.

"What is it," she said.

"Nothing."

"Ravi, why did you come here."

He hesitated a moment longer. But it was just for show.

"It's Demian."

Hannah raised her eyebrows. "Oh? What about him."

"I don't think he's good for you. I don't think he's good for anyone."

His earnestness made her smile despite herself. Nor was he entirely wrong. But like one professional maintaining boundaries with another she was forced to shake her head and deliver a short lecture:

"Ravi, I'm not sure if that's any of your business. And I'm not sure if I need your advice either."

"He's dangerous. And he believes in dangerous things."

"And you think I don't know that? You think I can't deal with that?"

Ravi only shuffled his feet and looked down at the floor. When he spoke again his words were badly mumbled.

"Well. There was another reason I was worried about you."

Finally. Hannah waited for the big reveal. But it came just a couple seconds too late. That was when she knew – or maybe she'd known it before, known it as soon as Ravi had arrived – that the conversation was about to sour.

"I was wondering if what they're saying is true. About what happened this summer. In Germany."

If she didn't hit him it was only because all the knives were shut away in drawers and there was nothing immediately to hand that could have delivered a killing blow. She banged her mug into the sink, pleased to watch it shatter, pleased to see Ravi jump up in fright. Displeased to see that he remained standing next to her, arms stretched out, embracing nothing. She tensed all her muscles and closed her eyes so she wouldn't have to see him.

"Hannah, I just wanted–"

"No, no, no, no, no." She took a breath and clenched her teeth and continued as slowly as she could: "*Leave. Leave. Leave. Leave.*"

She felt cold hands on her arms, felt breath stirring in front of her. She opened her eyes and ducked free, paced to the other side of the apartment.

"Ravi," she said, "this is *not* how it *works.*"

"How what works?"

"If you want a girl to sleep with you, it's usually best not to insult her first."

"But I wasn't...I didn't..."

"I don't know what else to tell you. Except leave.

Get out."

Ravi did as he was told. Didn't put up a fight, didn't even attempt it. Hannah threw the bolt when he left, loud so he would hear it. And spun around looking for something else to break. But she was too poor, everything was too necessary. She sat on the couch and dug her nails into her thighs. But it didn't feel like anything through her jeans. She was shot through with adrenaline, and she knew then that there would be no more sleeping for her tonight.

She always made it a point not to regret her past decisions. It wasn't just a self-help platitude for her. Because regretting one bad decision meant regretting all of them, and there were so many mistakes in her past that her entire life would topple on its foundations if she ever let even one get to her. She didn't want to regret having shown Ravi the way to her apartment the year before. But these people weren't happy until they made you regret it. That was why you had to be careful about the quiet ones. The stupid ones just disappeared after. It was the quiet ones who always came back.

She spun in a circle and fell back onto her couch. It seemed like she never used her bed anymore: she kept it only as a relic, a reminder of a bygone way of life. Ancient history, though it was only a year ago. But a lot had happened, and a lot could happen still. She thought about cooking some food – oatmeal, anything. It helped her sleep sometimes. But the idea of foreign substances in her body made her weak with disgust. She wanted to be clean and empty, a simple substance, without component parts, transparent and colorless like the night. She pressed herself back into the cushions and tried to clear her mind again. But the morning was still a long way off, and the day even further. Beyond that, the rest of her life. Eyes fixed upward, she watched the ceiling until the drama of morning unfolded on the blank space above her.


MARTIN HAD A HEADACHE. Andy fixed him a dark-and-stormy – "It's like medicine," he said – but it wasn't helping. Martin coughed and rubbed his Adam's apple with three fingers. His throat hurt too now.

"What's the secret ingredient," he said.

"Ginger beer."

"Ah." Martin took another sip and coughed until he couldn't talk. He waved his hands in surrender, forced the words out: "Take it. Take it. Anyone, take it."

Demian reached out and gripped the glass without taking his eyes from the computer screen, his head dwarfed by the cushioned headphones clinging to his ears. His body steamed in the cold, red and dripping. He got into a trance-like state when he performed, elsewhere and empty-eyed. Worse when they were recording: like he was trying to force himself in through the microphones, blip out of space and into the pure energy of sound. He took down half the dark-and-stormy and made a face. But forgot the pain a moment later and finished it off.

Andy took the empty glass from his hands. "Not too bad, huh."

Demian didn't answer. He was listening to the play-back so loud that Martin could hear it clearly from across the small concrete practice space.

Andy set the glass on the bar he'd installed in an empty speaker cabinet. Later in the night he'd rinse it in the bathroom sink and stow it again among his mixers and gagging-sweet liqueurs. He'd tacked some floral fabric onto the ripped tolex so that it would cover the empty cavity. In his own twisted way, working with only salvaged materials,

Andy could be very domestic. His priorities were mixed up like that; perverse in the purest sense of the word. He craved the sort of wholesomeness that could be achieved only on the fringes of a criminal underground. That was why he had agreed to participate in this second, illegitimate incarnation of Total Mobilization: he said he missed the sort of male bonding that could be found only in circles of the ironic far-right.

But Martin wasn't in it for the bonding. Nor was he in it for the politics, though these had always been a pose, mere means to an end. He wanted to produce; he wanted results. This was his least favorite part of the process: when it was too late to get any real work done but too early to go home without looking like you didn't care. Martin stuck it out, if only because he had little else to care about.

He waited until Demian removed the headphones. "What do you think."

"Needs work. We can use it though."

Demian was a formalist; an engineer, a perfectionist, at least when it came to technical matters. Useful to have around, especially since the technology had changed so much since the last break-up, and neither Martin or Andy had bothered keeping up with it. But Demian lacked ideas of his own; he subscribed to orthodoxy, and resisted deviations from the already-established template for Total Mobilization. When this new iteration of the band first got together – just as a trial, Martin told himself, just to get Demian to shut up about it – he discovered, as if by accident, an entire ocean of sound inside of him. Teeming, living, amniotic – what a burden it had been, carrying it all these years. He only realized once he started pouring it out. A lot had happened in the decades since Total Mobilization had disbanded. It was all there, fully present, inside of him. The difficulties of art had proved to be nothing in comparison with the difficulties of life. It was these that worked within him now, crushing and tectonic, grinding, shifting, exploding in ways so much more profound than than the juvenile angst of his earlier works.

Melodies had begun threading themselves through his walls of sound: melodies of feedback and sirens, shrill and fragile in the mix, close to dissolution and breaking into squawks and pops of static; just one note to form a bulwark against the surrounding chaos; one note, bent and sub-oscillated, which contained in it all the movements and modulations of unplayed symphonies. Everything he'd ever experienced, everything he'd ever thought: he put it all into that note, focused all his faculties on its willing-forth, until it was an almost solid, physical thing, gem-like and indestructible. Martin had never known before what he wanted from life. Family, friends, work, study – all was a disappointment to him. All he ever wanted all these years was to play one note; to witness something, however simple, however minimal, finally emerging from the dimmed existence of the world around him.

The record was still a long way from being finished. They were taking their time on this one; for all they knew they wouldn't be getting another chance at it. They had still not performed in public, they had still not finished a single track. But it was worth the hassle and the heartbreak and the thousand little internecine squabbles. It was worth much more than anything else Martin was working on at the moment, in either his public or private life.

Demian stood and began buttoning his wet shirt over his torso. Flinching as if stung when his elbow made contact with Andy's body: "Watch it."

"Don't worry. The doctors say I'm not contagious."

Andy was kidding, but Demian was not. He continued scowling and pretended that nothing had been said.

"So," said Andy, looking now to Martin. "Are we done here?"

"I think we've been done for a while now," said Martin.

"Then you should've said so. Goodbye, Martin. Goodbye, Demian."

"Goodbye, Andy," said only Martin.

Demian, coiling a cable around his arm, turned his head to make sure he had gone.

"Are you really sure we need him?" he said. "Do you really think he contributes anything at this point?"

"It's his band," said Martin. "You just live in it."

Demian finished his work and dropped the cable on the floor. "You busy tonight?"

"Is this your way of asking me for a ride?"

"It's my way of asking if you're busy tonight. I was going to ask if you wanted to come out with me."

"That depends. Are you going to be in the company of adults?"

Demian shook his head. "I don't make enough money to spend time in the company of adults. You know that."

"No thank you. I'm going home." And he added as an afterthought: "To see my family."

It sounded like a boast, though he hadn't meant it to be one. He certainly had nothing to boast about. And yet curiosity still nagged him: he wanted to know, at least, where Demian was going.

"But I'll give you a ride," he said. "In case you were wondering."

The wind pierced Martin's collar when they got outside, biting through the thinness of his jacket where it came together at the zipper. Demian was wearing only a hooded sweatshirt over his work shirt and wife beater. The vivacity of youth: something that Martin had never possessed, even when he was young. He sat shaking awhile after the engine started, and managed a few coughs.

"You gonna make it?" said Demian.

Martin shook his head no: no, you don't have to worry; no, I'm not going to make it. It was all the same to him. Eventually he gained his breath again, and pulled out.

"Where to," he said.

"Going to Sarah's place for a meeting. You should come."

Martin shook his head, still too winded to articulate why he wouldn't. There was no reason why a man of his or Demian's temperament would attend a Students For A Progressive Society meeting unless he were looking forward to spending time in the company of impressionable young women. Their small niche of the avant garde was good for a few things – male bonding, unfiltered expression, the forbidden thrill of samizdat communication – but it wasn't the sort of scene that attracted many, or any, attractive women.

They took Halsted all the way down: past the dot-com lofts and active warehouses, a couple restaurants lit like dim beacons along the black placidity of the river. The lights of the Loop soared into sight all at once, eye-filling and unbroken when viewed across the west-end lowlands. Only to vanish again behind overpasses and concrete condos, replaced in a moment by the thoroughfares and highways strapped like restraining bands across the city landscape. They passed Greektown and the UIC campus, and Demian started talking on cue when they reached the ungentrified neighborhoods to the south. He always did; maybe to ease his nerves, maybe because there wasn't much to look at besides sandwich shops and check-cashing spots.

"How's what's-her-name," said Demian.

"You mean my wife."

"Yeah."

"You mean Ellie."

"Yeah."

"She's doing just fine, Demian."

This was about as solicitous as Demian got. Martin should have been flattered. But he was not, and didn't care if he showed it.

"How come she never comes out?"

Martin almost said it was because she had a son to look after. But something stopped him. Something that felt like an instinct of self-preservation; he didn't know why.

"Because we've been married for a long time. She got her fill of Total Mobilization twenty years ago."

They caught a wave of greens: cruising easy southward on the empty weeknight streets. The tires thumped soft cadences over the seams in the concrete, lulling and regular like railroad ties.

"How was your break?" said Demian. "I haven't seen you."

"Let's just say it's good to be back."

"But you hate the city."

"True. But it's home now. I can't deny it."

His country town in Iowa wasn't the same as it used to be. It had lost the wild spark of his childhood, had become hopeless with a numbing and irreparable suburban hopelessness. People took drugs, watched TV, drove cars. Children stayed inside. Everything was on loan: the cars, the farms, the houses. Nothing belonged to anyone. As if the town had evaporated on the inside and only the shell was still in place. If he wanted wilderness, if he wanted authenticity, he could only find it now in the cities. And the same thing was happening there too.

"The book isn't coming along so well," said Martin. "In the city, in the country – nothing works. There's either too much or too little time on hand. It's like there's some sort of interference in the air. I'm blocked up no matter where I go. Frankly I'm wondering if it's worth it."

"You mean the book? Or life in general?"

Martin didn't answer at first. To him the two concepts were closely related, perhaps interchangeable. His work was his entire life. There was little enough joy to be had in the world; he had learned this long ago, and was content to bow out gracefully and let others fight over the scraps.

"I find myself running up against the inherent limits of language. Of thought itself. There's nowhere left to go."

"Sounds like a cop-out to me."

Demian got snotty when he disagreed with people. A side effect of youth: its energy, its naiveté. Martin had been the same way once. Demian went on:

"There can't be anything outside of language. If it's outside of language then it's outside of comprehension. If it's outside of comprehension then it's superstition."

Demian had the argument at the ready: loaded, chambered, primed to fire. His teaching-assistant brain was working overtime to figure out how to usurp, in whatever small way, the authority of the professor. And he was right: Martin had been flirting with entry to the noumenal. He didn't like using the word superstition. He danced around the concept: built a whole city of base camps at the foot of this vast abyss, planning for years the best way to plunge in. Yet he still could not bring himself to do it, and he was beginning to suspect that for him at least the preparation was going to be the entire point. Perhaps someone else could use his infrastructure for the descent – for the free-fall – but it wasn't going to be him. He was too old, had gotten started too late.

He didn't feel like explaining this to Demian; wasn't

sure that he could. If only there were a way to take the decades off his shoulders and lay them on Demian's – the exhaustion, the disappointment, the long, dragging hours of no fulfillment – then maybe he would understand. On further reflection, it had been a long and trying night. They had labored for hours over maybe sixty seconds of sound. Martin decided he could use a drink, even if it came at the price of undergraduate conversation.

When they got to the house Demian walked in the unlocked door and proceeded straight back to the kitchen. He peered in the freezer and asked if Martin wanted bad vodka or worse gin.

"Gin it is," said Martin.

"Mixer?"

"Anything."

Demian made two of whatever it was. They both tried it at the same time.

"Pineapple," said Demian.

"Nice. Adds a little sting on top of the sting."

A kid passed by the doorway dressed in neatly-pressed shirt and slacks. He glanced in, froze in place, dropped what he was doing to stop and stare at Martin. Martin stared back, wondering what sad circumstances had brought this young man to a house called Neverworld.

"Ravi," said Demian. "What the fuck are you looking at."

"Nothing. I just – I didn't know you were here."

"Here we are. You know Professor Hightower?"

The kid hesitated. "Sort of."

"Well why don't you say hi like a human being."

The kid extended his hand tentatively, as if reaching through the bars of a lion cage. His smile was pained: the smile of a man who feigns happiness for a living and forgets what real happiness is like. He shook hands with

Martin and withdrew as quickly as he could.

"Meeting starts in fifteen," he said, already walking away. "Twenty, tops."

Demian was mildly impressed. Which was the most impressed Martin had ever seen him. "Looks like you have a reputation, Professor Hightower."

Martin brushed it off. People got awed around him, mistaking reticence for some grand wisdom. But he always disappointed his proponents or detractors by being less than the black magic shaman they imagined him to be.

"Ravi's our 'community organizer,'" said Demian. Martin could hear the scare quotes in his voice. "Some weird birds in this place, man."

Demian fixed two more pineapple-gins, and Martin followed as he ascended the dark, narrow steps to the second floor. Demian proceeded through the corridor of closed doors, knocking finally at the last one, the light from inside casting a ghostly aura around its edges. There was no answer. Demian cracked the door to peer in, then swung it wide so Martin could follow him inside.

Sarah's room was in a state of ideological transition. It happened this way every time Demian attached himself to a girl: half the apartment was decorated with the objects of a past life – in this case, colorful flyers for feminist happenings, photocopied worker's manifestos – but encroaching on these like a disease were all the posters and records and books she bought to impress Demian, red and black and dour, stamped with pentagrams and runes of ambiguous provenance. It was always interesting to see how far the transition would progress before the girl saw through either Demian or his ideology. Usually, not very.

There were two beds in the room, set up parallel like a dorm: one empty, one occupied by the curled form of Sarah, a desk lamp shining on her like a spotlight. Her hair had gone from blonde to black since the last time Demian had brought her around. She was wearing only a night shirt, facing the wall, doing nothing. Not even dozing: her eyes were open and alert, hardly blinking. Demian gave Martin a look and sat on the empty bed. The look said: Let's approach with caution.

"Meeting in twenty," said Demian. Sarah said nothing. "Maybe you should get dressed."

Martin and Demian shifted their weight on the springs of the bed. Demian tried again:

"Where's Alanna?"

Sarah didn't answer him. But this time, at least, he had left himself room to continue the conversation unilaterally. He turned to Martin.

"Alanna's the roommate. You'd like her. I think she's your type."

Martin was unaware that he had a type. He nodded feebly, regretting his decision to come out with Demian.

"Sarah, I don't think you and Martin have ever met. He's the guy who runs the class I TA for. Maybe you've heard of him. But the stories aren't all true."

Sarah said nothing. Silence hung in the space where her reaction should have been. And when her voice finally entered the air it startled like words coming from a statue.

"Most people in this situation," she said, her voice flat and affectless, "would ask if anything was wrong."

"I'm not most people," said Demian.

He stared a moment, viper-like, at the back of her skull, then motioned to Martin that they were leaving. But Sarah could hear the creaking of the bedsprings, and spoke again as soon as they were standing.

"I heard Hannah doesn't come to the meetings anymore."

"I don't see what that has to do with me," said Demian.

"Everyone knows. We're not as stupid as you think we are."

"Right. You're so smart you spend all your time gossiping about my sexual habits. As if that matters."

"It's not about morality. It's about health. It's about common sense. She slept with twenty guys in Germany. That's not healthy for her. That's not healthy for you. And now, because you're such a whore, it's not healthy for me."

"That's just a rumor. The number of German guys is widely disputed."

"Alanna was there. She saw it."

"Yeah? She kept a tally? And who are you, miss feminist, to shame someone over that. Who gives a shit."

"It's not about shame. It's about being open and honest with your partners. Which you were not. And now you're down one more."

This time it was Demian's turn to be silent. Martin felt himself to blame somehow, as if his presence prevented Demian from unleashing his full measure of spite. He did nothing; just stood glaring tight-jawed at the tiny feminine form on the bed.

"Fuck you," she said. "Get out. Don't come back."

The lights were on in the stairwell now. SFPS members arrived from the outside world, carrying with them six-packs and homemade hummus and assorted grievances. Ravi, clipboard in hand, tapped his watch at Demian.

"Five minutes," he said.

Demian pushed past him without comment, heading for the front door. Martin followed, stepping apologetically around the confused community organizer. But a humongously tall girl thrust herself forward to intercept Demian before they made it out.

"Paul," she said, "I need to talk to you."

Demian sighed. "About Hannah?"

"No. What about Hannah?"

"Forget it. What is it."

The girl stretched wide her lipsticked mouth, paused before speaking; looked first at Martin and then at Demian.

"He's with me," said Demian. "He's cool."

She lowered her voice and stooped down closer to their level. "Cody got arrested again. He's out on bail, but he's not selling anymore. I've got clients calling and we don't have anything to give them."

"So don't give them anything," said Demian. "What do I care."

"But here's the thing. I don't think it's ever coming *back*."

"So what? You need the money?"

"Of course I need the money. Don't you?"

Demian could only play it cool for a second or two. "Yeah. Who the fuck am I kidding."

"I have an idea though. I just wanted to run it by you first. I have a friend who works reception at a doctor's office. She orders prescriptions all the time, she's got all the security codes. If we just—"

Demian cut her off with a motion of the hand. "We'll go over this some other time. I'm really not in the mood, Kim."

Kim's eyes went wide with concern when he turned to leave. "You're not staying for the meeting?"

"Not for all the Vicodin in the world."

Once outside, Demian lit a cigarette. He sucked it down and shook his head.

"What a fucking night," he said. "What a week. What a life."

They stopped at a bar a couple blocks from Martin's house. First for one drink, then two; then Demian said he'd take a cab home. There was too much to talk about. Over the fourth and fifth drinks he told Martin about Hannah.

Martin woke up alone in a cold house. Hungry, hung over; afraid to move and thus probe the extent of his pain. Ellie was gone; she worked the early shift at the campus administrative offices. His schedule was stacked with afternoon classes, his nights were occupied with his book or with Total Mobilization. She worked only part time, but sometimes it felt like they hardly saw each other anymore.

Fully awake the moment he opened his eyes, he lay in bed, waiting. He waited though he knew what was coming; waited and failed, as always, to fight the kindling of hope inside him. He knew it was childish: like waking from a pleasant dream and trying to convince yourself it was true. But hope moved inside him with a will of its own, against his every effort. Hope haunted him the way concupiscence haunted medieval mystics. And he had none of their countermeasures, either physical or metaphysical. Hope found a way in. Every morning it happened like this.

The sound reached its way down the hall: a distant foghorn, slowly building. The uninflected cry of a large and clumsy bird. George cried because he missed his mother. George cried because he was hungry. George cried because he wet the bed. George cried because he was four years old and still it was all he knew how to do. Closing his eyes against the pain, Martin swung his body out of bed.

He turned the thermostat up and started the coffee machine; then shuffled down the hall and paused outside the door to George's room. He felt no fear when lecturing extemporaneously for hours, when addressing hundreds from a podium, when sitting on a panel under intense scrutiny from his peers. But there was a constriction in his gut every time he had to confront his son. Eloquence, be it either the elucidation of difficult ideas or rhetorical smoke-screen, was of no use here. He lost his faculties of thought, his voice changed into something nasal and wheedling. He became hot and flushed if Ellie was around. It felt like someone was playing a trick on him. Like everything in the world and in his life had come together and conspired to play a trick on him.

But it was never as difficult as he feared it would be. The crying stopped as soon as he walked in. There were no tears on George's face. His crying wasn't an expression of anguish. It was more like a song: one note that droned through eternity, the hum produced by the whirring machinery of being. George was merely an instrument, giving voice to it.

He fed himself and the boy: a winter breakfast, hangover breakfast, rich and redolent. They ate in silence and, perhaps, contentment. But he couldn't be sure. He brought George to his study so he could keep an eye on him as he worked. There was no need for vigilance though: George sat where he was placed, either content or discontent or on a plane apart from such earthly commonplaces.

He spent time at his desk without results. His notes were scattered across the surface like a spilled deck of cards, gathering weight from dust. He was having trouble, lately, convincing himself that it was worth the effort. It was difficult to theorize about the world when there was no world about which to theorize. The physical was vanishing just as quickly, if not quicker, than the conceptual. Automated and synthetic, the world carried on indifferent to the input of mankind. Natural bonds meant nothing. Nations, races, wives, sons: more complications, external baggage without connection to the self. They weren't anything like you. How could they be – you weren't even anything like you.

The world was still in place physically, but man's words no longer corresponded with it in any meaningful way. Martin gave up after thirty minutes of stasis, anguish, blockage. He couldn't keep his concepts straight: the words blurred, changed, warped into others. It was all one; only a gray mush that resisted conceptualization, toxic runoff from the artificial manufacture of the phenomenal. He reached for a stack of student papers, two months old now, and began grading them by rote. Skimming them, looking for patterns of words and not cohesive thoughts. It all ran together.

He set aside the sheaf of papers and placed his head in his hands. Trying to resist the impulse; but he had already succumbed a long time ago. He switched on his computer so he could read the message once again. Old flames, forgotten friends: tangle of politics both party and personal. He read the message over and over, until the words were mere sounds, vocalized internally, lacking all meaning. Maybe they had never meant anything. This he could only hope.

He dropped George at the daycare center and parked in the faculty lot. And greeted the campus with what would have been disdain if the campus had had presence enough to produce a reaction in him. It was as if it had been designed not for beauty and not for functionality but only for alienation. In order to reach the flagstone walks and neo-classical facades of the old campus he had to trek through the concrete heaviness of the new one. Martin had lobbied hard for an office in the old campus. He didn't care how many stairs he had to climb, didn't care how drafty the room or how faulty the plumbing; all he wanted was a con-nection with the past that was visceral and immediate instead of merely theoretical. He wanted dust in his nose, splinters in his skin. When they forced him to take an office in the new campus he specifically asked for one without windows. He couldn't stand the sight of the place.

The buildings, high-walled and shorn of ornament, leaned and jutted at odd angles; built in the seventies to signal an international friendship of man, these gray and brown slabs of brutalism instead exuded menace from every vantage. As if they had been designed by extra-human functions, willed into matter by satellite signals and broadcast waves and the strange radiation thrown off by high voltage power lines. The campus was a cathedral of nothing, built out of nothing, for nothing; an uncannily faithful representation of the nightmare architecture of the contemporary world-spirit.

The sky over campus was always gray. Maybe it was just his imagination. But even the sunlight, when it came, was wan and filtered, as if it had passed through too many intermediaries and was robbed of all energy by the time it fell to earth. It was eerily quiet; all the students hushed and timid, their voices, their words, taken by the world as if by a thief in the night. The world could end and no one would notice. Not a shout, not a murmur, not from a single soul. He corrected himself: the world could continue ending. The years, now, passed much like this single day: gray and unlit, without sufficient differentiation between sunup and sundown. A sort of stasis which moved through time as if pulled by an outside force. Dead weight.

The mystics dreamed an apocalypse of flames and angels, of smoke and gaping hellmouths. But that wasn't how history had decided to resolve itself. The annihilation was slow and invisible; it crept, parasitic, into the heart of man, made its home in the spirit and from there carried out its work. Even mystics had nothing to dream of anymore.

All they could do was become professors, and lackluster ones at that.

Martin still had an hour to kill before his first class. He had come to campus early so he could get rid of George and pay a visit to Harold. But when he arrived at the old campus, its brick buildings held together with a webbing of leafless ivy, he found that it too was subject to the prevailing cultural rot: students were massed in the quad outside Harold's office, hoisting signs, attempting chants. Here, perhaps, was evidence of life: but it was a poor imitation, just a toothless reenactment of genuine outrage. Martin recognized several students from the house he and Demian had visited the night before. They appeared to be protesting the westward expansion of the university. But only because they didn't have words for what they really wanted to protest: the dearth of purpose or culture in their own lives, the meager job prospects afforded them by their liberal arts degrees, the creeping and unglamorous death of the entire world around them. Martin pushed his way through the crowd and walked up the steps to Harold's office.

He was standing with his back to the door, peering out the window at the quad. "The youth is getting restless," he said.

Martin picked a chair and sat in it. "That's what they'd like you to think. That's what they'd like to think too. I have my doubts."

"I don't see why they pick on *me*. I'm just arts and sciences. They should take it up with the dean. They should take it up with the school of engineering – they're the ones who are building the facilities."

"They don't want answers. They just want to make noise."

"Well, they do an excellent job at that. An excellent job, my friend."

Harold was the only friend, or even ally, Martin had on campus. He was a fossil preserved from a more sensible era: a time when academia had been a gentleman's pursuit rather than a tooth-and-claw struggle between overachievers, when a genial and rapidly aging specimen like Harold Rothman, his false teeth turned gray from red wine, could schmooze his way to the top and not do terribly much once he got there. Any actual improvement of the situation was out of his hands, he said. And he was probably right, which was why Martin respected him as a scholar, if not as a person.

Harold's collars were always frayed and wrinkled, his sweaters always stained. He kept liquor in the open behind his desk and always poured Martin a glass, even if he came to visit in the mornings. He was on his third or fourth marriage, but this one, too, was on the verge of disintegration. It was difficult for him to take anything seriously. When the students filed a complaint against Martin – that he had said something perceived to be insensitive, that he had the temerity to give them the grades they deserved – he always went to Harry so they could share a laugh about it.

"They take these things too seriously these days," said Harold. "They take *everything* too seriously these days. But that's not it, exactly."

He smacked his lips and plunged into thought. Physically plunged – shoulders hunched forward, frown pressed against a balled fist.

"They take all the unserious things very seriously and let everything serious pass unexamined. If only you'd been born ten years earlier, my son. If only you'd gotten in a little sooner, you really might have been something in this academic world of ours. As it is now, well…it's all shit. But we can always tip our glasses."

So that was what they did. Martin gagged slightly; it was still before noon. Harold poured himself seconds.

"I wouldn't worry too much about the protestors," said Martin. "I've seen how they operate. We've got a man on the inside."

"You don't say. Who is it?"

"My grad student."

Harold began shaking his head in disbelief: "Why on earth–"

"For the women."

"Ah, yes. Of course. I remember those days too. 'For the women,' we said. That was the joy of youth: not its variety of experiences but its plethora of excuses. But that was then, and this is now. We've no more excuses."

He poised the bottle over Martin's empty glass. Martin made a gesture of refusal; he had a class to teach. Harold, as if feeling sorry for Martin and not himself, shrugged and filled his own.

Five minutes into his lecture he regretted his refusal of the second glass of scotch. He could never escape the feeling that this was somehow beneath him; that the college experience had been expressly engineered to insult him. He stared into the face of the future ruling class: future managers, future administrators, future officials, future taste-makers. They all *appeared* to be thinking. They nodded earnestly, narrowed their eyes, chewed the ends of their pens – but this was all just for show, and had nothing to do with the production of actual thoughts. That was what they'd been taught; that was how they'd gotten this far in the world. They thought that the truth was something simply bestowed, something one could check off on a list, place forefront on a self-lauding resume. But truth did not work like that. It revealed itself only in the loneliest silence or the most terrible violence. This most important lesson was one he could never say; one the children were determined to never learn. The classroom was like a show trial, like any sort of psychological warfare: it humiliated insofar as he could never admit to being humiliated by it.

There was only one student who wasn't aping the body language of the would-be rulers of the world. But not because she was brighter or more attentive. Hannah Orenstein, Demian's star pupil and current bunkmate, was sleeping face-down on a cushion of blank notebook paper in the back of the room. He finished his lecture without drawing attention to her. And, struck with an unexpected barb of tenderness, lowered his voice so that he wouldn't wake her. He knew, better than anyone else, better than the GPA-chasers taking dictation in the front rows, that she wasn't missing much. When class was adjourned no one bothered waking her on their way out the door. No matter what their stated majors, they were all born bureaucrats, past masters at passive aggression, and it wouldn't bother them terribly to see her punished.

Martin stood behind the lectern, avoiding eye contact, waiting for the door to swing shut. When the room had emptied he walked to the back and sat in the desk next to Hannah, studying her first with amusement, then with a sort of pity. Then a deeper sense of fascination, as if puzzling over a painting in a gallery: searching for thematic patterns, probing inwardly for new ways of seeing, so that the false depths of his person might find harmony with the false depths of the composition. For a moment he wondered if it was really her. He never took attendance, paid little attention to his students. But Demian had shown him pictures – pictures she hadn't intended for public exhibition – and this girl didn't look anything like that girl. On the outside, maybe. But on the inside, in terms of presence, in terms of aura: not at all.

Strands of black hair fell in concentric arcs across the white paper. Her sleep was heavy and untroubled, as if she were guarding a deep secret between her cradled arms; the sleep of the innocent, but brought on by the exhaustion of experience. If he didn't wake her she'd sleep through the next class too. Maybe on into the night in perfect peace. And Martin imagined then that all the night in the world was living inside this girl, and only came into being when she breathed it out, sleeping.

"Hannah," he said.

Only the room heard it. He said it again, and listened closely this time to his voice:

"Hannah."

It sounded like someone else speaking. Not that his voice felt different as it left his throat and spread in the air; only like he was hearing it for the first time. Compelled by the novelty, he continued this dialogue with himself:

"Hannah. Hannah. Hannah."

He reached his hand out; hesitated a moment near her shoulder. Certain that she'd be startled – as if he'd seen it happen already – he shook her awake.

She looked up sleepily, blinked at him twice, buried her face again in her folded elbows. "It's too early," she said into the desk.

"It's two in the afternoon."

She kept her head down, hiding herself from the world and all it stood for. Martin was in a position to ruin her day if he so chose. Certainly it was what she expected. But why would he want that – what good would it do. If anything he admired her defiance. Even while sleeping she showed more character than the ostensibly conscious students.

"I don't blame you," he said. "I wish I could sleep through my classes too."

She rolled her head toward him and opened her eyes, but still did not sit up. "Yeah?"

"Yeah. I know all this stuff already. I wrote it. And no one else seems to want to understand it. Yourself included."

"I'm sorry."

She meant it; he believed her. There was no coquettishness in her voice, no duplicity; it was clear and bell-like, without undertones or ancillary inflections. Again he had to question whether he had the right girl. Maybe Demian was an even bigger liar than he thought. She leaned back in her chair, arranged her tumult of hair with a practiced shake of both hands, and smiled at him.

"So what did I miss?"

"Everything so far, I think. I haven't gotten any of your papers. I don't see you at many lectures. I can't pass you like this, you know."

"I know."

"So why bother coming at all? If you wanted to sleep you could have stayed in your bed."

"Just to be polite I guess."

Martin felt a flush of warmth in his face, felt his lips tighten to a smile as if shrunken by the blast of heat. He shook his head to try to escape her darting eyes.

"I can't pass you on politeness. I wish I could, but I can't. You can choose between private tutoring or failure. Those are your options."

"Okay. Who's tutoring me?"

The thought came at him like an attack: Demian. That would make for an easy grade. She was thinking it too. And then a pang of unexpected panic: anyone but Demian. He had girls enough. He could have any girl but this one.

"I will."

"Yeah? Do you tutor all your failing students?"

Already she had caught him out. He was not very

good at this: at concealing his motives, at advancing his agenda; at the thousand little duplicities inherent in the interaction of men and women. Ellie was charmed rather than off-put by his inexperience, and that was why they were married. He had to stifle the urge to explain this to Hannah. This: all of it. Ellie and him and love and the world. Yes: all his exhaustion, all his ennui – all could be given to her. All in a single word. Martin had already made his choice by the time he realized that here and now, for the first time in what felt like years, there was an actual choice to be made.

"HOLD ON. HOLD UP." Topher, eyes unfocused and fogged-over, reached his hand out. "Gimme."

Isaac hesitated, his sledgehammer held at mid-heft. He'd just met this guy, and didn't know yet if he could be trusted with instruments of demolition.

"Give it here. I have an idea."

Isaac glanced at Guy for guidance. Guy gave a thumbs-up: surreptitious, below the belt. Which was good enough for Isaac. It was Topher's apartment, after all; he could demolish it as he saw fit. Isaac surrendered the sledgehammer and stepped back without being told.

Topher had just moved into the warehouse. Now rechristened the Werehouse, it was currently being converted for use as a venue slash gallery slash illegal bar slash drifter crash pad. The first show was in a couple of hours; Guy had invited Isaac to help take out the last of the walls. Topher was said to go to school with them, though Isaac had never seen him around campus before. He apparently wasn't in the habit of attending class regularly.

Most of the debris had already been cleared out. There was nothing in the space now except some metal desks that were too heavy to move and some plaster walls around the corner offices. The previous tenants, a handful of either artists or teenage runaways, huddled over a hot plate, warming themselves and waiting for the water to boil. Topher's voice echoed off the bare walls:

"Hey, you kids might want to move. I'm gonna try something."

They either didn't hear or were too numbed with cold and hunger to care. On the bare floor beside them was their dinner: nothing but a carton of eggs and a shaker of salt. Topher shrugged and hefted his hammer. Wound up, three, four times, and at the fifth let fly, wincing even before the hammer made contact. It crashed through the wall above the kids, rained plaster down, bounced off and sent water from the pot racing in steaming snakes across the floor.

"Oh, shit," said Topher. On his face first levity, then concern, then anger: all the sociopath stages of grief. "Hey! I told you kids to fuckin' move!"

Silent, submissive, they stood and shook the sheet-rock from their rags and matted hair. Topher marched over and swatted their clothes in a sort of attempt to clean them up. Nudging the egg carton with his feet, he watched the yolk and broken shells run out. He sighed and hesitated, wondering what best to do; finally, took out his wallet. The kids seemed to be expecting this.

"Buy some McDonald's or something," he said, "you don't look too good." He poked with agony around his empty wallet and finally produced some bills. "Have a coffee too, stay out of the way for a little while. We'll be done in a couple hours."

"Where are they going," said Guy, watching them shuffle out the door.

"McDonald's," said Topher.

"I mean in general. Where are they going tomorrow."

"I dunno. Sounds like their problem."

Topher picked the hammer up and spun it in his hands to reacquaint himself with its center of gravity. He wound up, swung it sideways, and dented the metal piece that joined the walls at the corner; spinning around back-handed, made contact again and broke it in two. Guy had to jump back to keep from being clipped. Topher didn't notice.

"Who would've ever thought," he said, panting with satisfaction. "All my life people have been telling me to build stuff up. Turns out I was meant to tear it down."

Isaac learned to work the sledgehammer; learned to heft it with two pulls and let it topple gracefully with its own weight. His shoulders burned and his hands went numb from the  shock. He ended up taking down more walls  than anyone else. So far, one and a half years into his college ca-reer, his every effort, academic, romantic, otherwise, had come to nothing. At best, embarrassment. The rubble un-derfoot was the only mark he'd been able to make on the world; this was all he was good for. Breathing heavy, sweat-ing now under his layers, he propped the hammer in the corner and returned to the others. Topher clapped slowly, the impacts ringing hollowly through the open floor.

"What's his deal," he said to Guy, just loud enough so that Isaac could hear.

"Girl problems," said Isaac.

"What girls," said Guy.

Isaac shrugged. "That's the problem."

Speaking of which, Guy had to split; he was going to fetch Blue from a nearby warehouse and bring her back once the show started. He trotted down the stairs, whistling, problemless, and Isaac and Topher just sort of looked at each other a moment.

"Let's get rid of these desks," said Topher.

An industrial-sized door, caulked up and painted shut, took up most of the wall on the side of the building facing the abandoned lot. That was probably how the desks had come in, but it was uncertain if the door had seen any use since then. Topher rang the hammer against the metal latch and popped it open on the first shot; the mechanism fell to pieces and tinkled on the floorboards. But the epoxy held between the two halves of the door, and the paint stuck on the hinges, and all his hammer did was dent the metal on impact. He put his shoulder into it to distribute the weight better; still nothing. He looked at Isaac and flicked his wrist at the door. Isaac didn't understand.

"Together," said Topher.

"What if it opens."

"That's what's supposed to happen."

"But we'll fall out."

Topher put his hands on his hips and sized up the problem like an engineer, his head cocked as he worked out the solution.

"We might not though."

Isaac agreed to go on three. It wasn't that he trusted Topher; he just had very little to lose.

They knocked a crack in the caulk on the third try. The smell of the cold came in from outside and an edge of murky light shone through between the doors.

"Next one should do it," said Topher, and he tapped his left shoulder. "Fresh shoulders this time."

Topher didn't wait for three, though he was the one counting. He hit first and went flying, feet bicycling through empty air. But Isaac was there too somehow, and his hand found Topher's collar without him telling it to. They both ended up on the floor, more or less intact. And in front of them, framed like a photograph: the low rectilinear Pilsen skyline, warehouses and factories breathing smoke into the gray wash of light above. A hidden world revealed, though it had always been there. It was like they owned it now, having found this way of looking at it.

The desks were a two-man job, squealing against the floor and leaving trails of wood shavings where the legs had gouged a path. Isaac and Topher worked together until gravity took over and the first desk hit the lot below with a gonglike sound, hollow and sustaining. The last desk sounded a defeated note, less sonorous, as it clanged atop the other three. Isaac anchored himself to the wall while Topher held his hand and reached over the open air to shut the door. Friends now, or at least accomplices, they drank away the hours until Guy returned and the guests arrived.

The floor crowded slowly with assorted misfits, most of them in their thirties or older, all of them male, none of them very threatening. Isaac wasn't sure at first if they weren't looking for a model railroad convention that was happening on some other floor. Topher left him to mingle with the others, and he found himself wishing there were something more to destroy. And certainly there would be if he looked hard enough for it. He planted his back against a wall and scanned the crowd until he saw Guy, who had returned empty-handed except for a six-pack.

"Where's Blue?" said Isaac.

"Blue blows. Where's Cordelia."

"I don't know."

"Are you saving yourself for her or something?"

"No."

"Can I have her then?"

"No."

"Next time you see her give her my number."

They eyed each other warily, smiling and not smiling at the same time, each trying to figure out how much the other was joking. But Guy should have known better:

this was something Isaac never joked about.

"I would *murder* you," he said. Just the thought of it made him want to kill. Guy opened his mouth but the swelling crowd jostled them apart before he could respond.

The room was filling up with younger people, friends of the residents, prospective tenants, more interested in partying than fascist aesthetics and nihilist praxis, and the die-hards in the back grew blotchy and sweaty in the increased heat. They plucked at damp shirts and shuffled their feet, waiting in discomfort for the show to start. Then came a shift: the older crowd sidling forward sheepishly, almost reluctantly, as if the ground beneath them were giving way. Topher and a kid covered in zits and some fatter, older guy were setting up tables of audio gear in the corner of the room designated for the stage. The younger people moved to the back to chat and the mob of older people ringed a semi-circle around the performers. Isaac wavered somewhere in the middle, identifying with neither, belonging, as always, nowhere.

The music started. Or something started. Isaac wasn't sure what to call it; wasn't sure if it wanted to be named. It was the howling of a vacuum, the amplified screeching of never-satisfied need: the screaming of the spirits of the world as they labored in the endless turning of the globe. He scanned the room, wondering what everyone else made of it, wondering why they were there. The older people nodded dutifully, somewhat enthusiastically, to the non-beat of the non-music. The younger people just looked annoyed that the volume had forced them to stop talking. Isaac's eyes halted then, as if fixing reflexively on an imperfection in a pattern. He focused his eyes in the darkness, his sight improved by the imposition of deafness: tucked against the back wall, silent as a totem, blending chameleonlike in the grime and shadow, was Hannah.

His mind worked to assess the situation. She was alone. She didn't seem to want to be there. So either she was meeting someone there or this someone had left her alone for some reason. It had to be a man – Isaac wasn't sure if he'd ever seen her in the presence of another female. The question was who: he hadn't thought that she was within six degrees of separation to a scene like this. But he wouldn't have thought that he was either. So he decided to do what he always did: decided to wait. Half conscious, as always, that his window of opportunity would shortly close, and relieved already by this reprieve from action.

But whole minutes passed and no one returned to her side. No one seemed to even notice her there, and she, as if fading from existence, withdrew into herself, leaning forward from the wall with her hands pinned behind her back, looking like a figurehead mounted on the prow of a doomed ship. Isaac's pulse picked up with the ticking of the seconds as fate imposed itself on him. To refuse to act now would only invite regret or overcompensation. And as he approached Hannah, as he felt with strangled horror his feet moving beneath him, he understood, but from the opposite side, how it felt, and what it meant, when a girl was seduced by a man. There was choice in the matter, yes. But the shame of not choosing was enough to render this choice nominal at best.

"Hannah," he said.

She didn't hear him; kept staring straight ahead, numb to the noise and tumult.

"Hannah."

She stared.

"Hannah. Hannah. Hannah."

It took the form of an incantation: just a breath slowed by a touch of the tongue, chanted to the empty skies and vanishing without leaving so much as an echo. Isaac reached out to touch her, slowly, haltingly, as if afraid that his hand might pass straight through her shoulder. And what would he be left with then?

She staggered slightly when he made contact and blinked as she left her trance state. Isaac wondered if he'd be recognized in the dim and unfamiliar surroundings. It had been a long time since they'd last seen each other. She'd probably met a lot of guys in the meantime. But her eyes grew wide and pleased, black like deep water, sparks of recognition flashing in her irises. He asked what she was doing here. She pointed at her ear: she couldn't hear.

"Who are you here with?"

She kept her finger pointed at her ear and mouthed something. Every time Isaac spoke she mouthed the same thing. To him it looked like "I can't."

*I can't. I can't. I can't.*

He pointed at the roof: "Upstairs?" he said, slowly so she could read his lips. He put two fingers to his mouth to mime the act of smoking. Hannah, maybe relieved to finally understand him, maybe grateful that someone was finally talking to her, maybe just genuinely glad to see him, nodded her head yes, and in doing so shook her hair in her characteristic way, darting her eyes from side to side as if to watch it move.

Isaac found the emergency exit in under a minute. This was one of the few things he was good at: in social situations he could sense the path to higher ground like an animal escaping a flood. He stuck a spare brick in the door to prop it open and climbed with Hannah to the roof of the warehouse.

Across the industrial wastes, seen from that height as an unbroken lake of black, the towers of the Loop glowed in golden columns, their red beacons fading and unfading in the swallowing night. Smoke hung in still plumes from nearby factories as if frozen in the cold, and Isaac and Hannah, revolving awed in the panorama, released small clouds of their own humble production. Hannah held out a lighter in her striped fingerless gloves.

"Do you have cigarettes?"

"No," said Isaac. "I was hoping you did."

"No. I don't."

She pocketed the lighter and stood there shivering, tremors audible in her pattern of breath. Leaning forward as if expecting him to warm her somehow. There was a time when he might have tried. But bitter now from past rejections, keenly aware of chronic personal failings, he let her go on shivering. She never wore enough layers. Her nose and fingers always turned red from the cold, and seeing this again, reminded of the body blanketed deep within her coat, Isaac was struck with new tenderness at the sheer fragility of the thing.

"What are you doing here?" he said. "I didn't think this was your scene."

"I didn't think it was yours either."

"Good point."

Hannah said nothing. Her attention was already starting to wane. Isaac was never very good at keeping her entertained. As the months went on it became harder and harder to understand what she had ever seen in him. He tried again:

"I should have at least brought something to drink."

Hannah reached in her coat and produced a small flask, only half as wide as a normal one.

"In case of emergencies?" said Isaac.

"It's always an emergency," said Hannah.

She took a swallow and passed the flask to Isaac. He placed his mouth on the lip and left it there for a moment, tasting cold metal, before taking a drink. When he handed it back he could see Hannah's whole hand trembling.

"It didn't work," she said. "I'm still cold."

Isaac blinked. And wondered for an instant if that wasn't an invitation to something. He wasn't sure what. But by the time this thought had petered out it was already too late to act upon it. Hannah scuffed her shoes over the desert of pebbles and crushed glass and leaned her hands forward on the ledge of the skyline-facing side. Isaac shuffled to join her. And just waited: without tension, and without expectations, waited. The city around them hushed, deferent, waiting too. There was a crystalline quality to the air itself, as if the two of them and everything within sight were suspended in the glass of a paperweight. There was no wind, for once; Hannah's hair, hanging in still ringlets, rippled mirrorlike with reflected moonlight. Isaac watched the beacons on the towers arrive and depart from the world, breathing deep the salty-fresh scent of a frozen city, and was reminded of their friendship the year before, when everything was new and the world was only as big as the two of them.

But the time came to consider his next move. He didn't know why. He was happy where he was. Or if not happy then close enough; closer than he had been in a long time. But it was a voice that came from outside him, the received wisdom of a thousand generations of men. Guy, Topher, everyone but Cordelia, and maybe her too, would say the same thing. Though Hannah's back was turned to him, he could feel his cheeks grow hot with the pressure. He didn't want to break the stillness, but knew already that he would. And in the seconds before he acted took some time to mourn the passing of the moment. His voice was strained and artificial, hitting only wrong notes:

"You should get new gloves."

She didn't respond. He half suspected that she

knew what was coming and was doing what she could to delay it. Her fingers were poised on the ledge as if preparing to strike a chord on a piano. Like she was orchestrating the silence, playing it, and at her command it would cease and everything would go back to normal, as loud and fast and meaningless as the tumult downstairs. Her hands went slack and slid back from the edge. Isaac pounced before they disappeared from sight: put his hand on hers and felt it wriggle warmly underneath, pliant, assenting at first. But it drew back in an instant, collapsing like a cat that didn't want to be held, and then her hands were hidden safely in the pockets of her coat.

"Not you too, Isaac," she said without looking at him. She leaned over and touched for a moment his arm with the side of her head. It reached to just below his shoulder. "Not you too."

Isaac stayed on the roof for a long time after she left. He was hot despite the cold: every molecule vibrating, directionless, burning with agitation. His mind crowded with inarticulate rage like the white noise pouring from the speakers below. He stayed still, still as the skyscrapers, still as the night, until the excess heat left his body, until his pulse slowed and the cold brought numbness to the extremities of his face. He waited just a minute longer – forced himself, mortifying the flesh – and by the time he got inside was genuinely glad to feel the heat and smell the sweat rising up the staircase.

Topher's band was still onstage, though no one else was paying attention to them. They'd played for too long, exhausting even the autistic focus of the noise aficionados. Topher, microphone in hand, jumped into the crowd to stir up hype. But this didn't work either. Most just brushed him off, staggered awkwardly away. These weren't the most graceful people when it came to physical interaction. Someone, bored with the show so far, stepped up: circled sharklike and shoved him from behind, and Topher, wheeling around, acting on animal instinct, clocked him just below the eye. Immediately the sound cut out. The fat one killed all his switches and pulled the plug on the kid with the zits. He shoved a finger in Topher's face and shouted, his thick-rimmed glasses fogging with perspiration. Topher kept trying to apologize, but the other guy wasn't looking for an apology; it took three people to hold him back. His arms broke free now and then, swiping in clumsy arcs in Topher's general direction. Topher backpedaled, hands held palm-out in supplication. The rest of the crowd melted away to give them space; the spell was broken, the show was over. Isaac scanned the far corners of the room: no sign of either Guy or Hannah. There was nothing left for him here. Regretting now the body heat he'd squandered on the roof, he descended the stairs and walked back to the train.

Hannah didn't want to wake up. Consciousness dawned in her mind but she fought to keep her eyes closed. Trying to remember where she was and what she had done. Some faded impression in her mind told her that she had met up with Demian, that she had gone home with him. That was why she didn't want to wake up. That was why she didn't want to open her eyes and find out the truth.

Just as her eyelids began to flicker the pain cascaded again in the front of her skull and she shut them tightly. She tried to think about something else, tried to feel the texture of strange sheets upon her bare legs. Inching them further and further, searching for a presence, a warmth, not her own. It didn't matter who else it belonged to. It was like being suspended in a solution, a specimen of observation; like only in that context, in the presence of a silent other, could she begin to understand herself.

But the pain came creeping back again; slowly, like memory; no avoiding it. She held out as long as she could, then sat up and opened her eyes in one sudden motion, doubling the pain in order to get it over with quicker. She was in Demian's room but Demian wasn't there. It was quiet all throughout the apartment. She was relieved at first, then disappointed. Not because she wanted to see him – because it suddenly seemed like it was all a waste of time. Like she could have just stayed at her apartment and imagined it all and spared herself the trouble of being hungover, spared herself the humiliation of being undressed and far away from home. She didn't even know where all her clothes were. She was tempted to shed a quick few tears. Just because her head was hurting and she didn't know what to do about it. Because she didn't want to be there but she didn't want to have to go through the process of leaving. The thought of tears tempted her, that was all, and brought some water to the eyes like saliva in the mouth. But she couldn't take the chance; she didn't want Demian to see. She held them in and breathed deeply until the feeling passed. Breathing still, she swung her naked legs out from under the covers and proceeded on bare feet across the cold floor.

Demian was eating a plate of eggs at his kitchen table. It was visibly difficult for him to chew: one half of his face had swollen to twice the size of the other one. He didn't notice her, or pretended not to, until she spoke:

"That bruise looks terrible."

"It's fine," he said, still without looking at her.

"It looks like you should go to the hospital."

He shook his head.

"If something hurts too much to sleep, that's a good

sign you should go to the hospital."

"I wasn't tired. It doesn't hurt. That faggot sucker-punched me."

"Language."

"Faggots are faggots."

"Enough."

When silence fell once more she took a few halting steps forward. She wanted to get closer to the wound; wanted to press her fingers against his cheek. She didn't know why. She knew it wouldn't help him. But she felt compelled like a pilgrim in front of a relic. She kept approaching until she was in reach, but still she didn't touch him.

"Have you taken anything?" she said.

He shook his head and chewed his eggs with a funny sideways motion of his jaw.

"I'll get you something."

"Better not do that, Hannah."

She stepped into the bathroom and looked in the medicine cabinet. Stared a second until everything made sense again. She carried all the bottles back to the living room and threw them at Demian as she read off each label.

"Percoset. Klonopin. Adderall. Oxycontin. Adderall. Adderall. Adderall."

None of them hit their target. Demian stayed still, the bottles went wide. One landed in the eggs; most banged off the table or hit the cabinets behind.

"I told you not to look," said Demian.

"Jenna. Cheryl. Sarah. Caryn. Sarah, Sarah, Sarah."

"My friends look out for me."

"I know all about your friends. Everyone does. They don't come to the meetings anymore. They leave with you one day and then they never come back."

"Kick me out then."

"I'm not saying you should be kicked out."

Demian put his fork down. "Then what are you saying, Hannah."

She didn't know. She hadn't thought this far ahead. But she could see what he was getting at. She was just another one of the girls. The only difference was that she didn't have any useful prescriptions.

"You're not saying anything. Tell me. Have I done anything wrong."

"It's not about right or wrong."

"No no no. No obfuscations. Use clear language. It's all we have. Tell me. Have I done anything wrong."

Demian always did this. He always acted like he could take the floor out from beneath her feet if he wanted to. He always forgot that she didn't depend on him for anything. But, thinking this, she didn't have time to think anything else, and she still didn't know what to say to him. She wished she were wearing more clothes. She wished she could disappear. Demian picked up his fork again and continued forcing himself to eat.

"You don't have any answers, of course. Which doesn't surprise me. Are you going to the soup kitchen today?"

"I wasn't going to."

"You never go. I wonder why. I never see you cook. You know, I never see you around food at all. I wonder why that is."

It should have been the easiest thing in the world to leave. She didn't care about him and he didn't care about her. They had said as much, and in as many words. But still she couldn't move from the spot.

"I guess it's always a good idea to stay in shape," he said, trying to look disinterested as he pushed the eggs around his plate. "I guess you never know when one of your friends will hop on a plane from Germany."

Her clothes had scattered themselves all over the apartment. It was like there had been an explosion. Painfully conscious now of Demian's eyes following her as she picked up all the pieces, she paused behind a wall to make sure she had everything. She didn't; was missing a sock, a sweater, and it was cold outside. She pulled some of his things from his drawers just to layer up and tried not to look at him as she went out the door.

The sun was so bright that she mistook at first the bite of cold for the sensation of heat on her skin. The strong rays of late afternoon melted the ice in the road, reflecting the scene above in fluid mirrored blue and gold and white. The world was sudden in its presence, startling in its clarity, and she wasn't up to the task, today, of standing up to it. She veiled her eyes behind her lashes and stepped onward as the wind drew watery tears from her ducts. Something in her was bent to the point of breaking – and yet it wouldn't break. She didn't know what it was. She didn't care; just wanted it to break and then be done with it.

Hangovers were tough for her. She was smaller than most girls, and didn't drink often. Only when she was nervous, which she always was when she went out; when she was with Demian, who knew this, and who liked making her more nervous, though he still didn't think she could tell. Her headache was so strong it made her dizzy, but she couldn't imagine any way to get reparative nutrients inside of her. Her stomach was empty and full at the same time: empty with a hard kind of emptiness like air frozen solid. All the space was already taken. Her heart was leaking emotive fluid and there was no room in her for anything else. It wasn't true, but no other explanation did it justice. It wasn't just words, wasn't just a metaphor.

Cold water from the sidewalk nipped at her one bare foot through a hole in her sneakers. She kept marching forward. Men watched her: from across the street, from behind the streaks of glare on car and restaurant windows. She didn't turn her head to confirm; didn't want to make eye contact. She didn't want to exist for them anymore. But the thought opened up a bottomless feeling within her: she didn't know who else she was going to exist for.

She made coffee when she got home. It was a reflex, just something to busy her hands. But also what she genuinely wanted: another summary of her life, another living metaphor. The coffee slithered down her like a living thing and sat warm and filling in her empty stomach. When it worked its way into the blood her headache would be better, and maybe the nausea too. Already her stomach twitched with a second pulse in the dark cavity of her body. But until the caffeine spread further, awakening the other organs, she sat at her desk, upright and attentive, feigning productivity. Because even when she didn't have anyone to perform for she still had to perform somehow.

A few times she had dropped by Martin's classroom after his last class of the day. Skipping Demian's discussion section now and attending Martin's lectures instead of the other way around. She had to write a paper: that was the deal. One paper, he said, and he'd pass her. And still she couldn't do it. She asked him what she should write about. Half-vamping, but she couldn't help it. Maybe just because it was so fun to watch the role he played after, the sententious, unsmiling elder.

"Look inside yourself," he said. "Find the one idea that holds the whole mechanism together. Go inside that one idea and break it into pieces. Into molecules and sub-molecules. Put it under a microscope and try to figure out what it's all made of."

"And have you figured out what it's all made of?"

She hadn't meant the question seriously. She hadn't

known what to say, so she'd retreated into her usual irony. But Martin never joked about these things; he pursed his lips and weighed his words, and Hannah didn't have the heart to tell him she was just kidding.

"I can see the component parts," he said. "But I'm missing something. I still don't know what's holding it together. Everything just floats. And right now everything's floating apart."

The coffee working now, brain humming with activity, she rested her forehead on her closed laptop. If only there were a trapdoor she could open and make everything pour out. But even then it wouldn't help. The circuits of her mind raced in closed loops, without unifying theories, without any sense of purpose. As soon as she joined two together another two slipped apart again. The trapdoor would have to be somewhere else. But there was nowhere that would do any good. Nowhere even to start. Empty mind, empty heart, empty stomach: there was nothing there.

Warmth from the coffee flushed all through her body, plumed up into her skull with a pleasant lazy dizziness. She shed her layers, stood and cracked a window wearing only Demian's clothing: a pair of boxer shorts and a sweater, both too big for her. Her limbs moved free in the tentlike folds of fabric, and she was happy to have her imperfections hidden for once from herself. She thought about changing, but all her other house clothes were also taken from boys she used to know. Sort of like trophies, only she was ashamed to have them. There hadn't been many outright heartbreaks in her life – she'd learned, at an early age, how to avoid them – but there hadn't been many amicable splits either. She took from them and they took from her until one of the parties could give no more, or lost the will to take. Most of the time this was her, and so she took their clothes just to take something.

Already night was falling; she had missed the day again. The day whose eyes she fled, the night whose blindness beckoned her. The twilight and its enchantments; the lure of freedom which led her always back to the sticky web of daylight. Trailing with her second-hand clothes that poisoned the air with the brain-bespinning scent of men and their unwashed bodies, unclean houses, unkempt lives.

Martin had given her his cell number – his "mobile phone number," he called it, drawn simultaneously to archaic and Continental forms of speech. In case she ever wanted to discuss things further. A phone number that circumvented the lines which had been strung over the earth and terminated at the table beside the bed he shared with his wife; a signal that instead beamed its waves through ethereal space, without any intermediaries, be they either copper wires or suspicious wives – further evidence, if any was needed, of the both literal and metaphorical floating-apart of things. He had not given her the number as an incentive to discussion but in order to confirm that which was already known. And he was waiting, for some reason, for her to confirm it for him.

She was waiting too. She didn't know what for. Waiting until the switch flipped in her that would tell her what to do next. Holding her phone in front of her, flicking it open and closed, on and off, searching its illuminated face for some sort of spark that was lacking in herself.

THE LIQUOR STORE WAS CLEAN, orderly, Asian-run. Isaac knew it wouldn't work as soon as he stepped inside. But Cordelia was counting on him, watching him from the front window. For her, he would humiliate himself. He had done it before and would certainly have to do it again. He slid his fake ID across the counter and rose up on his tiptoes, as if that might make him look older. The clerk looked down through his glasses and shook his head, disappointed by the effort.

"You shouldn't have spent so much time deciding what you wanted," said Cordelia. "It looked suspicious."

"You shouldn't have been watching me through the window! *That* looked suspicious too!"

They were blowing with the wind around the periphery of campus, where the university made clumsy overtures to the real world and the real world attempted to siphon what profit it could from the university. But neither the dorms dressed up as apartment buildings or the buffets dressed up as cafeterias had managed the synthesis: the cross-pollenization had rendered the product sterile, and no real experience could ever be born here. Bars, restaurants, full-service laundromats, clothing boutiques, all with an uncanny property about them, too bright, too clean, too empty, shed a surreal and colorless light onto the salt-chalked sidewalks. These weren't for them – weren't for Isaac, at least. It was his inability to fit in at these places that, even more than his inability to fit in with his classmates, had made him realize he wanted no part in their glorious future. Cordelia looked in at the mannequins and paused to read the menus mounted outside the doors, pretending as always to belong to the world of the living. But she didn't really, and maybe she knew it too, and this was why they got along so well together.

"Let's forget about it," she said. "I'm freezing."

"And do what else instead?"

"I don't know. Go somewhere warm."

"Like where?"

"I have a room. So do you. Use your imagination, Isaac."

He didn't say anything. He kept walking. He would rather walk forever, through whatever type of neighborhood, through whatever type of weather, than pass the night alone in a room with Cordelia. He had made that mistake once, and he didn't even like to be reminded of it anymore.

It didn't seem to bother Cordelia as much. She never flinched, as he did, when the conversation veered too close to a reminder. She, as well as all women, Isaac was slowly noticing, always kept potentially significant things in their proper proportion, and only got worked up over the insignificant.

They walked, without plan and without aim. The streets grew wide and dark as they proceeded away from campus, the parallel rows of streetlights converging to Vs down the lengths of the endless midwestern lanes. At the end of the horizon everything sparkled dimly like the stars above the country to the south and west. But there was nothing they could do but keep walking. Farther from campus, into a world of uneven sidewalks and abandoned lots and falling-down houses. All the windows had bars on them and most streetlights were dark; when cars whipped by they lit up the night like prison searchlights. Isaac and Cordelia kept quiet, as if they might attract predators if they raised their voices too high. And yet they pressed on. Death, mugging, embarrassment, fear, the claustrophobia of their own torrid friendship and the loneliness of mutual exile: these were small sacrifices compared to the thought of spending another Saturday night alone.

They found a strip mall. A liquor store with a glowing yellow sign sat between a used furniture store and a shuttered hot dog joint. Isaac pointed to a flask-sized bottle of whiskey and placed a ten dollar bill on the bulletproof glass carousel that communicated with the interior of the store. Several men outside watched, silently, this transaction. Cordelia waited beyond the parking lot, pivoting uncertainly up and down the street.

"Let's go," said Isaac, and they fell into step together.

"What did you get?"

"Terrible whiskey."

"But I don't like whiskey. You know that."

"I know. I panicked. I'm sorry."

Without breaking pace she turned and pushed him softly. "Go back! Get something I like."

"No way. That was the last time I ever do that for you."

The trip back to campus seemed to be passing much quicker than the trip away from it. Cordelia hummed to herself, bouncing her steps, unconcerned. Isaac didn't know what was supposed to happen next, and felt that his options were dwindling with every block. He took a swig of whiskey to help him think, and the tips of his fingers were already numb by the time he returned them to his pocket. Finally they reached the gates of the campus. He halted while Cordelia went on ahead. She spun on her heel and arched her eyebrows.

"Well?"

"One second," he said, flipping his phone open and dialing Guy.

It was good timing: he and Topher were just about to go out for booze. Guy lived in a single-occupancy room where no one would narc on them for drinking liquor or complain about them smoking cigarettes. Isaac could imagine worse ideas than bringing Cordelia around; at least, it was no worse an idea than drinking alone with her in a warm room on a cold night.

"Let's see the goods," said Guy, shutting the door behind them.

Isaac pulled the bottle of whiskey from his pocket,

but it looked very small now with three pairs of eyes upon it.

"Sorry," he said.

They sat on the floor since the chair and bed were piled high with clothes and papers. The boys sent the bottle around in a circle and Cordelia sipped contentedly from a glass of tap water. The bottle only lasted a few revolutions, and then Topher wiped his lips and tossed the empty plastic over his shoulder.

"So," he said. "Now what."

"I don't know," said Isaac. "This was my big plan, to be honest with you."

"Some plan," said Guy, who was learning how to talk like Topher.

The carpet smelled like three decades of vomit and body spray. The boys lifted themselves up and Guy handed out some cigarettes so they could add smoke to the mix. They lit up next to the cracked window and Cordelia, blushing from a small coughing fit, said she was going to go stand in the hallway for a minute.

"Who's the chick," said Topher.

"She's Isaac's," said Guy.

"No she's not," said Isaac.

"Then she's up for grabs?" said Topher.

"No," said Isaac.

"Why not," said Guy.

"Because I said so."

He glared at Guy to make sure he had been heard and understood. But Guy was looking up at the ceiling, blowing smoke from the corner of his mouth, apparently unconcerned.

"You heard me?" said Isaac.

They fell quiet when Cordelia stepped back inside the room. She found a seat on the bed between two heaps of laundry, and Isaac pitched his half-smoked cigarette out the window, followed by Topher and Guy.

"I know a party we could go to," said Topher. "Might as well do something with this buzz before we lose it."

"Where is it," said Isaac.

"Who cares," said Guy.

Topher shrugged and gestured out the window: "Out on the west side somewhere. We might have to take a train or two."

"It's too cold," said Isaac. "No way I'm waiting around on el platforms all night."

"Maybe we could take a cab," said Cordelia.

"Too expensive," said Isaac.

"We'll split it four ways," said Topher.

"Two ways," said Isaac.

He looked to Cordelia, but she was already pulling her scarf and hat and jacket on.

"Either way," said Guy, tossing him his coat, "you can't stay here."

Together they descended the cinderblock staircase and started walking through the light snow brightening the black asphalt footpaths. But Isaac didn't know where they were walking to. Everyone was facing forward, no one was talking, and he felt like he was intruding on something when he tried to get Cordelia's attention.

"Cordelia," he said. "Walk you home?"

At first there was no response; only the crystallized breath pluming from her mouth and evaporating before he could read the secrets encoded therein.

"No," she said, still staring straight forward. "I'll be alright."

Already they were approaching his dorm building. Cordelia's lay somewhere in the dark distance, past a further junction of the campus footpaths.

"Guy," he said, trying to stall them, "can I bum a

cigarette?"

But Guy handed it over without saying anything, without giving any indication that he was going to stop to smoke with him. They reached the dorm and Isaac let them go on without even thinking to ask for a light.

For a second he closed his eyes, not wanting to see what was going to happen next. They were still in sight when he opened his eyes again; walking together through the snow which now swirled violently across the bluish-white spheres of illumination cast by the lights lining the footpath; walking towards the turn leading to Cordelia's dorm, walking past it, walking on in the direction of the campus's west gate. Bass throbbed dully from Greek Row like the heart of the world lost somewhere in space, floating around in the cold expanses of the sky and trying to find its way back inside. Girls in skirts, jackets clutched tightly around them, approached from the direction of the music, shivering, pallid, cold as ghosts in their bright lamé minidresses. Isaac looked past them at the three figures receding into the darkness. His fingers were burning with the cold, and he remembered the presence of the cigarette in his hand. He still didn't have any way to light it. But if he could burn his whole life down in an instant – as surely he had done before, as surely he would do again – then surely he could light a cigarette with a touch.

MARTIN DROVE THROUGH GALAXIES of snow descending in parallax, falling in sheets like slow rain, caught in drafts and floating again upwards as if to escape the terrestrial world. Where was he going, Ellie had asked him. Out for band practice, he said. It had been so long since he had told a lie, even a small one, that he was shocked at the sensation it caused him, breathless and shy like a little boy. But Ellie would believe anything he told her. She was a woman who was born to believe, so much so that even after all these years of life in this world she still had not realized that there was nothing believable in it.

He had pecked out an answer to Hannah's message on his phone's eight-digit keypad. Impossible to convey subtlety, true intentions, any type of nuance whatsoever. A tiny digital signal floating through the winds like an SOS. He told her he could pick her up and take her somewhere – a bar, maybe, or a restaurant. Do you always tutor your students at bars, she said. He hadn't bothered answering her. It wasn't worth the effort. The whole situation was something of a lie, and she knew it, and this relieved him of the pressure of lying further. The words they used did not matter; the words were not the point.

He pulled to the curb outside of the address she had given him. For a moment he held his cellphone in his hand, wondering what he was supposed to do next. He was not used to having one, and his relationship with Ellie was so regular and domestic that he did not often have to use it. He opened the phone and scrolled through to her number – hidden under the name "Demian 2" – and hit the dial button, aware that young people were not in the habit of answering these phones which they carried on their person at all times, unsurprised when the call rang six times and then went to an automated voicemail. He closed the phone without leaving a message. He would lie to his wife, he would flee his responsibilities, but he would not be made to look ridiculous. And yet he still waited there – he didn't know how much longer. He kept the engine running, kept the lights on. But he didn't have any intentions of leaving either. And he still did not, minutes later, when the passenger door opened and a small dark figure slid into the seat beside him.

"Hello Hannah," he said.

"Hi," she said, shivering, drawing her seatbelt over her shoulder. "Where are we going."

"I don't know." He hadn't bothered thinking this far ahead. Still the whole situation felt unreal to him. Inauthentic, as if he had been placed in it by an agent far outside his control or comprehension. "I don't imagine there are many bars around here."

"No. I'm not old enough to go to bars anyway."

"Oh." His mind idled like the engine humming before him. "Are there any cafés?"

"No. Not at this hour."

"Or anything."

"No. There's nothing. That's why I like it here."

He reached out and turned the key to kill the engine. First as a gesture of defeat, and it was only after this that he realized what it meant, or could mean. He stared straight ahead through the windshield, which was already frosting over at the edges. He still had not turned to look at her. She clicked the release button and the seatbelt slid with a hissing noise across her body.

"Okay," she said. "Let's go."

The words came out like a sigh of resignation. How different this was from the adventurous women he had known in his youth, fired with idealism, filled with utopianism, so overbrimming with verve that they had no choice but to share it with others. How much the spirit of the world had changed in only a few decades. This girl truly believed that she had no other choice. He wondered, with a sinking heart, what the world had done to her.

Together they shivered as she searched for her keys. Together they mounted in silence up the narrow stairwell. Whatever it was he had been looking for, he was not going to find it here. How different from what he had expected. But maybe that was the point, if there was one. She opened the door to her apartment and disappeared into the interior without turning on any lights.

He followed her inside and the door closed by itself when he let it go. Somehow he was able to follow her without knocking into anything. Somehow he knew where she was going. Particles of dark swarmed in front of his middle-aged eyes, black on black, like the snow moving with other-worldly intelligence through the air outside. He heard the rustle of cushions as Hannah fell onto the couch. He remained standing where he was, a short distance away. He began to speak, but had to stop and clear his throat and start again.

"What would you like to go over, Hannah."

"Excuse me?"

"What aspect of the course. What would you like to talk about."

His voice diminished in volume, rose in pitch as he talked. He was nervous. Even in close proximity, even in this intimate setting, he still did not want to touch her. Not because he was afraid of corrupting her, or because he was afraid of being corrupted. Because he wanted to tell her everything, and he did not want anything to get in the way of telling her everything.

HE TOLD HER EVERYTHING THAT NIGHT. He told her about his pastoral youth and about his short stint in the Catholic seminary system. He told her about the disillusion that followed. Was it a philosophical disillusionment, she asked. At the time it was. At least, that was the form the disillusionment had taken. But it was a sickness deeper than philosophy; at least, deeper than any philosophy he had encountered up to that point.

He told her about his wife and child. Not everything – something stopped him, closing his throat, halting his voice, before he was able to tell her everything – but he made a start. He made an effort. He wasn't unhappy – he made it a point to tell her this. He wasn't unhappy because of his immediate circumstances. The sickness went deeper. He told her about the band he formed with Felix and Andy all those years ago. He couldn't justify it; he didn't even try. It was the sickness that had made them do it, the sickness that lived in everything. He told her about Regina and the emails she had been sending him recently.

Felix had known her since his childhood. He had been fawning over her for a decade. Only at a safe distance, though, so she wouldn't notice, or so he thought. They were too young then to know that women always noticed things like that. They were too young to know that there was no safe distance.

This was back in their undergraduate days, when Total Mobilization was just taking off, after they'd pressed their first LP and were starting to get major write-ups in the sort of minor publications that cared about bands like them. Back when the city had some character and the world some solidity to it, when books stood in racks at newsstands and newspapers were inches thick and the smell of slag and slaughterhouses still hung in the air. Felix didn't want her knowing about the band at first; was afraid it would scare her off. But he couldn't keep her away after they got their loft in Old Town, across from the abandoned church, so close to the river you could spit into its sludge from the roof. Felix tried to dissuade her with stories of bums and muggings and gunshots in the night, but that only stoked her suburban lust for adventure. She wanted to be part of the "downtown scene" like the one in the New York music magazines, and didn't care that in Chicago there was no such thing. But no one did much to disabuse her of her illusions. These were the first years of recolonization after decades of urban blight, and its adherents welcomed any warm body willing to give itself to the cause.

The air burned liquid-thick that summer. Coupled with the energy and exhaustion of youth it had an almost psychotropic effect on him. All Martin could remember from that period of his life was running. They ran everywhere, him, Felix, Andy: fled from gangbangers, charged at skinheads, jogged to parties because they were too broke for the bus, ran just for the hell of it down the empty corridors of the city. Their tennis shoes clapped stereoscopically through the air, multiplied in echo from off the rows of crumbling warehouses, the night glowing swampy green in front of them and the air choking their lungs with supercharged oxygen. They sweated. No AC in the apartment: they hung around in briefs and ran cold showers when they couldn't take it anymore. The only way to sleep was to get stumbling drunk first. There was no question of intimacy: Andy, like a fat praying mantis, kicked his lovers to the curb as soon as he was done with them. It didn't matter if they were lost, if they didn't have cab fare, if there was a gang war going on in the streets below. He removed them by force if he had to, dragging them by the hair and throwing them down the stairs.

Regina lowered herself willingly into this hissing cauldron of sensation after she got into art school. She told herself she wanted it; and to her credit bore her bruises and hangovers as well as the boys. They spent days in bars and nights in crowded warehouse lofts; took drugs together in the old church across the street and chucked fallen brickwork through the broken rose window. Before the summer was halfway over her weekend stays started lasting weeks. She became a de facto fourth roommate and the subject of many serious talks on the roof in the quiet hours before dawn.

"I think she likes you," said Felix.

"What makes you think that?"

"She told me."

"Oh."

Martin dipped his hand in a puddle of rainwater and ran his palm over his shaved scalp. They were out of beer and too shaken by a recent burst of gunfire to go out for more. The towers on Lakeshore Drive stood out now from the morning gloom, silhouetted by the sun rising in the east. Martin hadn't made any special efforts to impress Regina. Ellie was off at the local state school, pursuing a degree she would never use. They were still a couple, technically; had always been, technically, since Martin was fifteen. But it was hot that summer, and he was a long way from Iowa.

Martin tried shrugging it off at first: Regina wasn't his type. He said it out loud as if to reassure himself. But Felix wouldn't hear of it. Go for it, he said. He kept saying it; not just that night but other nights too. Go for it. Go for it. Go for it.

Somehow just the thought wounded Martin. And not just because of Ellie. Hardly because of her. It was the thought of Felix's cluelessness, his strangled self-effacement; the thought of Regina's body and all the rest. There on the roof, coming off a bender in the dewy cool of dawn, as the moon hung in a haze of creamy peach near the horizon, he trembled with empathy. The body's rebellion: don't bring me any closer to a soul not my own. One was too much for it to handle most of the time.

Martin had never planned on it, of course. But

nothing was planned out that summer – the days ran in open infinitudes, without constraints, without landmarks or horizons, and sometimes they had to make something happen if only to take their minds off the constant sensation of freefall.

Two decades later, he'd become accustomed to not thinking about it. Maybe this meant, in layman's language, that he'd forgotten about it. But he wasn't a layman, and nothing was ever so simple for him. Time, in his mind, was a living thing, an external organ of the body, and not just an arbitrary means of marking the blank space between events. The body absorbed a man's desires and victories and defeats, and everything he ever experienced became an inextricable part of his being. That was why the thought of him and Regina, twenty years after the fact, could still cause a twitch in his spirit like the ritual beating of a breast.

"It just happened." That was the official explanation. That was what they'd both told Felix without even convening to get their stories straight. It came naturally to the tongue. It was the spirit of the age speaking through them: "it just happened."

Except it hadn't. In retrospect it was easy to see the traps that they'd laid for themselves and for each other: buses missed, cans emptied, doors closed. Even at the time it was difficult for Martin to ignore the piled contrivances. One went through the motions of significance – literal motions, tactile, involuntary, as if that were enough to validate the process – but in the end it was as arbitrary as everything else in the culture surrounding them; an example of affection insofar as a freeway overpass was an example of a civic wonder. A generation or two previously they might have called it liberation, called it "free love." But by the late eighties it was no longer important enough to deserve its own name. It was just nothing, the same as everything else.

Felix didn't take it well, though he said he would. They all lied that summer, to themselves and to each other.

"You don't have to feel bad for him," said Regina. "We don't have to apologize for anything. He does this to himself. He's always been like this."

There was one more tour after that, another short record. Some magazines outside of the photocopied underground took the time to blurb them, if only as a curiosity. And then the original lineup for Total Mobilization was finished. There were the surface reasons: Andy going to grad school, Felix breaking his arm at a show, some threats of legal action lingering on the horizon. And then all the real reasons. Felix disappeared as completely as a man could disappear in the twentieth century. For the first half decade Martin still heard about him through friends of friends. Rumor was he'd gone out of his mind; just how far out, and in what direction, was still open to speculation. Martin could certainly see it happening. Toward the end of their nominal friendship he'd witnessed Felix take daily psilocybin-fueled walks in the ruins of the church. But he didn't entirely trust his sources. Their definition of sanity was idiosyncratic at best.

The surface grievances passed as all superficial things do; replaced gradually and silently like a new coating of skin. But the real grievances were never resolved, never flattened entirely beneath the weight of accumulating time. He could tell the truth about the universe, but when it came time to tell the truth about himself all he could do was lie.

He still missed Felix, though he wasn't generally in the habit of missing people. Regina had recently contacted him via email, asking if he wanted to catch up. It seemed as though history was repeating itself, or trying to, though he did not know why. He told all this to Hannah, though he was not generally in the habit of telling people things.

Hannah listened in silence. His eyes had adjusted to

the dark, but the shades were drawn against the streetlights, and all he could see was her silhouette. He thought he could hear her breathing, but maybe it was his own. Somehow he was sure she was awake. Somehow he knew the night was over and the gray dawn was rising outside the closed blinds. His mouth was dry and his legs were weak from standing. It had never occurred to him to move closer.

He didn't know what was supposed to happen next. The obvious thing had not happened, and neither of them knew what to do about it. Doubt crept in: maybe she was sleeping after all. Maybe he had spent all night talking into the darkness. His knees trembled from fatigue and anxiety. He waited, standing, studying the figure sitting up on the couch. He didn't have any way of knowing. But he was not going to leave until he knew for sure.

RAVI ALWAYS FOUND EXCUSES to stay late: he met with professors, joined clubs, attended lectures, holed up in libraries with books too esoteric for circulation. He kept binders at home, meticulously indexed and cross-referenced, filled with assorted bits of knowledge, scraps of conversation, insights that popped up on him when he was in the shower. It was like he mistrusted his powers of memory and wanted to make sure everything he experienced was assigned a place in posterity before he had a chance to forget it; like he mistrusted his powers of experience and wanted to entrust his life to a more worthy medium before he had a chance to ruin it. He never used the binders for anything, though he often daydreamed that he would. They grew like maggots gorging themselves on the decayed matter of his life. He didn't have time for anything else, he told himself; for friends, family, girlfriends. He had to work harder than the other students to get the same grades, and if he looked hard enough there was always something to work on.

The classrooms were empty and the only sound in the halls was the hollow rolling of the janitors' carts. The Arts and Sciences building emptied out early. Anyone serious about their studies – engineering majors, pre-law and pre-med students – had buildings of their own the congregate in, and Ravi seemed to be the only one who wanted or needed to work hard at the soft sciences. He kept his head down and tried to focus. But there was little to focus on; there wasn't much he could do to improve his sociology paper, and Sandra, his professor, had said as much. Really he had just stayed after class to kill the sad winter hours between night and day. Really he had only sought an audience with Sandra because he was trying to figure out whether or not he was attracted to her. It shouldn't have been that difficult, but it was. She was younger than most professors, which was what had put the question in his mind to begin with. But her figure was too wide at the hips and too narrow at the shoulders, her clothes too frumpy and unflattering; there was something gawky and off about her poise and posture. In trying to figure out whether he was attracted to her he wondered what other people would say if they knew he was, and imagined how he might answer them. In trying to figure out whether he was attracted to her he wondered if he wasn't just acting under the pressure of the subconscious societal obligation which dictated that college students were supposed to be attracted to their young professors. He didn't know what to think, about this and so many other things; hadn't even found the first steps necessary for thinking, and was beginning to fear that he never would. Instead he was doomed to blow back and forth across the face of the world driven only by the prevailing currents of ideology and these strange upwellings of passion which on closer inspection were only the desire for such.

Sandra was reserved and professional, her legs hidden under her desk and her figure hidden beneath a shapeless fleece sweater; maybe annoyed that he was wasting her time, maybe intentionally cold in the face of the confused signals he was broadcasting. She left him alone as soon as she reasonably could. And because that was the last block of classes for the day and they never locked any of the buildings he didn't see any reason to leave. He didn't have anywhere to go; didn't want to do anything but sit still and avoid the cold and wonder, not without a subcurrent of satisfaction, like a hangover that melds perfectly with a dreary winter day, when he would start feeling things the way other people felt them, or seemed to, or spoke as if they did.

He heard footsteps coming down the hall. Solitary footsteps, briskly moving. He knew even before he knew. The intuition visited him an instant before he saw her in the doorway. So certain was the intuition that he was made to doubt the sight: maybe he was mistaken, maybe it wasn't who he thought it was. But when he ran the tape back in his mind there could be no mistaking. There was Hannah, flashing for a second through his vision; Hannah afterhours though she could never find the time to make it to campus during the daylight.

He didn't get up right away. He waited first for the sound of footsteps to fade, and then their echoes. And waited longer still after this. He still had a choice. And he tried to savor this sense of agency, as if he knew already that he wouldn't always have it with him.

He knew he had to follow her. He didn't want to, but he had to. As if by looking into her present he would be able to discern exactly what had taken place in her past: peel back the skin of her entire life and dive deep into the mystery waiting within. It was a physical sensation close to panic. It didn't feel like he used to feel about her. More like there was something living in him that was not him, and that was what was telling him to get up and follow her. And he knew he had to listen to it, and that was what so frightened him. Because it was so much bigger than he was, so much more powerful; because he knew already that he needed to welcome it, to channel it, in case he one day needed to draw upon its strength.

He was careful not to let his sneakers make any noise against the tiled floor. He wasn't himself anymore; he didn't have to be. He was a wraith now, a spectre without body or personality, intent only on fulfilling its purpose. All the lights were muted and dim, the hallway murky like a grotto leading to the underworld. In one room, though, the lights were on: a stain of sick green fluorescence fell on the floor outside the room where Hightower and Demian held classes. But Ravi didn't have enough strength to look in; he was new at this, and didn't know how to make it look like he wasn't spying. He stayed where he was, waiting, unbreathing. Dreading the future, though he knew already what he'd see when the door opened: Demian in full swagger, cocky with the strength of his latest conquest. The minutes passed, but he wasn't counting. He was at the mercy of whatever power had led him here; everything else that happened would be in its hands. And though his senses tensed themselves when the door opened, he was no longer frightened, no longer nervous.

The two figures never saw him. They stepped into the hallway and headed immediately in the opposite direction. He waited until they turned the corner, and took a minute or two to collect himself, and only then did he feel up to the task of getting himself home.

Neverworld was colder and messier than usual. Ravi had been on campus all day and hadn't had a chance to clean up from the meeting the night before. And when everything was scattered around it always made the house seem colder to him, as if its molecules were coming apart, drifting so far that they no longer produced any friction, any heat.

There was a smell of cooking coming from the kitchen. A smell of burning: Kim still wasn't the best cook. But she was working at it.

"What's going on tonight?" he said.

"What do you mean?"

"Who's coming over."

"No one," Kim said absently, throwing a mixing bowl on the counter and crossing the room in two arching strides to check the oven. She had three out of four burners going, one with no pot on it. The food that was finished and recognizable, steaming in uncovered tupperware containers, was already enough to last a week. Most of it rotted on the refrigerator shelves or adhered permanently to the block of ice on the bottom of the freezer. Kim never ate anything but fried chicken from the corner store, and no one else in the house was close enough to her to feel comfortable eating her food. In a month she would be back in the kitchen, glum instead of manic, spooning mold into the garbage. Though struck often with the urge to provide, she still hadn't found anyone to provide for.

"You hungry?" she said, smiling over her shoulder.

"No," said Ravi, and he sat down. He felt like he might not eat for days.

Kim lowered the heat of the burners to quiet the bubbling of the broths and stews and sauces. "Is everything alright?"

Nothing was alright. Everything was wrong. It wasn't just self-pity; wasn't just the feeling that he didn't fit in with the rest of the world. That was high school stuff, strictly for amateurs. He'd passed through all those fires long ago. This was more piercing, more insurmountable: the awareness, reached too late, that the world itself was wrong on a molecular level, that injustice was the invisible force holding the stars together and keeping everything from falling away into nothing.

It was all still speculation. But speculation had never contorted him on a physiological level before. There was no more air in the room or in the house or the city beyond. Breath was theft; life was crime. It was more than just a symbol. It was too true to not be true.

Kim had her X-ray eyes trained on him, reading the cellular activity beneath his skin. There could be no further harm in telling her what she already knew. And he needed to tell someone. If not to make himself feel better then to set forth a chain of events that might bring the situation to a close. He didn't know how yet, didn't know why. He would have to move the earth, trigger a landslide big enough to carry him along with it. All the way to the end or buried somewhere in the rubble: it made little difference to him. Kim was waiting. All he had to do was begin, and once he did he felt, almost immediately, the ground startle and shift beneath his feet.

Her name was Ludmila, and she was not returning Topher's calls. Neither was Yvonne, neither was Katya, neither was the other Katya. Maybe he had developed a reputation among them. Like his money wasn't good enough. Like he was so physically repulsive that even when he paid for it women wouldn't go near him. The hurt of this was joined in a way that he couldn't explain with the physical hurt of his hangover. He'd been bluffing anyway when he called them – he didn't have any money left. But somehow that just made it hurt more.

"I think we need a few more roommates," he said. "Split up the rent a bit."

"I think we've got plenty," said Michael Reality.

They had put up plywood walls and curtains to subdivide the loft into as many rooms as the floor space allowed; one of their new tenants, who Topher had not yet met, had pitched a pup tent in the middle of the room. Had they been smart they would not have knocked down the walls in the first place. Topher swept his eyes over the space, making a rough estimate of how many more tents they could fit, doing some quick and exaggerated calculations of how much money that could potentially bring in. His parents had threatened to cut him off unless his grades improved, and this semester they showed no sign of improving. Knowing that he'd never get any more of it, he'd spent the last of his money the night before. It was an indirect urge to purity, he told himself, one befitting an artistic personality. That was why he'd taken so much molly, that was why he'd left Ludmila a series of voicemails, that was why the world didn't seem entirely real anymore, that was why all his feelings, even the bad ones, didn't quite feel like real feelings. That was why he was tempted sometimes to make his mood worse on purpose.

"So I guess we're about done here?"

Andy had packed all his gear up. The practice had only lasted half an hour, and Andy had sulked through the whole thing. Now that Total Mobilization was back together he didn't have time to waste on them. Their band was just an imitation, but Total Mobilization was the thing in itself. Someone like Topher, who'd never had an original thought in his life, could never measure up against the band that had invented the genre. He had enrolled in Hightower's class thinking that this might spur him on to take schoolwork seriously for once. Instead it only laid bare his poverty of thought: he had nothing to say, and didn't want to make himself look ridiculous in front of Hightower by trying to bullshit him. So he didn't bother writing any papers, didn't even bother showing up to class anymore. The rest of his classes he could probably salvage if he wanted; but Hightower was going to sink him.

"Yeah, sure," he said. He didn't mind terribly; his head was killing him, and band practice had not helped with this. "I guess. Mike, we done here?"

But Michael Reality had already left the room. Topher stood in the middle of the empty floor with nothing in his hands and nothing to do.

"Hey Andy," he said.

Andy was just about to walk out the door without saying goodbye. Reluctantly he turned around.

"Something I wanted to ask you."

Andy said nothing in reply. He did not smile or blink. He just looked at him.

"I'm having a bit of trouble in Martin's class."

Andy stared, waiting for him to go on. Topher knew already that it was a lost cause, but he couldn't back out now.

"I was wondering if you could talk to him about it."

Andy watched him a moment longer, and then opened his mouth in slow motion before he began to speak.

"Talk to him about what."

"About changing my grade, maybe."

Andy shook his head unenthusiastically: "Unlikely. Martin's an altar boy from way back. Believe it or not."

"What about Demian then."

Andy blinked some slow, heavy, disbelieving blinks. "What about him."

"Could you talk to him, you think?"

"About what?"

Topher clenched his teeth, then unclenched them to speak. "About my grades."

"Demian and I are not exactly what you'd call best friends. He's no Felix Kulpa. Neither was Felix Kulpa, now that I think about it, but that's a story for another night."

Topher didn't have anything to say to that. He knew that Andy was just playing with him at this point. Otherwise he would have left already.

"Why don't you ask him yourself?" he said. "Don't tell me you've still got your dignity. Of course it would've helped if you hadn't punched him in the face." Andy smiled for the first time all afternoon. The sight of his tongue, thick and candy-purple, filled with blood, produced a small convulsion in Topher's empty stomach. "And besides. I'm not running a charity here. What can you do for me?"

And with that, his smile broadening to show all of his small square teeth, Andy left him alone. He stood in the middle of the empty floor for a moment longer and then lay down on his mattress to try to get rid of his headache. But it was too painful to sleep. Too painful to think, too painful to be alone. He rolled over to claw his phone from his pocket and called Guy.

"What are you doing tonight," he said.

"I can't hang out."

"Why?"

"You know why."

A wave of pain passed through his head, and Topher thought for a moment that he might cry. He didn't know why. Either the innocence of it or the lack of innocence. Both/and. The molly had crossed all his wires, confused all categories. Everything meant everything, everything meant nothing. It was because they were the two most innocent people he knew, because that was the most innocent thing happening in his life, and it wasn't very innocent at all. He hung up and lay there a while staring at the ceiling.

A series of rhythmic knocking noises came from the rooftop above him. This also did not help with his hangover. He closed his eyes to wait it out, but ten minutes later it still had not stopped, and he pulled himself up the stairwell to see what it was.

Michael Reality was swinging at a piece of ductwork on the roof with a broken piece of timber, pausing after each stroke and listening to the resonant tone dissipate into the cloud cover. He had worked up a sweat, and he was steaming gently into the atmosphere when Topher came up beside him. He wiped the moisture from his forehead and offered him the board, panting faint plumes of breath into the air.

"No thank you," said Topher.

Michael Reality let the board fall from his hand and sat down, leaning his back against the roof ledge. Topher followed him, waiting for something, waiting for nothing – waiting for whatever was supposed to happen next.

"I know a girl who can help you," said Michael Reality.

"No one can help me."

"Maybe I don't really know her. But I've been trying to get to know her."

Again the strange pang of jealousy within Topher. He was jealous of Michael Reality for being acquainted with this stranger. He was jealous of everyone who wasn't him, who had even the smallest remaining shred of hope.

"Mrs. Reality?" he said.

"It's up to you. You can make jokes or come check it out. Doesn't make any difference to me."

"And how do you think she can help me."

"Because she knows things. She knows things that

other people don't know."

"Don't they all," said Topher, forgetting for the moment that Michael Reality was not supposed to see the side of him that was unguarded and without irony, forgetting also that this was not an authentic reaction, that he did not know enough about women or about life to know this first-hand, that this was only an imitation of a human response to something, that his brain was just a burned-out place in his skull where nothing was ever going to happen again.

Isaac had been in love only once in his life, though he'd attempted it plenty of times before. He'd always thought, growing up, that all romantic gestures and techniques had already been developed within the dialectic of history, had reached their final and ideal forms, and all he had to do was enter himself as the male variable in these behavioral equations in order to reach the desired result. It seemed to work for everyone else: courtship in American high school was as stereotyped as that of the troubadours and knights errant, only with handjobs and misunderstandings in place of sonnets or deeds of selfless good. But it didn't work for him. The algebra was sound, but he was a faulty variable. This was beyond mathematics, beyond self-deception: the problem was him.

Of course he kept trying. But even if he did all the right things, they were somehow wrong when he did them. He studied the techniques of his competitors on campus, gym-built and phrenologically enviable, and found that they worked sometimes in a negative register. They could do something like cheat on their girlfriends and it would make their girlfriends like them more. They did everything wrong, but consistently and expertly so, so that everything still came out positive in the end.

Isaac tried to give assertiveness a shot, but was only brave enough for passive aggression. He stood up dates, or told himself he did when he got too nervous to leave his dorm. This didn't make them like him more; this made them sit at the opposite end of the room when class came around on Monday. He decided that maybe his subconscious was trying to tell him something. Maybe he didn't want love at all; otherwise he already would have had it. How could he not, when he had all the fundamental mechanics of it figured out. Maybe he was just smarter than everyone else. Maybe love was only for suckers.

This was the attitude he adopted as he shivered bitterly through his first Chicago winter. He told men whose girlfriends he'd never met that they'd be better off single. He sneered at the sight of elderly couples helping each other walk down their icy stoops. He couldn't keep his supercilious smile to himself when he saw punk-rock dads emasculated behind their powder pink baby strollers. His condescension extended to expressions of fondness or acts of devotion to anything at all, living or dead, manmade or natural: neighborhoods that changed, sports teams that lost, jobs that ended. *That's what you get for trying to love something,* he would tell himself.

He met Hannah during a tornado warning. Funnel clouds had been sighted over the lake: Judgment Day vortices come down to vacuum up whatever little was left of what the world once was. The winds were so high they whipped snow and dust and pebbles and twigs into a dirty mini-blizzard localized mostly on their campus. Isaac imagined it was something like being caught in the tail of a comet. Students sprinted from door to door, taking shelter in interstitial alcoves when the wind was too strong to walk through. The quad was empty except for a small figure wearing only a turquoise sweatshirt, her hands in her pockets and her face hidden behind the hair blowing around inside her drawn-up hood. She was leaning motionless against a wall, her eyes shut tight against the blasting particles. Isaac passed her by accident, and said something by accident, forgetting that he wasn't interested in talking to women.

"What are you doing out here?"

"I'm going to class."

"No you're not. You're just standing there."

"I'm waiting for the wind to end."

"It's not going to."

"I knew you were going to say that."

This girl still hadn't opened her eyes to take a look at the person she was talking to. But already she knew what he was going to say. Already she knew him better than anyone else.

The cold was always what had bound them together. Their friendship lasted only those winter months; he never knew what it was like to spend time with Hannah in temperate weather, strolling together through the open air. He wondered if she'd be a different person entirely. Every time he saw her it seemed like she was on the brink of transition, about to segue into another self that she never let him see. But then she'd fix her eyes on him, look through him as if at a distant focal point, and that way return from wherever it was she was going. She'd look at him and remember that she knew him better than anyone else; remember, at least, who she was that day when she was frozen stiff in the miniature blizzard.

They never went out. The world was too big, too busy, and they were too small and lost to navigate it successfully. She hid out in Isaac's room when he wasn't there and took naps between classes. In a single month she'd become better friends with Isaac's roommate than Isaac had in five. She was the only person he knew with an off-campus apartment that first year, when everyone was scrambling to make friends in the dorms and settling for what they could get. This girl couldn't cook anything but cereal, and didn't own a winter coat, but was still adult enough not to care what anyone else thought of her. She'd call him up at night when she couldn't sleep, and he'd take the bus out to her place. They played cards and talked, eventually losing track of the game and forgetting the rules, throwing down and picking up cards at random as they continued on with the conversation. At an arbitrary point one of them would declare themselves the winner, and the other would accept it without contest and deal again. Isaac couldn't remember what they talked about. Never anything important. But somehow it was never hard to find things to talk about.

He resisted it for as long as possible. She didn't seem to love him, and wasn't trying to elicit love from him either. There were no warning signs; there was no escalation. Whatever it was – though he knew it was not nothing – it could not have been love. The equation did not allow for it.

Cordelia got jealous. Not that she admitted it. But she was never any good at dissimulation. She catalogued rumor upon rumor pertaining to Hannah, related each one in detail to Isaac. When it came to other women in his life she was always happy to be the bearer of bad news. But the rumors couldn't have been true. That wasn't the girl he knew.

One night was different from the others. The call came later than usual and cut off abruptly, Hannah's voice wavering and unstable. She didn't answer when he tried to get back to her. And because he wouldn't be able to sleep anyway he pulled on his clothes and took the bus to her apartment. The doors were unlocked, as if she were expecting him.

She was still up, still dressed, puttering absently around the room in order to keep her back to him. There was a fragile quality to her cheerfulness, and her eyes when they landed on him sometimes turned dull with a sort of dread. She was trying to remember who she was on the day they met and she couldn't do it.

They sat together on the couch. Conversation did not come easily: Hannah was distracted by something. He'd never seen her this vulnerable before. And even if he knew it wasn't true, he flattered himself to think that maybe he was the cause of this vulnerability. They talked softer and softer until all he could hear was her breath between words, drawn slow in and sighed heavy out, constant and crushing like the susurrations of waves. All throughout the encounter she maintained that determined cadence of breath. It was like exercise for her.

The days got longer and the weather got warmer. Isaac stayed away a whole week without thinking what that might mean. By the time he saw her again she'd already moved on, and the person she'd been when she met him was gone from her forever.

Isaac didn't know what to tell people – tell Cordelia – when they asked him what was wrong. It wasn't like he had lost a girlfriend. And he'd only known Hannah for two or three months. There weren't any words to describe what she was to him or what he was to her. There weren't enough words; try as he might to explain it the definitions slipped through his mind like breath through a punctured lung.

Cordelia was still jealous. Jealous of the hold that Hannah still had on him months after they stopped hanging out; jealous of her constant presence within him, and the fawning attention he gave it. It was almost solid, the feeling. It had carved out a tangible space inside his chest, and he had grown accustomed to its parasitic presence. Had grown to love it more than he loved Hannah herself, and felt pregnant now with something that had little to do with love or what love, in the popular imagination, was supposed to give you.

What Hannah had done – everything, from first to last – produced a resonance with Isaac's past and the entire makeup of his character, so much so that it was an almost familiar occurrence, like a grand synthesis of something that had been scattering pieces and preludes throughout his entire life. It wasn't as though he had brought it on himself; more like the forces which had influenced everything in his life, both inner and outer, within and without his control, which had bent to their will everything subservient to prevailing tendency, had finally completed their work, and rendered him a living metaphor for what he actually was. That this turned out to be a caricature of self-negation and pure failure was besides the point. At least he knew now what he had been built for. And since he had only one function in life it was inevitable that he found himself in a position to perform it again and again. As he fell through the clinamen of the world the particles sorted him accordingly: failure, failure, jealousy, envy, frustration, failure. And now it was happening once more.

It had been too long since he'd seen either Guy or Cordelia; too long since either of them had tried to talk to him. It had to mean something. It was the longest he'd gone without seeing them since he had gotten to college, and he only realized in their absence that he had not bothered making any other friends.

Topher picked him up without telling him where they were going or whose car they were driving. These were minor details. He was introduced to a large silent pimpled man named Michael Reality and packed into the back of a beat-up beige sedan. Smoke-stained fabric lining drooped in tents from the ceiling. The check engine light blinked on and the floor shook as Topher, with both hands on the wheel and a cigarette in his mouth, accelerated down the avenue. They drove without talking, with no music on, and came to a halt on an empty residential block in Little Village. Empty except Isaac could sense disembodied eyes watching them from the bent and leaning frame houses lining the street. Topher turned around.

"We'll be right back. You stay here and watch the car."

"You're leaving me?"

Michael Reality turned around also. They were both staring at him now. "For five minutes. We're losing time as it is."

"Take this." Topher held something out to him. "But don't call me unless it's an emergency."

Isaac took it. When he opened his hand he saw that it was a screwdriver cut into a crude shiv about halfway down.

The other two left the car, and by the time it occurred to him to check his watch he had already lost track of how many minutes had gone by. Probably close to five already. He gripped the screwdriver in his hand and slouched down lower in the seat. But he picked his head up just enough to watch one side of the empty street. Early twilight was coming on, and the horizon, visible at the other end of the avenue, was banded by bright red fading to the orange of burnt embers. The first stars had just come out above the crooked houses: somewhere high above the atmosphere there were heavenly bodies which had been made a billion years ago so that they could now shine upon these forgotten latitudes of Chicago. A raccoon or large cat crept along the sidewalk and into the basement of a condemned house. It was cold in the car with the heat off, and he began to wonder if the others were ever coming back. He didn't really know them, and the car couldn't have been worth much. Cast off like the unfit babies of Troy; a sacrifice bound and offered to a god he had never heard of. Boutique gods, built to designer specifications, esoteric and niche like sub-sub-sub-genres of underground music. He wasn't terribly relieved when he saw the two of them coming back to the car.

"Maybe it'll work anyway," said Topher. He blew into his hands and started the car.

"She said a trance state. That's what she's going for. You ever heard of cocaine putting anyone in a trance state?"

"Maybe it's better than nothing."

"Maybe Dan is gonna be pissed we spent his money on drugs that he didn't ask for."

"So we'll just give it to him. He can cut it and resell it. We don't have to do it all tonight."

Michael Reality looked to the back seat for corroboration, then looked immediately away again when he saw who was sitting there. "Sounds like you don't know a whole lot about doing cocaine."

A police siren blew a short whoop in the distance. Topher jerked his head reflexively and made the next turn. "If this girl can do magic anyway what does it matter what kind of drugs we're on."

An engine revved behind the car and an undercover cruiser with its lights flashing pulled ahead of them, speeding off to some more serious business happening elsewhere. Michael Reality turned around and held his hand out. "The screwdriver." Isaac handed it over. Michael Reality turned the shiv lovingly in his hands as he spoke:

"It's not just magic. But it's not just drugs either. It's a synthesis of the two. Something she's been working on for a long time. A synthesis of all energies. Consciousness and unconsciousness, being and non-being. An attempt to undo all forms of capture and alienation." Michael Reality stared wistfully out the window. The city slid past like a bad museum video installation: empty, deadened, drained of all color by the night and the winter. "You're the one in Hightower's class. You should know this stuff better than I do."

"I can't understand a word he says. That's the problem."

They pulled up outside a three-story brick building in a block of chop shops and warehouses and humming tortilla factories. Topher dialed a number and hung up without getting a response. A few minutes later a thin man with glasses and long straight hair marched outside and opened the door. Isaac had to scoot to the other side so he could get in.

"Did you get it?"

Topher pulled out into the street. Michael Reality stared forward through the windshield.

"Yes or no?"

"Yes and no," said Topher.

"What the fuck is that supposed to mean."

"We got something," said Michael Reality. "They were out of the other stuff."

The man gaped in disbelief at the two headrests in front of him. He glanced briefly at Isaac but didn't bother addressing or acknowledging him. "What does that mean? What the fuck did you buy?"

"It's no big deal," said Topher. "We got a bag of coke."

"No big deal? That was *my* fucking money!"

Topher shrugged and searched for words: "You can do some if you want."

"Like I haven't done enough coke in my life. Like I don't have anything better to do than rail lines with a bunch of fucking eighteen year olds. Pull over. Stop the car."

"Dan," said Michael Reality. "Chill."

"I said pull over."

"We made a mistake. We were nervous."

"I don't give a shit. This is my car. Pull it the fuck over."

Topher hesitated only a moment longer before doing as he was told. His eyes wandered over to the passenger seat.

"You're not gonna make us get out, are you," said Michael Reality.

Dan didn't say anything. Topher killed the engine and sat there.

"This neighborhood is sketchy as hell."

"Fuck you," said Dan. "I live here."

They shivered on the curb with their shoulders slumped and their necks bowed. Isaac, thinking he'd be in the car all night, hadn't worn a heavy enough coat. But who was he kidding: he didn't own a coat heavy enough. Not for tonight, not for Chicago. Dan had trouble starting the engine, leaning in close to the steering column and firing the ignition again and again. Topher tried to shout through the window:

"We didn't even spend all the money."

Dan had to lean over to the other seat in order to roll the window down: "So use the rest to call a cab. And don't act like you don't owe me."

Still swearing under his breath, he rolled the window back up. The car stuttered to life at the next turn of the ignition and he pulled away fast from the curb.

"Might as well call a cab then," said Michael Reality.

"No," said Topher.

"What do you mean, no."

"I was bluffing. We did spend all his money."

They set off walking, in what they thought was the

right direction, and Isaac followed behind. Michael Reality gave Julia a call to tell them they would be a little late. No problem, she said – she was just waking up.

They stalked through the empty Chicago streets, unnoticed, unimportant, unmolested. They looked down at their feet when police cruised by or when groups of young men brushed past them on the sidewalk. They reached Cermak and watched the block numbers count slowly down as they trudged their way back east, their black shoes sparkling with salt and their toes numb within by the time they reached Julia's place. Michael Reality rang the buzzer and they waited for an answer in the vestibule of chipped rust-colored paint.

There weren't any decorations in the apartment, hardly even any furniture. Julia was an average-looking girl with an average-looking wardrobe: shapeless hoodie and sweatpants, flip-flops, hair pulled back unflatteringly. She was on her knees within a circle of candles, a preoccupied expression on her face as she struggled with the safety mechanism of a long black barbecue lighter. All the ceiling lights were still on, and they glowed with a sterile fluorescence off the bare white walls and empty bookshelves and new appliances. It looked more like a sound stage than an apartment; it looked as if an alien intelligence had set up a habitat for a human woman to live in. Michael Reality stooped toward the candles with his cigarette lighter turned upside down and Julia stepped into the bathroom to finish applying her makeup.

Topher reached for his pocket. "So, you wanna…?"

"What," said Michael Reality.

"Cut up some lines."

Michael Reality checked over his shoulder for Julia, dropped his voice: "No. Trance state. Trance state."

"So you really think this shit is *real?*"

"Look. We have to pay Dan back eventually. And we don't have any way of doing that unless we cut and sell the shit we bought. So just hang onto it for now."

Topher was about to argue further, but Julia entered the room again with her hair down and a long black dress flowing forth from her bare shoulders. She shut the lights off and the rest of them watched in silence as she stepped barefoot into the circle, taking care to lift the hem of her dress over the many little pearls of flame struggling up into the air. They intensified the darkness instead of alleviating it; they increased the contrast between light and shadow, so that the pale skin of Julia's arms and head seemed to float disembodied upon the ambient sea of gloom. The room was more quiet than it had been only moments before: nothing else had changed, but the potential for sound had been somehow dampened. Isaac wanted to make a joke to relieve the tension, wanted to ask where they were supposed to sit in the furnitureless room, but the thoughts could not be translated into speech. He found to his surprise that he was shaking slightly, and tried to lock his knees to stop it. He had never bought a pack of cigarettes in his life, but he suddenly needed to smoke. He needed a drink. A black hole of need was opening up inside him, sucking all other thoughts and feelings into its pull. Julia's body had disappeared behind the shadowed folds of her dress, but he badly needed her too. She sank slowly into a cross-legged pose on the floor, and the men, watching, sank slowly with her. Topher's mouth was hanging open and his eyes were glittering with reflected candlelight. She closed her eyes, and after a moment she began to speak.

"Tell me what you want," she said. "And then we can work on trying to get it."

The silence was like solid mortar displacing all the free molecules of air around them. It filled their lungs and bowed their heads low. It weighed heavily on Isaac's shoulders and made them tremble from the strain. His hands were cold and sweating. None of them said anything.

"What is life but a great want. That's why things grow. That's why things live. Your cells want something, and that's what makes them pulse with life. Your neurons thirst, and that's where thoughts come from. The earth wants, and that's why it keeps turning. There is an ache at the heart of all things. If it were possible for it to be fulfilled it already would have happened by now. And even if we were to stop wanting, by some trick of magic or discipline – that wouldn't change anything, would it?"

Isaac closed his eyes and felt her voice move over him. Her body had disappeared, but her voice was more flesh than sound: deep vibrations, and the slow wet movement of the tongue in her mouth. He wanted to ask her something. He wanted to ask her everything. He could feel the want living, growing within him. He wanted to know if Hannah was happy. He wanted to see into her heart and know why she did the things she did. He wanted to look into the life of Cordelia and see what she was doing at that very instant.

"There's no use fighting against it. The want is what exists before everything else that we are. In the beginning was this hunger. So what are we going to do about it."

Isaac's head kept sinking lower, lower. It was becoming hard to breathe in this pose. Or maybe it was something else. The evaporation of breath from the air, all oxygen sucked out of the atmosphere by the great want of the stars. Their hands were slack, their feet were heavy. There was nothing left for them to do but be taken by whatever it was that wanted them. When her voice came again it was hard and clipped, cutting through the silence like a threat:

"Tell me what you want. And then I'm going to get

it for you."

"This is bullshit. Bullshit." Topher was trying to free his legs out from under him. He tried to pull himself up on the bare wall but his hands kept slipping. He wobbled unsteadily on his feet, his pupils swollen and black, his tongue clumsy in his mouth: "You can't do shit."

"We'll never know until we try," said Julia.

"No." Topher slapped his hand against the switch and flooded the room with plain white light, extinguishing the mysterious ombre glow of the candles. The caking of Julia's makeup was clearly visible upon the creases of her face. Topher was shining with sweat and panting slightly. "It's bullshit."

"What are you so afraid of," said Michael Reality.

With trembling hands Topher spilled a bag of coke onto the dust of an empty bookshelf. "I'm not afraid of anything. I'm afraid of wasting my time."

"Then why didn't you say so before we started," said Julia. "Maybe I could've worked with you."

But the spell was broken, the mystery was gone: with all the lights on she was just another undergrad in a poor apartment with a headful of ideas that were much too big for her. Topher ignored her and did the first line.

Everyone gathered around the bookless shelf. Topher held out the rolled-up bill to Isaac, but he turned it down: he had had enough excitement for one night, and he was pretty sure he had a test tomorrow. The rest of them talked at great length, at great speed and volume. Julia was saying something about tinctures and active reagents. Michael Reality said something about deity and altered consciousness. Topher went down to the corner store to buy some beer and said he was just trying to get through another night.

Isaac tried to turn down the Old Style that was

thrust upon him, but Topher wouldn't take it back: he kept holding it out, the open can shaking almost violently in his unsteady hands.

"Why not," he said. "Where are you going."

"I have a test tomorrow," said Isaac. "I think."

"A test in what?"

"I don't know."

"And how are you getting home anyway?"

Topher used his head to point at the darkness outside the window. Isaac looked around for a clock but couldn't find one anywhere. Too much time had passed; if he left now he'd have to wait around at freezing bus stops and el platforms all night. But he knew that Topher's place was only a short walk away. He took the can and drank from it, the beer so icy cold that it had lost all taste and texture. His grades had been slipping from too many nights like these. But though he always came to regret them in the daylight hours, by the time night fell again it always seemed he had no other choice. It was already too late, it had always been too late.

They walked back to the Werehouse in silence and began drinking warm beer that they found in a corner of the room. No one offered Isaac a place to sleep. There was nowhere to sleep, really, except for the floor or the couch they were sitting on. It was looking less and less likely that he would make it to campus in time to see if he had a test. It had always been too late.

"So what did you think," said Topher.

Though they were the only ones in the room, Isaac still had to look around to make sure he was the one being addressed. "About what," he said.

"Everything. Julia. All of it."

"I don't know."

Michael Reality leaned forward to talk past Topher:

"Don't bullshit us. You must have been thinking something. What were you thinking."

Isaac was too tired to resist. Too tired to lie. Too resentful also: as if he might as well try to learn something or feel something if he was going to be held hostage all night.

"I was thinking about Cordelia," he said.

"Why," said Topher.

He shut his eyes and forced the words out: "I wanted to know if she was sleeping with Guy."

"Oh."

It was spoken so plainly and matter-of-fact that it dispelled everything ominous or occult from the atmosphere. All the cocaine mania had left Topher's expression. And when Isaac could read pity there, real concern, he was, for the first time all night, made genuinely aware of a force far more powerful than he was.

"Of course she is," said Topher. "I could've told you that."

RAVI THOUGHT AT FIRST that he was sick. Physically sick, with physical symptoms proceeding from physical causes. He was all choked and twisted-up inside. There was a burning in the back of his skull that he couldn't figure out how to vent. All the passions he'd ever felt, or thought he felt – the resolution of common cause, the solidarity of the picket line – couldn't compare. Maybe he'd known it too; known he was only going through the motions for the time being, keeping up appearances until the moment came when a current of sentiment would carry him to a different level of reality, a higher consciousness of purpose. That was always the dream, though no one ever said it; that was what all the slogans were for. Yet now that it had happened it wasn't anything like he expected. It didn't ennoble him, didn't spur him to action. It only convinced him that action was worthless, and that nothing could be done to fix his broken brain or right the wrongs of the world.

He clutched his pamphlets close against his chest and leaned into the wind so it wouldn't knock him back. It was the coldest day of the year so far, so cold that it felt wasteful to care about anything but keeping warm. He stood outside the student union and pushed pamphlets on everyone coming and going, buried in hoods and scarves as they hurried through the wind. Nobody made eye contact; they accepted the papers without comment and then crumpled them a moment later. Some pamphlets were crushed into pockets, some dropped on purpose, some torn from gloved hands in the next gust of wind and shot like bottle rockets across the quad. But Ravi didn't mind seeing his seeds scattered through the world. He was sure at least some would find their marks. He couldn't afford to lose hope. All preventive measures had failed and the warmth of his body was seeping quickly into the wind-blasted waste: belief in his purpose was the only thing keeping him upright.

There was a lull after lunch. All the serious students scheduled their classes for the morning, and the unserious students didn't make it outside their dorms when the weather was bad. He stood alone in the howling wind because that was the only way he could feel like his inner suffering meant something. He wasn't sure it was working. But sometimes, when his hands and feet got so numb it was like they were detached from him, remote-operated appendages, he could almost convince himself that he was healing, convince himself it wasn't true. Hannah and Demian, Hannah and Hightower: it didn't make any sense. Lambs did not copulate with wolves. The world could not be that ugly.

A group of men approached through the swirls of snow eddying off the flat roofs. Their heads were uncovered, and Ravi could see the skin where their jackets ended and their T-shirts began. Huge men, bald and bearded, carrying shovels and icepicks on their shoulders and buckets of salt in their swinging hands, their chests square and their laughter loud. The oppressed classes for which he so often clamored. But they didn't look so oppressed when you got closer to them. They passed him by without a glance, without a care, content with their cars and their overtime and their small urban lawns. He needed them more than they needed him.

He knew that if he went inside to warm up he'd never go back out again. That was the only reason he'd stayed out as long as he did. But as the light failed to muddy grey and the campus crowd dwindled to nearly nothing he forced open the door against the outside pressure and stepped into the artificial heat and fluorescent light and enameled tiles of the food court. There was a buzzing in his ears and extremities, and he had to halt and hunch into himself to deal with the pain when they started stinging. Blood surged and pricked them back to life, and the burning increased past the point he thought possible. He shut his eyes against tears and felt the other students, healthier in both body and mind, brush past him on their way outside.

He bought soup and coffee, both too hot to touch, and stared into them, savoring the steam against the cold bones of his face, while he waited for them to cool. His hands and feet were quieting down. Despite all its difficulties, he liked the winter. He liked the comfort of the short days and the exhaustion they brought: was never struck with restlessness like on those long blue summer evenings with nothing to do and no one to love. In winter the dark came down early to tuck him in, obscuring all his most intractable problems and veiling all that was worst in the world.

A shadow fell across his table. He looked up only in time to see his whole sheaf of pamphlets snatched and scattered in the air. And a kid with a puggish nose and a carpet of zits for a face sneering down at him.

"The fuck is all this about."

Ravi didn't have an answer for him. He'd put himself through too much in too short a period of time. All he felt was an unexplained urge to give him all he had: his soup, his coffee, his money, his coat. Not from fear but from pity. He didn't though. He didn't do anything.

"You got something against Hightower?"

Not the man himself. Just some of his ideas. Just the way some of his ideas could be construed by people like the one looming above him. The way they could corrupt student teachers and mislead impressionable young girls. But Ravi didn't know how to articulate this on such short notice. The kid leaned in closer, his face shining with grease in the overhead light.

"Hightower knows things that we don't know. He's seen things that we'll never see. Hightower can peel the skin of the world aside and see the future written in its guts. What the fuck do you have. What the fuck can you do."

Ravi didn't have any answers to give him. He felt his neck bending down against his will, the blood rushing to his cheeks. Surely this person could not be right. And yet, if he had no way to answer him, and if he could feel the strength of his argument in his very body, who was he to say he was wrong. The other person couldn't have been much older than him, but he spoke with an authority that belonged to the ages, the law written into the miles of compressed stone beneath them, the millennia of birth and growth and death behind them and before them and all around them.

"You're out here playing checkers while we're playing chess," he said. "I don't want to see you around here anymore with that shit. I don't want to see you wasting your time."

Still he was waiting for a response from Ravi. Ravi held out as long as he could before he gave one. Just a nod of the head, not to say he agreed, only that he had heard and understood, but this was enough. The kid rapped his knuckles on the table like a judge pronouncing a sentence and walked away. Ravi waited until he was gone, and then stooped down to pick up the pamphlets one by one. Once they were all collected he put them in the nearest garbage and left the food court.

He boarded a bus heading west instead of going home. He didn't need to check maps or schedules anymore; he had it down to a science. He got off automatically at the correct stop and began walking the necessary blocks. So far he still hadn't seen anything. Not even a light in the apartment; nothing. He wondered sometimes if he had the right place after all; wondered if maybe she'd moved out. But he stayed true to his instincts, because he was in a situation beyond reason and instinct was all he had left. He'd wait for hours, circling the block, standing sentry, the cold stealing into his joints and bones. He told himself he'd get used to it eventually – he never did. But there wasn't anywhere else for him to be. He couldn't read, couldn't study; couldn't bring himself to care anymore about the SFPS. He was held captive by his lust for certainty. And he saw now that this was the only reason anyone took seriously the pursuit of truth. It wasn't because they wanted to but because they had no other choice. It wasn't a pursuit at all; it was a sort of escape.

Every time there was a party at Neverworld a group

of academic anarchists drank too much and debated the concept: maybe there was no such thing as truth at all, only shifting matrices of intersecting values, a primordial soup of metaphysical concepts which evolved or died in the struggle for dominance. But Ravi knew now that that wasn't true. Truth was real, and it could be felt even if you hadn't yet come to comprehend it. Truth could keep you up at night. Truth could make you sick with rage. It was something physical, tactile, inescapable. It was like something lodged inside Hannah's body without her even knowing. He could picture it: calcified somehow, a black pearl, small and shining, deep deep in her innards. He needed to get closer to it. He needed to *know*.

Streetlights speckled with white an all-purple canvas of late sundown. Snow that had been churned brown in the streets froze into a gnarled mass at night, opaque black, reflecting nothing. Ice reached in shelves off roofs and crusted into permanent deposits on the underside of cars. Everything was slow, heavy, sluggish; hostile and alien; the world burdened and without hope of relief. Ravi pushed forward, shuffling through the bleak shoveled walks between him and Hannah's apartment.

She lived on the attic floor of a house in some residential neighborhood where no one else lived. No other students – only the solidly middle-class in their small solid houses, families of cops, firefighters, teachers, teamsters, metalworkers. He walked past her building once, his head down, too afraid to look up. But hated himself for it – he'd be conspicuous now if he passed by again soon. This was how it went every time: blushing and frustrated, stumbling and graceless, like trying to ask out a girl when you knew the answer was going to be no. He turned around to look at the end of the block: there was light in Hannah's window. One of them. He couldn't remember which was the bedroom. He strained his eyes to pick out silhouettes in the blinds; disturbances in the light; stopped breathing as if that would help him see better. But there was no making it out. He'd have to wait for whoever it was to leave. Wait until morning if he had to. He might not get another shot at this.

He didn't feel the cold anymore. It was a physical high, adrenaline-charged. It was *real*; not a pose like his prior activism, the pre-planned, committee-vetted, legally-sanctioned transgressions of the SFPS. This was something bigger than himself, something he could experience but never explain. This was something he could never tell any-one else about. He couldn't come up with any reasons why Hannah and Demian or Hannah and whoever shouldn't have their fun together. Only a couple weeks before he never would have fallen back on such conventional cate-gories. But he didn't have anything else to fall back on any-more. A boy who had never believed in goodness or even justice – only advantage, tactics, change by painful incre-ment – now longed for the purity of vengeance.

The sidewalks, gritty with crushed salt, grew smooth and slick again in the overnight chill. All color had fled the sky except a rusty brown smear of light pollution showing wanly on the underside of the clouds. Ravi kept watching. Sometimes he stood still and sometimes he walked around the block to keep warm. But he always made sure to maintain a line of sight on the door to Hannah's unit. It didn't bore him. He trembled beneath his coat, but not from cold. From anxiety, excitement, the thrill of the un-known; the force of reality as it flooded finally his dormant body. The icicles reaching their long teeth from the eaves; the hardly perceptible hush of the sleeping suburb; the light pouring from windows, drawing yellow squares in the street, so bright they almost warmed him: all this banality captured his attention like a sea of dazzling jewels, infinitely variable, infinitely valuable. Everything mattered. He mattered too, for once. And when the door to Hannah's unit cracked open he focused all his senses as if on a vision from an oracle. But instead of telling him the truth about the future this was going to finally reveal to him the hidden truth of the present.

It was still early, relatively. The man had somewhere else to be. He was hunched and small in silhouette, as if aware of being observed. He shuttled through patches of lamplight on the way to his car. Ravi, at first, tried not to see. Like the mental equivalent of watching a horror movie through your fingers. He hoped against hope: please be Demian, please be anyone. The man passed by Ravi on the other side of the street. It wasn't Demian, the student, the imitator. It wasn't any random nobody, a piece of meat plucked from campus for temporary companionship. It was Hightower, the professor, the thinker, the true believer. Who was so much older than her, who was married, which made it so much worse. Ravi didn't know why. He'd given up on explaining things to himself. He could see in his mind the two of them laboring together, wrinkled and unnatural. She would settle for anyone. Anyone who she'd never settled for before; anyone who wasn't him. Ravi froze in place, watching Hightower fumble for his keys, start his car. Ravi stayed there until the car had pulled out, and waited until the light in Hannah's room blinked off. It took about an hour. And then he was alone in the dark and quiet of the residential street, where the men and women who worked the morning shifts were already waking up.

He lay awake in the daylight wondering how he was going to get to sleep and how he'd ever return to his old life. Maybe he never could anymore. And after the worst of the pain was over the thought of this so excited him that it almost made all he had seen, all he had passed through, seem worth it.

THE CAMPUS CALLED THEM OFFICES, but really they were more like cages: partitions of rigid wire walling off one wing of the library's top floor and subdivided into several six by six sections. Demian used to be able to work better under these panoptical conditions, but not anymore. His pen had developed a habit of moving by itself. A nervous tic at first: then he began to cultivate it in case anyone happened to be passing by. And now that he'd started he couldn't stop. He didn't make words, just lines. Lines that could be mistaken for words at a distance. The pages filled up all by themselves. He began running off dummy copies of his students' papers so he wouldn't mark up the originals with gibberish. He was becoming aware that it was a problem, but he didn't know yet what kind of problem it was.

His face was still hurting him. He thought it might be fun to conduct classes with a shiner, but the picture in his mind didn't match up with the image in the mirror: the bruise was yellowish green instead of smooth Hollywood blue. It spread all down his face instead of halting at the eye socket. It hurt when he sneezed, when he smiled, when he squinted from holding a cigarette in his lips. It hurt when he sent his fingers probing through the cushion of flesh; pushing only lightly for fear he would discover a piece of bone or gristle floating in the mass, knocked loose, inviting infection. He was running low on girlfriends and Vicodins. Running low on money also, which only made it harder to procure the first two. But there was always hope. Except hope was such a cheesy word. There were always opportunities.

Hannah had been avoiding him, of course. Avoiding

his class, which made sense – with all the absences she'd already accumulated she didn't have any chance of passing anyway. When the end of the semester came around she'd come back to try to make the best of her grade. He was sure of it, and that was why he had no problem waiting until then. When he spotted her around campus it looked like she'd grown thinner and yet more skittish: motions sudden and birdlike, as if the next breeze might compel her to flutter over to the nearest lawn or rooftop. But he could see through the act so clearly that he suspected at first it was adopted for his benefit, or for the benefit of other men like him. He could see the weakness, the woundedness just beneath the surface, and that was what had first drawn him to her. It was like she wasn't even trying to hide it; like her attempts at normalcy were actually intended to highlight how damaged she was. Maybe intended was the wrong word. Or maybe there was no difference between intentional and unintentional when it came to Hannah. He didn't know which way was up when it came to that girl.

He had signed up to perform one of his poems at a Neverworld open mic later that night. He could picture the performance in his mind; rehearsed his lines, anticipating the reactions. Maybe Hannah would be there. The thought produced an anxiety in him that he couldn't quite place. Readings had never made him nervous before, especially in bullshit little rooms like the one at Neverworld. He took Hannah out of the equation – she'd been spending less and less time at the house – but that didn't make the anxiety go away either. He tried to lose himself in his work. "Work": his pen moved over the page, jotting out alien hieroglyphs. They didn't mean anything, they never would.

He heard a noise above him and saw, when he looked up, pink fingers wriggling like worms through the mesh-metal cage walling him off from the rest of the university. He snapped to attention with a small physical jolt; like the kid had been reading his mind, like all his thoughts had been written clearly on his face. But in the next moment he saw there was no reason to be intimidated. It was just some skinny ginger with a bad attempt at a beard. He looked vaguely familiar – a student, he decided. No one else would have known he spent his office hours at the grad student petting zoo on the top floor of the library.

"How can I help you," said Demian, hiding papers, shuffling papers, trying to look busy.

The kid hesitated, and his voice when it came wasn't much more than a nasal whine.

"I just wanted to apologize."

"For what?"

"The other night."

"What night?"

"You know. Last Saturday. The show."

Demian hesitated just a moment too long. Usually he was a good enough liar, but he had been slipping lately. "Kid, I have no idea what you're talking about."

"I was the one who hit you."

At first a pang of fear: their cover was blown. This had been Martin's biggest objection when Demian proposed that he take Felix's place in the resurrected Total Mobilization. But they had gone too far to turn back now. He had gone too far to turn back now. He let a smile grow across his face until it started to hurt. "Then why are you apologizing? Why are you *here?* You could've just not told me. That way I never would've known."

"I know. But I thought–"

"No no no no no." Demian cut him off with a wave of the hand. "Never apologize. Never back down. That's rule number one. If you want to survive in this game, I suggest you remember it."

The kid nodded and cocked his head to get a better look at the bruise. "Does it hurt?"

"Of course it hurts. But if you're afraid of getting hurt you don't have any business in the scene in the first place. If you're afraid of getting hurt you don't have any business being alive."

Demian stood and paced his small office space with his hands tucked behind his back. He would have to take care to navigate this situation correctly. But it was like anything else in life: it was all just one long con. He acted for a moment like a man lost in thought, then looked up at his visitor.

"You a student?"

The kid nodded.

"Are you one of *my* students?"

The kid thought about it. "Sometimes."

"Ah. And were you afraid this little incident was going to hurt your grade?"

The kid dropped his eyes and said nothing. Already Demian knew that he had him. The rest was mere formality. He flipped open a nearby binder with an air of authority and scanned the lines of gibberish with his finger. "What's your name?"

"Topher."

He stopped his finger at an arbitrary point and put a pained expression on his face. This was not so difficult, because it caused him actual pain.

"It's not looking too good for you, Topher."

"I know."

"You know. That's why you came." Demian shut the binder loud enough to send an echo through the top floor of the library, and the violence of this motion was somehow connected to the birth of a new idea in his brain. "I can't help you. That is, unless you can help me."

"Help you how."

"I don't know. Use your imagination."

"I don't have any money"

"That's why I said use your imagination."

"I don't have anything."

Demian, frustrated, opened his hands and let the binder fall to the desk. "Then I guess I can't help you."

The kid nodded and turned his sloped shoulders to leave. Then, just before taking his first step, turned back again.

"I'll see you Friday then."

"Are you sure about that?"

"Yeah. You guys are playing a show at my place."

Demian had to do some quick calculations. The kid was right: the first show of the reunited Total Mobilization was booked for this week.

"That's not gonna help with your grade either," he said.

They weren't prepared for the show. Every week it was getting harder to schedule practices and recording sessions. And it certainly wasn't because of him and Andy. Martin was always calling out to spend time with his family – never a priority before this month, it was now his favorite excuse. His kid was always "sick." Sick how, he never said. Demian never looked any deeper into it until Andy spelled it out for him.

"His kid's practically a vegetable," he said. "You didn't know that? Of course Martin would never admit it. In the past he was known to be very vocal about the importance of maintaining good eugenic health."

A silence fell over them like a cloud, a fog, a physical presence when he said it. There were no taboos in the world of Total Mobilization; in reaction to the kitsch and sentimentality inherent in the manipulations of mass culture they devoted themselves unflinchingly to the disembowelment of everything sacred to the popular mind. But sometimes the popular mind struck back, and this was something they were never prepared for. They thought the popular mind was externally constructed and merely theoretical; they didn't think it could become tangible, didn't think there was any trace of it left in them. But they never brought up Martin's son again after that.

Demian rode the bus as far as it would take him. It stopped only at the outskirts of Neverworld's neighborhood, like a guide who brought travelers to the border of a haunted forest but would not accompany them into the interior. He turned his collar up and walked with brisk steps the rest of the way. Tree branches, sheared by the wind, lay scattered in the street, their bark twisted open and the wood beneath showing bright yellow like a wound in the colorless world around them. The wind found him, crawling down his neck and billowing up the bottom of his jacket. It pressed itself in deeper, through the legs of his pants, and sucked with vampiric wetness the warmth below. It was like a personal assault: the wind swept the length of the whole world, yet was intended only for him.

He halted in the vestibule at Neverworld, warming himself and listening to the doors banging gently in their frames. Listening for signs of life and wondering why he didn't hear any. He was right on time – that is to say, much too early. It was too cold a night for poetry. Too cold for revolution. A night to stay in and stay warm and be glad for what you had if you had anything. Demian thought for a second about turning around and going home while he still could. But there was nothing waiting for him at home, and at Neverworld there was at least the possibility he would see Hannah. He had to take the chance.

There was no one sitting in the mismatched semicircle of chairs arranged in the living room. He crept unseen through the kitchen and the pantries and the closet-sized bedrooms of the first floor, listened unbreathing to the voices emanating from the second. Listened longer: none were Hannah's. He searched the basement and attic, poked his head in every makeshift tent and sleeping bag, finding only cobwebs, broken furniture, the deep sleep of dreaming anarchists. Kim was greeting the first guests when he got back downstairs, taking their coats and leaving lipstick smears on their cheeks. He drew her close by the elbow and guided her over to the wall. He didn't feel like prevaricating. Kim wasn't worth the trouble.

"Is Hannah coming?"

Kim didn't betray any disappointment; was flattered enough by his eagerness to grab her. She craned her neck over her shoulder and peeled the lids from her big egg-shaped eyes. In her mind it probably looked elegant.

"I thought you'd be the one to know."

"I'm not kidding around with you."

"I'm not kidding around with you either." Her teeth flashed in a smile: a smile of the purest girlish joy, which she had to twist and contort to give the appearance of cunning. "You mean you don't know?"

"That's exactly what I mean."

"I hear Hannah's graduated from teaching assistants to professors."

Demian crowded her closer; felt the pliancy of the skin gathered in his hand, felt her yield, liquid, to the pressure of him in front and the wall behind. He tried to ignore the electric charge given forth by the compression of her body. He wondered if any of the other Neverworld kids were watching. He hoped they were.

"I already told you. I'm not playing games."

She milked the moment just a few seconds longer, wringing every drop of pleasure she could from the situation. There was a new fullness and life in her drained and pale body. Like she was stealing it somehow from Hannah, or maybe from him.

"Martin Hightower," she said, and she watched him scowl, studying him closely, barely able to keep her lips together.

"So you and your friends heard a rumor. So what."

Her face became serious then. And he knew women well enough to know that he was about to hear something he didn't want to hear.

"Don't be so sure of yourself," she said. "That girl would sleep with anyone who asked her nicely."

Demian, composed up until then, both outwardly and inwardly, felt his face flush purple, felt his heart rate double. Anyone who asked her nicely: that was why it had to be true. Because Martin was the only one dumb enough to actually do that.

He let her go and watched her jellied limbs bounce back to stability; added his coat to the pile in her arms and walked away without another word. There was nothing he could have done to his advantage. Even if he wounded her, either mentally or physically, it only would have given her more satisfaction. He planted his back against the wall and sized up the room. Sarah had made it downstairs. Her hair was growing blonde at the roots; she wasn't dyeing it anymore. Also in the crowd: Jenna, Cheryl, Caryn. Like an intervention of all his undergraduate lovers. An intervention except they all ignored him, and that was how they were going to cure him.

He had been to plenty of readings before. But this was the first time his hands ever shook. Standing up in front of a room of nobodies, and it made his hands shake. He joined them together, hid them behind his back, but this looked too obsequious. He had a bottle of wine with him: he drank it too fast, and it burned on the way down. The bruise throbbed with his pulse and stretched his face into a permanent sneer. His eyes ran over the page, from top to bottom and back, searching for the real poem hidden behind this phony poem in his hands. He was saying the right words, he was sure of it, but they didn't seem to mean anything after he had said them. Maybe they never had. The audience talked over him, and by the time he was done he was glad to be off the stage.

Once seated he took another look at his scribbled poems. But they were unintelligible now: his sweat had fused the paper together, blotted the ink to smears. He wished the whole thing would melt away in his hands; wished he could slither into liquid and be anywhere else but here. Now, suddenly, he was the old guy in a room full of kids. There was always one; he'd spotted plenty in his time, and marked them all as rejects, defective. He never thought it would happen to him.

He remembered the wine at his feet; finished it off and felt the grapes complete their rot inside his stomach. He scanned the room and saw Kim, turned in her chair, watching him. Watching the whole thing: all his inner drama unfolding publicly. He pretended not to see her. But this in itself was only another maneuver in the game they were playing. After a sufficient interval had passed he moved to the seat next to her and whispered through the next poet's set. Just business, he told himself; just to earn some cash, just to take his mind off things.

"That thing you were talking about last time."

She nodded. "I already did it."

"You got the doctor's codes? Everything?"

She glanced around as if wary of someone overhearing. But she couldn't help it; was enjoying too much the middle school thrill of trading secrets with a boy. She leaned in close and blew hot breath on him:

"You want to go for it?"

Demian paused to give it thought. It wasn't an act like everything else: he actually hesitated. And not at the criminality of it either. But his options were running out. Kim grinned wide and eager, gummy like a little girl with all her baby teeth. It wasn't just the thrill of the perfect crime that was making her so happy.

"Alright," he said. "Let's do it."

Snow was piled halfway up the windowsills. The world outside swallowed as if by glaciers, drifts of earth, thousands of years – smooth and smothered, silent and waiting forever for rediscovery. The world of man receded, and with it their noise and machines and endless empty busyness. Classes had been canceled, and Martin was still in bed with Ellie. In any other circumstances he would have gotten up already. But he didn't have much to do. And it looked good: spending time with the wife. From now on he would have to be very careful. How much wrong had he done, really. Probably nothing that could get him convicted in divorce court. But he had no idea how these things worked. Ellie, of course, did not believe in divorce. Neither did he, if he took half a moment to think about it.

He found George and seated him at the table as Ellie mixed the batter for pancakes. The snow gave a bluish tinge to the light coming in the window. George was still partly asleep, his head lolling on its neck, his eyes roaming vacantly. Martin smiled at him, smiled for the cameras, close-mouthed and strained, and then looked at him no more.

Ellie asked him questions by rote and he did his best to answer. Yes, the show was still tonight, as far as he knew. Yes, the practice sessions were keeping him out late. He made a polite noise – hm? – and cocked his head to indicate that he had not heard. But this was not something he usually did; he was trying too hard to be cheerful. Usually Ellie didn't mind when he was morose. She knew him too well. But now he felt he couldn't chance it. Yes, he said when she had repeated the question. The recording sessions too.

She sat with her plate and asked if he wanted to go for a walk after breakfast. Yes, he said, smiling. Yes, yes, yes. It was all he ever said to her anymore. Always with an unpleasant hammering of the heart, as if he knew that she knew that he didn't mean it. George was tearing his pancakes with his hands and rolling them into little balls on the plate in front of him, thoughtfully engrossed in this task, or at least as thoughtful as he ever was.

They wrapped themselves in colorful boots and jackets like a family from a magazine ad and made their way slowly to the park. Already, with the morning wind off the lake, a gloss of ice had formed over the sculptured drifts of snow. They shone with a dull blue under the overcast sky, as if each flake retained within its phenotype an image of its unspotted ancestry above the clouds. Martin pulled a sled as he crashed his boots through the frozen toplayer of snow; George slid behind him, mouth gaping, failing to take in the scene around him. Ice hung in frozen torrents off gutters and electrical lines; ice encased with perfect workmanship the smallest intricacies of each tree's branchings; ice sent vapor into the air and reached with pricking urgency the depths of Martin's lungs and the coursing cells of his blood. He walked faster: away from buildings and people, closer to the lines of trees stained dark by dampness and the untroubled expanse of the frozen lake beyond. Ellie couldn't keep up; red-faced, panting, she lagged behind them. Martin, checking on George over his shoulder, pretended not to notice.

The runners of the sled hit a curb that Martin's feet had missed. George tilted like a felled tree and slumped over, his frame so slight he didn't even crack the snow. Martin watched him. He knelt down and pretended to reach out; but really he was lost in observation as his body performed the motions. The boy didn't have any interest in getting up; didn't seem to understand that anything was wrong. Martin felt neither concern or anger. No pity, for his son or for himself. His hands met the boy and placed him back on the sled. He would have done as much for a stranger.

They made hot chocolate and sat around the house. More model family life, pretend-family stuff. He couldn't remember – hadn't they used to do things like this? Or was it only in covering his tracks that he had begun acting like an actual father? He smiled at his family and they smiled at him. Ellie didn't seem to think he was pretending. Maybe, in truth, he was not. Or maybe he was, yet this was all that she, or the world, had ever asked of him.

Ellie caught George in one arm and settled down on the floor with a picture book. She blew ripples over the surface of their shared mug.

"Careful, baby," she said. "It's hot. See? Blow."

He was her baby. He would always be, no matter how big he grew physically. Martin didn't know whether it was because she truly didn't mind or because she was still in denial. Maybe it didn't matter. Maybe it didn't make any difference; maybe there was something to be learned there.

George just stared at the book. Words were nothing to him. Books were objects. When Ellie read aloud the richness of her intonation was enough to keep him calm. But as soon as she stopped he began to struggle, and his limbs flailed with such violence that she couldn't turn to the next page.

"George," she said. "Please. Honey."

But reasoning did no good with him. She should

have known that by now. George started to cry: that one note, droning and mournful. As if he were conscious, like an artist, of its effects, its minimalist aesthetics: complaint, unarticulated; grief that could not be managed. He had a good enough life. Well fed, well clothed, well loved. There were no specific causes for his misery. Simply existing: that was the problem.

"Georgie," said Ellie. "Sweetie."

He bucked in her arms, reared his head back into her nose. She dropped him; dropped the book, spilled hot chocolate across the floor. George landed in it, rolled, splashed the walls. All the while intoning his cry, moaning at great volume, his eyes wide open and without understanding. He ran into a corner of the room and huddled under an end table. His voice grew hoarse: a beast at bay, sounding its desperation.

Ellie grabbed at tissues, tearing up from the blow. George was getting older; he didn't know his own strength. One day he would be a man, full-grown. Martin had known this in an abstract way but had never before felt its effects in reality. Ellie, as far as he knew, had never given the slightest thought to the matter. It took her a minute or so to recover. All the while George's cry sounded continuously, like an air raid siren, stopping only when he paused to suck down breath. She kept her red eyes fixed on Martin, waiting for him to do something.

"Come on." Martin seized first one and then both arms; drew the kicking mass out from behind the table legs, held him like a volatile substance at arm's length. "Come on. To your room."

It was a stage whisper, for Ellie's sake: words were less than useless. He dragged him through the hall and into his room, shut the door behind them. The boy slid easily on his heels; wasn't bright enough to resist effectively. Martin stood over him, studying him, and the crying dropped in volume until it became a sort of labored breathing. Even for Martin, with all the advantages of age and experience, and with all his faculties intact, the world made little sense; what hope, then, did this small person have of making sense of it. He didn't have the heart to be angry with him. It was punishment enough just being alive. Just being. For the average person, yes; much moreso, he imagined, for his son. When he went back to Ellie in the living room he closed the hallway door to better block the noise from George's room. Ellie was more composed now: kneeling on the hardwood, passing sodden paper towels over the spill with a slow and meditative motion. Sniffles escaped her only occasionally, during the regular cadences of breath. Martin took a seat, exhausted already by the conversation which had yet to take place. But he'd known for a long time that it was coming.

"Maybe," he said, "we should seek some outside help for him."

"What kind of help," said Ellie.

"I don't know. Some sort of therapy. I'm sure there are plenty of options."

She kept her back to him as she balled up the dripping paper towels; he couldn't read her face. But the tone of his voice sounded false in his own ears. He knew he wasn't getting through.

"The doctors have been saying it for years," he said. "It would be cruel to keep him away. Cruel to him and cruel to us."

"But what do you expect these people to *do?* Are they going to *cure* him?"

"No. But they could help him. So he could get better. So we wouldn't have to take care of him forever. So he might be able to take care of himself after we're gone."

She didn't answer. Maybe he had taken a wrong turn somewhere. But he couldn't figure it out; reason was of no use here. He tried again:

"We'll set up an appointment for our next day off. All three of us, together. Don't you want that? Don't you want him to get better?"

He watched the back of her head; watched it move side to side as she shook it.

"I don't want him to change," she said. "I hope he never says a word."

She spent the rest of the day in George's room. She could watch him for hours like a devotee at the feet of a guru, engrossed in the simplicity of his presence. To her he was perfect, self-contained, already complete. It scared Martin, in a way, to witness that measure of devotion. To see firsthand the thoughtlessness of it all. But he was at least honest enough to entertain the idea that she was in the right and he was in the wrong. Thoughtfulness had never profited him anything.

He sat in his study because it was an excuse to remain behind a closed door. It had been too long since he'd worked on his book; he'd lost the breadcrumb trail of scribbled notes, and he wouldn't know where to start. Or he could jump in at random and prove what he'd always feared: his system of thought, such as it was, was merely an ouroboros in which each point was equally valid insofar as it was equally invalid; each proposition predicated only by what it was superseding and what would in turn supersede it; and though it might produce in the reader the illusion of movement, of revelation, this movement did not proceed to or from any definite point. Revelation into revelation into revelation: on and on the process stretched. He would have to find another way.

He swept the papers aside and opened up his laptop

computer. Finally, after months of planning, agonizing, fantasizing, he sent a reply to Regina: typed it with the hands, not the head, not the heart, tapped it out and sent it without thinking a thing about it. He shut the laptop again before he had a chance to ask himself what it was supposed to mean. Maybe she would know where Felix was; maybe she was the only one who did. Maybe there were other things she could do for him. And he was reminded, in a flash of recollection, of his childhood religious observances: if his parents had allotted time for confession later in the week he would do his best to cram as many sins as he could into the time before absolution.

He said goodbye to Ellie. Dutifully, husbandly; came close to her and bent down to kiss the side of her head. She was sitting on the floor, across from George, trying to communicate with him, play with him, capture his attention for just a moment. She would hold up one of his toys and then another, awaiting his reaction. Over and over again: every time it was something entirely new. *This is a truck. This is a cow.* This is cowness. This is truckness. And Ellie had become lost in it too, entranced by the repetition, seeing everything in eternities. She hardly noticed him approaching, hardly felt him kissing her. Fair enough: he hardly felt it too.

Demian was already drinking when he got to the warehouse. The kids who lived there were in the last phases of constructing a makeshift bar out of crooked, greying pieces of salvaged wood: adding reinforcements to faulty joints, bending back the most dangerous of the protruding nails. Demian was leaning forward on a flimsy cross beam, balancing a whisky on the plywood surface. He gave a look to Martin and made a small stonefaced nod of recognition before turning back to his drink. Martin dropped his equipment in the heap of speakers and wires in the corner and poured himself a drink at the unmanned bar. It would do him no good now to be hesitant. He could still feel the aura of Hannah's warmth around him, short film clips of her still played beneath his eyelids, and he was proud to be carrying with him more of her presence than Demian, smug as if concealing a weapon. He fought down the attack of jealousy when it came: of course Demian had gotten closer to her physically. This he knew. He didn't know how many times, or where, or any other circumstances. Through an act of will, almost superhuman, he chased the thought from his mind. It wasn't about that. It never was.

Demian was still leaning forward on the bar, not saying anything. Maybe ignoring him intentionally, maybe not. Maybe he was just in another of his lousy moods. There were always plenty of reasons for him to be in one.

"No date tonight, Demian?" said Martin. Trying to be jovial, fatherly, but he didn't know how it came out. It was like back at home, with Ellie: his good cheer, however artfully expressed, however genuinely felt, only made him seem more suspicious.

Demian shook his head slowly, barely moving his neck. "The well has run dry."

"You're young. There will be others."

Martin said it as a sort of threat. That was how Demian took it too: Martin could read his thoughts through the subtle deepening of creases in his inexpressive face. Demian could be very smart for a person who took so much trouble to live stupidly. Martin raised his glass as an after-thought, and they drank to that, or maybe to nothing.

Martin closed his eyes and listened to the sound of the room. Dueling stereos behind the curtain walls, hammering of light construction. Murmured conversation growing in volume as the room filled with warm bodies and their youthful sweat-smell. His fans, his followers, his people. He didn't want anything to do with them. He didn't even want to look at them anymore.

He kept his eyes closed and moved his hands over the sliders on his rig, reading the notches like braille. He took a breath and plunged deep into the work, stewarding the waveforms through Andy's wall of sound and Demian's intentional distortions – squeezing, by any means necessary, a hint of music through the wreckage of noise. Heat came in a constant blast from the spectator side of the room: red stagelights and massed bodies beaming warmth into Martin's skin as he nudged the knobs and sliders up, up, testing the capacity of the PA system, trying to see how far over the edge he could push it. He could almost picture it: the walls between brain cells melting down, everything aggregated into oneness, finally whole. No more disconnect between thought and action, between thought and thought, between thought and thought and thought on into infinitude. The brain turned liquid and coursed through the veins and the blood bubbled up to the skull to dictate thoughts of its own. Everything became sound: his thoughts and the world around him. And yet it was a sound that produced the same effect as a deep silence; the first silence, before the creation of that which made noise. As if they had pulled down the silence of the atmosphere, millions of cubic miles of still air, and compressed and condensed it until it exploded out into music. The walls shook with bass and the glasses sang with the treble. The sound wanted to break it all down: return matter to dust and dust to dust's precondition. Wanted to peel back the scrim of the created and hum with the energies of the yet-to-be. It opened like a portal: wider and wider they willed it. Until they and the audience would finally melt into continuance with all that is.

This, thought Martin. There were no more words in his head. Only this, this, this, this. No longer a word but only a placeholder for one; the last boat to be burned after he built his home on these shores beyond language.

He didn't know what it would look like, exactly, when he saw, unclouded, the world-as-it-was, the world-before-man; but he knew now that he'd know it when he saw it. He was reaching for it – a spiritual appendage emanating from the center of his heart, the center of his center – could sense its nearness – but he didn't see it. Not that night. There was still that one word – that thisness – clutching his ankle as he ascended. But he knew now that one day he'd see it. Somehow – at all costs.

It was a night like any other. A show like any other. But Hannah was with him still. She was in his blood like a sickness; glowing on his skin like a fever; airborne and all around him; inescapable. All these years of searching and he'd collected all the reagents required for transcendence except for the last one. He swallowed her like a pill and waited for the drug to kick in.

He tweaked the oscillations, maxed all his sliders out. The gain in the high registers exploded a PA with a dull internal pop. Andy, expecting formal precision from Martin, glanced over, confused. But this was something Andy would never understand. Martin willed the waveforms larger, faster: they ate static and swallowed the room. Still the second PA held out. Demian understood without a word or a glance, bound to Martin by something deeper now. He seized the PA stand with both hands; lifted the tripod over his head and threw it into the crowd. It sailed over the heads of the small congregation and caved in the side of the newly-built bar. A pop and a fizzle, and all that was left was the low tinnitus-whine of feedback. But the sound remained: the crowd, roaring, jostling, surging, exploding from the arbitrary confines which held them. They fell upon the fallen PA as upon the body of a martyr; many hands, working in wordless unison, picked it up and sent it flying again. Wood from the shattered bar sailed through the air, popping lightbulbs and catching tents with their nails. The curtains dividing the rooms were torn down, mattresses and shelves upended. Windows shattered one after the other: a hurricane of flesh swirling through the room, breaking all that could be broken. The residents grappled with the rioters upon the sea of splintered glass. One kid tried to set fire to the wall with a cigarette lighter before he was stepped on and throttled. Demian and Martin looked at each other without saying anything, their eyes glued together, unable to be parted. Whatever it was that had them wouldn't let go. Whatever it was had gotten into everyone else also. They tried to sweat it out, tried to tear down the walls. It didn't matter. Nothing worked. The sweat, the destruction: all that was Hannah too.

"But this is really important," said Ravi.

"You say that about everything," said Isaac.

"I mean it this time."

He did. Isaac, driven often to desperation, could recognize the signs in others. Ravi wasn't howling his cause from the rooftops like he usually did. This time he'd pulled Isaac aside in a dark alcove in the Arts and Sciences building and had gone on in hushed tones about deposing Martin Hightower.

"I don't even know who this guy is," said Isaac.

"He's a fascist."

"You'd call someone a fascist if they cut you off in traffic."

"It may not look like it, but that's only because he's good with words. Because he talks in code. But he's infecting the whole student body. We have to stop him before it's too late."

Ravi's cheap polyester middle-manager outfit was pilled and wrinkled, hanging in shiny folds off his skinny body. His skin was pale, his hair greasy, his eyes dim, red, watery; he bore all the hallmarks of a compulsive masturbator. He'd never been the most self-assured person on campus, but he usually looked as though he washed himself.

"You look like hell," said Isaac.

"That's not the point."

"Yes it is. You can't save the whole damn world, Ravi. Save yourself if you can."

Ravi just shook his head, his neck limp, a crooked smirk spread across his face. Isaac saw it then: conviction, terrible conviction, shining through into a world of make-believe. To a make-believe person like himself it just looked like insanity. But it resonated within whatever part of him could still recognize real things when it saw them.

"I don't care if it kills me," said Ravi. "I'm taking him down with me."

Isaac went to the library and laid his books out in front of him without any intention of studying. He never did any studying anymore, he never did any reading. His only object of cogitation was his life: where it had gone wrong, how badly, and so forth. But it was all wrong, and had always been. Ever since he came into the world, drawing his first breath from the smog clouds of New Jersey. Condos, subdevelopments, industrial parks; shopping malls next to tacky mansions next to fenced-in fields of derelict grass; highways and highways and highways: these were the aesthetic influences which had shaped him from his protoplasmic beginnings. As such he felt powerless to resist the zeitgeist into which he'd been born. He watched, with mingled pity and satisfaction, the successful people among him equivocating desperately as they fulfilled their filial duties. They picked up hobbies and pet causes; changed their zipcodes, changed their haircuts; but they couldn't really change anything about themselves, and never would.

Isaac, who lived in a haze of daydreams, was unable to deceive himself when it came to things that actually mattered. There were no solutions: he was sure of it. You didn't go to college for solutions, only to exchange one set of problems for another. Everywhere was New Jersey, or pretty close to it, or would be soon. The campus was New Jersey, the city was New Jersey. The library was New Jersey, beige and bright-lit, without features, without purpose, fulfilling its quota of existence out of obligation to the past and not hope for the future. And if he were to part his skin and crack his ribs and look at what dripped out: it would be colorless, odorless, without heat or chemical properties. Not blood, not even water. New Jersey was inside him and everyone else.

He met up with Topher at the dining hall so he could swipe him in; Topher's card had run out of money a long time ago. He, like Ravi, looked terrible. Worse than usual. The bags under his eyes had turned purple like a bruise, and the skin of his face was so thin and white that Isaac thought he could see all the way through to the veins and the bones.

"What's up with you," he said.

Topher was eating slowly, too anemic to even lift his fork. He halted it midway and let the heavy end droop. "There was some damage at a show the other night. Couple windows got knocked out. It's too cold to really sleep."

"It looks like you've lost weight."

"I think I'm losing more than that."

He chewed and swallowed with apparent effort. It was like talking to an invalid – Isaac wasn't sure how to go on without coming across as disrespectful of the situation.

"Do you remember Julia," said Topher.

"Yeah."

"Me too. Can't stop remembering her, in fact."

"Maybe she put a spell on you."

Topher had been rubbing his eyes with his hands, but removed them so he could stare back at Isaac. This was no longer a laughing matter to him.

"I'm going back there today. You're coming with me."

"Why?"

"Because of that favor I owe Dan Drugs. He's got another little job for me."

"I mean why do I have to go with you."

"Oh." Topher hesitated, the lids half drawn over his tired eyes. It was the first time Isaac had ever seen him display shame or shyness or any reticence at all. "So it won't look like I'm trying to sleep with her. Even though that is in fact what I would like to do."

Julia was bored, preoccupied, dressed down when she opened the door to her apartment. She looked at them like a government clerk who had just clocked out for the night.

"'Do my thing?'" she said, still standing at the threshold. "You want me to 'do my thing?' And what 'thing' would that be?"

"You know," said Topher. "The candle thing."

"The candle thing."

Topher opened his mouth but no sound came out. He looked to Isaac for help, but Isaac had no help to give him. He was only an accessory in this, much in the same way that he was only an accessory in everything else.

"You think I can turn it on and off like a switch?" she said. "You think it's just an act? One big joke?"

"No," said Topher. "I just thought–"

Julia spun on her heels and disappeared into a

nearby closet, then emerged with a large envelope. She held it in front of her like a shield for a moment before pressing it into Topher's hands.

"There," she said. "That's what you came for."

"What is it?" said Topher.

"Just one of my creations."

"What does it do?"

"I think you're about to find out." A smile appeared on her face as she read their expressions. "Or did you not know?"

"No." Again he looked to Isaac, who had even less than usual to say.

"Dan told you to come pick it up, right? And what did he tell you to do with it afterwards?"

"I don't know."

"Well." Again the mysterious smile appeared, broader this time, showing a row of rich-girl teeth, remarkably straight and white. "I do."

Topher told Isaac he didn't have to worry about it — he was the one who'd spent Dan Drugs's money, so he was the one who'd earn it back. He removed a bottle of clear liquid and a pipette from the envelope and poised the dropper over his tongue after it was filled. He held his head back and pointed his eyes downward, waiting for a signal of assent from Julia. She let him stay in that pose for a moment and then gave him one.

"Five drops," she said, and she watched each one fall onto his tongue. "Six," she said, and Topher complied before the word had slithered all the way out of her silken mouth. He lowered his hands, leveled his head, and they locked eyes with each other for about sixty seconds.

"Guess we should get going then," said Isaac.

"No," said Julia, and she moved aside so they could step past her. "Now I'm curious."

Julia had found a couch somewhere since the last time they'd been there – second-hand black imitation leather, the white netting showing through where the upholstery was flaking away. She stretched herself out upon its full length and watched the others with her cunning eyes, waiting to see where they were going to sit. They slid down to the floor with their backs against the wall directly across from her, where the TV would have been in a normal person's apartment. She lit a cigarette and sort of swished her hair behind her shoulder. Nothing special about her still: no ritual, no incantation. But she was a type of magic all by herself. Topher fixed his eyes on her and watched her without blinking; his pupils, filled entirely with her image, grew into placid black lakes. She spoke slowly, the words spilling forth from her mouth along with a thin stream of smoke:

"Tell me what you want. And then maybe we can try and get it."

"I just want to pass my classes," said Topher.

He spoke with trancelike persistence, but he was still putting on a show: he wasn't all the way gone yet, and Julia knew it.

"I don't believe you," she said, shrugging and smothering her cigarette to death in the ashtray. She turned her attention on Isaac, fixing him with her eyes, waiting for him to speak. "Now the other one. You."

"I don't want anything," said Isaac.

"Don't make me beg." It was both a request and a command. "Don't waste my time."

"But I don't."

She shook her head slowly, smiling with only one side of her mouth. Her voice was all in the throat, almost whispered, yet still powerful enough to fill the room: "Tell. Me what. You want."

He almost did. He would have, but he didn't have

the words for it. Not yet – and he knew that if he tried to start he would go on talking for years without finding them.

"I don't want any of this. I never asked for any of this. I just want a normal life."

"Really? Do you really, honestly think that?"

Isaac didn't have an answer for her. It hadn't felt like a lie when he said it the first time, but he knew it would be a lie if he had to say it a second time.

"I don't think that you're normal, Isaac," she said. "I think you're one of us."

Somehow it frightened him to think that she knew his name. And yet he was also proud to hear it come out of her mouth, as if that made his existence that much more valid, as if that made him that much more real. She held him in her gaze for only a moment longer before something – mercy, perhaps – compelled her to look away.

"How are you feeling," she said.

"I feel great," said Topher.

"Any visuals yet?"

"No. Just you."

She smiled at first and then made up her mind to frown. "Michael's gonna swing by here in a few minutes. It would probably be best if you two left."

"Okay." Topher labored numbly to his feet.

"And you," she said, turning her eyes on Isaac. "Isaac." There was the smile again, twisting her lips as she turned the name over in her mouth. "Make sure you stay with him. Just in case."

"Just in case what."

"Just in case he goes for any sharp objects or open windows." She smiled once more, just as cryptically, this time in Topher's direction. "Just in case he needs someone to hold his hand."

"For how long."

"Yeah," said Topher, lagging a couple seconds behind. "How long."

"No one knows," said Julia. "Estimates say ten to twelve hours."

The two of them descended the dark staircase and squinted into the sun. Isaac had forgotten it was still daylight out – had forgotten what day it was. He'd been planning on going back to the library and getting started on a paper, but it no longer looked very likely that this was going to happen.

"After we do this," he said, "are we square with Dan Drugs?"

Topher shook his head. "Not by a longshot."

Topher took one step toward the street and then halted as if facing an invisible wall. He leaned back until his palm made contact with the bricks of Julia's building and rested in this pose a while.

"Whoa," he said.

Isaac waited there with him. They had figured out an easy way to get to Julia's by bus, but he wouldn't be able to find his way back without Topher. They were in it together now, for better and for worse.


It had not been a pleasant trip. Topher was not a neophyte, and hadn't been since middle school. He gladly ingested substances and substrates he had heard of only minutes or seconds before, he could manage to have a good time taking the pills he found between couch cushions at parties. But last night was different. He still hadn't slept. One long nightmare with his eyes open: the walls leaking bugs, the walls decaying into living gristle, the meat moving with a will and a mind of its own, creeping across the floor, reaching up for his ankles. He climbed on top of a chair and spent the night making sure the floor didn't come too close. He ransacked his roommates' tents looking for cyanide pills. The only type of drug he wanted, the only type he couldn't find.

He was sick to his stomach after his head had cleared: there were stabbing pains in his gut that kept him from sleeping. He didn't have enough blankets to keep warm; no one had made any efforts to repair or patch the windows. No one had even swept: the floor of the apartment was still a minefield of glass and nails and splinters. There was no food in the kitchen because there was no kitchen. He couldn't remember much from the night before, but he could remember what Isaac had told him on the walk back to the Werehouse. He still had the address and the phone number written down somewhere. It wasn't the neatest solution, but it was a solution. He put in a call and gathered some things together and boarded a bus heading to Neverworld.

He parted the beads hanging in the doorway and tripped over a cat. Agitprop posters of unsmiling dictators hung on the walls between sagging tie-die tapestries. Yellow stuffing poked from the couch, its fabric slicked black with wear. Eyes looked up at him: some in surprise, some in a daze. Some frightened, as if it were a raid of some sort. Topher lit a cigarette and ashed into the pile of ash on a nearby saucer. He'd heard of Neverworld before but only from people he hated, either on principle or from experience. Never in his life had he imagined he'd find himself here. But it seemed appropriate somehow. A phrase he'd heard somewhere: revolution makes strange bedfellows.

"Cody's not here," said a male or female with bleached blonde dreadlocks. "He doesn't sell anymore."

Topher grinned wide and ashed on the floor this

time. "I'm here to see Ravi," he said.

Ravi lived in the basement, past the pile of broken bicycles, in an improvised shelter abutting the furnace. It was like a fort a kid might build on a rainy day: a floor of dirty pillows, half an old bedpost for a wall, and the light from overhead bulbs glowing through a pink sheet draped overhead. Ravi turned the dial up on his hissing gas lantern when he saw he had a guest. It took a while for Topher to recognize him. They'd never been introduced before, but Topher knew who he was. He was hard to miss: he was the only kid on campus who treated worldwide revolution like the most boring of all office jobs. But though Ravi dressed in public like a tool and a narc, he was shrouded now in a shapeless poncho like a medicine man living out at the farthest edge of the settlement, holding his lantern up near his head and squinting suspiciously through the light.

They sat cross-legged with the dossier between them. Binders, folders, zines, CDs, record inserts, thumb drives – Topher had dug deep in his archives and amassed a mountain of evidence. Mostly textual except for some badly blurred black and white photos. Nothing to condemn, but plenty to implicate. Which was good enough for their purposes.

"Here's the thing," said Topher, sifting through the papers. "He always uses pseudonyms. Bardamu, Azazello, Stavrogin. But he uses them consistently across a number of platforms. That might be where we get him. If you compare his underground writing to his course materials you can see the similarities. Sometimes word for word. It's not much. But it should be enough."

"Enough for what," said Ravi.

"I don't know. You tell me."

Ravi shook his head. "No. *I* asked the question. Either you're in a hundred percent or you're not in at all. So tell me. What are you looking to get out of this."

"I want Hightower gone."

"Yeah? Why is that. You seem like a pretty big fan."

Topher smiled: as much from nervousness as admiration. And he was sure this kid could see it too. He was pleased to have so underestimated him.

"It's personal," he said.

The kid nodded grimly and stared into the glowing bulb of flame at the center of his lantern. He tried to laugh but it came out almost without sound, just a grunt to relieve an inner impact.

"And you?" said Topher

"What do you mean, you."

"What do you have against Hightower."

Ravi grimaced and hunched himself protectively over his memories. "It's fucking personal, man."

He ran his hands over the documents; picked them up and fanned them until the tent was filled with the smell of old paper and new printing.

"Okay. Say the word. He's finished."

Topher hadn't expected the interview to end so soon. He hadn't expected it to go so smoothly. But he hadn't stooped this low just to boost his GPA. There were more immediate matters to attend to. It was as fair as life ever was, he told himself. He was paying a price too, though he didn't like to admit it.

"One more thing," he said.

"Yeah."

"I'm not giving this up for free."

"How much."

Topher ran numbers in his head. "Two hundred."

As soon as Ravi reached for his pocket Topher knew he blew it.

"Four," said Topher.

"Fuck you," said Ravi.

"Four hundred."

Ravi glared back at him. A strip of blue flames ignited at the base of the furnace, casting shadows where his eyes should have been.

"Fuck you," he said again, and again reached for his pocket. He had to empty both this time.

Topher counted the bills in the otherworldly blue light. Heat from the furnace drew forth from the basement all its subterranean smells: musk and mildew, mingled body odor and machine oil. Here, in the bowels of the building, was housed the burning hate that allowed Neverworld to lift its turrets skyward and pose as a place of love. It was like a fungus spread in spores from the Werehouse, thriving rhizomatically in all the coldest and darkest and most unlikely places. Or maybe the other way around: like it was only a dark energy radiating from Neverworld's twee antennae that allowed places like the Werehouse to exist.

He stood to show Topher outside the tent.

"It's a shame," he said. "You have good instincts. Maybe you want to drop in sometime at an SFPS meeting."

"Unlikely," said Topher. "But who knows. Maybe I'll see you around sometime."

THERE WAS WARMTH IN THE SUN where it cut through the buildings; the late-winter warmth of Chicago, wan and fleeting in the afternoon declension, restricted to long rectangular lengths of auburn that implied heat more than they imparted it. For the first time all week it was clear enough to see the towers of the Loop, pale blue in the mists of distance, from the top levels of the library. It was the first time in months, maybe years, Martin had been able to work. Scribbling in notebooks until his hand cramped, blind to consequences and criticism, the way he used to work before experience had taught him the futility of effort and the emptiness of enthusiasm. Age had imposed moderation on him, and moderation had aged him prematurely. He was glad to have broken from the cycle. Everything came back to him; he worked by muscle memory. The only difference was these were the tendons of the spirit and not the body.

These were only rough drafts. Later, at home, he would revise them, type them, send them to Hannah. He didn't know if she read them; he never asked. He didn't write to her because he thought she would understand, but only because she was the one who was drawing the thoughts from him. Almost as though they were really her thoughts, however hidden, and he felt obligated to return them to their rightful owner.

The last time they were together she told him about her dreams. Her visions, whatever they were. Just like Ellie, just like plenty of women before or since. The ones with good dreams wanted to share their splendor with this man who had no dreams of his own, and the ones with bad dreams thought that he with his immunity could exorcise whatever was haunting their sleep. But Hannah's dreams were of a different order altogether. Her eyes went blank when she talked about them, her muscles fell slack. Even her voice was low and throaty, as if she didn't have the energy to raise its pitch or inflect it with life. She went limp and let the voice of the world speak through her. All explanations, all metaphors – all the facile tools of literature and psychology – were of no use. Her dreams were too unambiguous for interpretation; their images were too primordial to be contained within any larger system of existing symbols. There was no way to talk about them. There was only the image they presented, and a great silence surrounding.

He had held the suspicion for years now, but she had confirmed it: the world was dying or perhaps had already died. All fashionable eco-apocalyptics were only an outer reflection of this inner state. An inner state that Hannah embodied, that bodied forth in her dreams, her hallucinations, her visions. Hannah, without knowing it, lent validity to Martin's entire schema of thought. All had been conjecture; but she was the proof.

He was coming close, he felt, to identifying the kernel of the problem, the black center from which spread the omnipresent rot. He tried to go back a step further and identify the cause of the crisis. But unrelated elements of the system were failing simultaneously, as if a breakdown had been coordinated by an outside force. There was no way to isolate a world-historical culprit. All anyone could do was try to fashion an escape. But how, if the rot was present in thought the same way it was present everywhere else. Uncompelled by any particular thinker, lying latent in the very structure of the mind's processes – present invisibly but most importantly within the mind, and from there radiating its influence outward to touch all things. This was not a crisis of technology but of perception. The world, like a virus, grew resistant to human means of perceiving it. All the TV stations and all the internet servers could burn tomorrow and the problem would still persist.

His post at the school, the return of Total Mobilization, the appearance of Hannah: it was all of a piece. It was as if his life were being uplifted by the same nameless will driving the world to its doom. So it felt to him like an obligation, a duty: he had to find a way out of this invisible prison. No matter what it would cost him, no matter who he would have to leave behind.

The sun dipped behind a science building bristling

with antennae and the library fell into dull bluish dark. Martin sat still, lost in thought, until all color drained from the sky and the stars failed to appear above the light-washed city. And when he came back to himself he remained still to avoid triggering the motion sensor overhead. He flicked his wrist to put pen to paper and the room flooded with pale white nothing-light. All his thoughts were disrupted, banished from his mind like the shadows from the room. He could still sense it inside, the nervous energy, worn-out momentum, from the lucidity of the day. But he could draw no more from it. His legs were unsteady when he lifted himself from his chair. This was how he had worked in his youth, his mental activity so intense that it drained the body as well. He needed to stay strong; he was the only one who could act as a medium for the truths he was approaching. Every day it would have to be like this. But for today his work was done, and he was satisfied, as rarely before, at the depth and the breadth of it.

Next he had a meeting with Harry. He hadn't been given much notice, but he wasn't surprised either: Harry was a man who was prone to emergencies. There was a good chance, statistically speaking, that his fourth wife had come to the same realization as the first three. Martin sent his shaky legs downstairs and into the bite of the cold. Across the empty campus, where the neo-classical buildings breathed silence through their columns and cafés leaked coffee-scented air when their doors swung open. He walked with a quick pace, hatless, his heart rate up, as if, like a marathon runner, his body would go into shock unless he cooled it down gradually.

The Arts and Sciences building was dark and empty. The elevator droned as it lifted him to the fourth floor. Something was off about the whole situation. Or maybe that was just an effect of the quick succession of exhaustion and exhilaration. His boots sent muffled echoes through the hallway as he approached the light glowing through the marbled glass window centered in Harry's door. It opened out on him before he could touch his hand to the knob. Harry stepped through the crack, wedging himself between the door and the world outside.

"I'm sorry, Martin," he said. "I tried to talk them out of it. You know I always do. But they wouldn't listen this time."

And with a defeated shove he swung the door the rest of the way. Martin saw faces in semi-circle, stern, their necks bent unnaturally, and a dozen eyes glaring at him. He recognized some from academic ceremonies and formal functions. Board members, presidents, lesser deans. The list went on: sub-clerks of sub-heads of sub-departments. The university had an endlessly supply of bureaucrats at its disposal. He stepped inside and let Harry close the door. He waited, unfrightened, resolute like a soldier. He willed up images – of Ellie, of George – like those his father and his father's father might have carried in their wallets. He clenched his jaw so that the bone popped from his cheek and everyone could see. He knew exactly what these people were after. There was only one thing they ever wanted. But they weren't going to get any blood from him.

He was trembling faintly when he next walked outside. A light snow was falling, as if the darkness of the sky was flaking off and drifting in specks down to their streetlit city world. It was still early; he still had plenty of time to get home. Plenty of time to figure out what he was going to say before he got there. But he had to get going before the streets became impassable. Snow in Chicago piled up like age, so gradually it couldn't be noticed until it was much too late.

He tried to sort it out as he drove; reasoning against

himself as if bargaining for hostages. He could keep his job. He could provide for his family. Could continue his work at this crucial juncture. There had to be a way, however degrading, however humiliating. Man never lacked for means of compromising himself. It wasn't a matter of how; he was willing to do anything. The only question was when, and to whom. Which earthly or unearthly power wanted the most to see him grovel.

*A number of documents have been brought to our attention,* they said. *Do you now have, or have you ever had, an affiliation with a musical group known as Total Mobilization?*

Ice streamed down his windshield, leaving bright black trails of water in its path. He drove by instinct, adrenaline, the same way he had answered the people in Harold's office. Neither conscious or unconscious, neither lying or telling the truth. Arranging words to signify nothing. That was all they ever wanted anyway. His heart beat with the memory: he had gotten away with it. So far. It wasn't yet the end of it. There might never be an end to it. But so far he had survived.

*If proved true,* they said, *do you have any idea how serious these allegations could be?*

He drove past his house without realizing it, then hit the brakes and skidded to the curb a couple blocks away. Like he was avoiding an accident. He kept the heat on and waited for his hands to stop shaking. They felt steady on the wheel, but fluttered uncontrollably whenever he took them off. And he couldn't drive forever. He could hide very complicated matters from Ellie, but he could never hide something as simple as that.

The snow came down clear and fast, heavy and needlelike; late winter snow, close to rain, dense and colorless. It pinged audibly on his roof and spattered hard against his windshield. Vapor rose from sewer grates like the soul of the world as it gave up the ghost. He killed the heat and the engine as if the cold might help him think better. He felt his cells slowing, accreting, hardening. Maybe he wouldn't have to tell Hannah anything. Maybe he could just disappear, like he had never been, like they had never happened. It probably wasn't the first time she had been through something like this. The more he thought about it the more certain he was. She was a smart girl, and she'd be able to figure it out on her own.

The wheels spun on icy marbles when he put the car in drive. But it satisfied him to at least be leaving a mark, however superficial, on the world. The tires dug until they hit pavement and the car jumped from the curb. He swung around the trafficless street and pulled up his driveway the same way he did every other day.

Ice came down in sheets, slowly encasing his car, his house, the whole street of sensible modern duplexes. If he stood out there long enough the same thing would happen to him. And beneath the ice and beneath the world was something else still. Humming with invisible life and warm with a heat that was not heat. The hail placed hard cold kisses on his skull when he stepped out of the car. Banging repeatedly as if trying to drill it into his head: the reason behind the hail, the cause of storms and earthquakes, tragedies, whirlwinds. The ice melted on impact and licked down his cheeks and behind his ears. His hands had stopped shaking. He would be ready for whatever came next. He didn't know yet what he was going to do, but he knew he would know it when he saw it. Intuition had carried him this far, and intuition would carry him farther still.

*And if you're not involved in this project, Professor Hightower,* his accusers had said, *do you know of anyone affiliated with the university who is?*

Martin opened the door and stood in the vestibule

as the ice dripped off him. He wanted to see how long he could remain there without being noticed. Something prevented him from moving any deeper into the apartment. He listened closely until he knew what it was: the sound of plastic wheels moving over the tile. A sound coming from the main hallway, where someone was pushing a toy car forward and back, forward and back, forward and back.

Isaac did not want to take action. Nothing had ever frightened him more. And yet he could feel it: living, growing, turning inside him, whispering into his ear all the world's many promises and taunts and incitements. In the end the realized, with an inner quail of the spirit, that he didn't really have a choice. His roommate was getting sick of him hanging out in the dorm room, unshowered and unmotivated, and he was getting tired of hanging out with Topher.

He avoided Cordelia for a week longer as he put the final touches on his plan: what kind of tone the conversation should take, a list of major points to hit, possible responses to likely objections, a whole tree of branching conversational paths which he schematized and memorized and sometimes rehearsed in his increasingly plentiful private time. He skipped all of his classes to ensure that he wouldn't see her on campus, hoping secretly that by withholding his presence from her he might loom larger in her mind. And yet, when the time came, he was still afraid to act. There was no real urgency; he knew she wouldn't forget about him completely like Hannah did. Their friendship, because it so often waxed and waned, could never flare out or diminish completely; it lacked the potential energy to effect a permanent change of state. There was no real danger of abandonment, and maybe this was why, above all other reasons, they had never been scared into loving each other. He would either have to force it to happen or continue to endure the shame of nothing ever happening. And that was something he was no longer willing to do.

He planned on intercepting her on her walk from the Arts and Sciences building to the dining hall, where she sat at the same table every day to drink tea and get started on the reading assigned by her early classes. The cold clear light glowed off the snow and fatigued his eyes, leaving green trails of distortion when he looked away. He had come too early because he was afraid of coming late, and had nothing to do but stand in the quad with his hands in his pockets, fidgeting around, fearing the worst.

Something in the corner of his eye compelled him to look closer: a small figure with her head down, moving slowly and erratically over the path as if blown by the wind. He was sure of it long before his vision adjusted to the glare: it was Hannah. But he froze as she came closer. No matter how often he thought about her, he still had little to say to her. Her magnetism was of an entirely different kind. He stepped aside to let her pass, and she didn't notice him standing there. She looked like she didn't even know where she was going. She looked like she had forgotten once more who she was. He turned his head to watch her pass, and kept watching even after she was far away.

"Isaac."

Cordelia was standing next to him, trying to smile. Wanting to smile, masking the effort, but aware already that he was not going to make it easy for her.

"Where have you been?" she said.

"Where have I been? Where have *I* been?"

Already the script had been disrupted. Isaac hadn't expected her to see him before he saw her, and this was enough to collapse the entire plan he'd laid out. He abandoned all subtlety, all cunning, all goals, all purpose: all he wanted, now that the conversation had begun, was to burn it down and be done with it.

"You think I wouldn't have picked up if you called?" he said. "What, you think I had anything better to do?"

She shook her head and cast a glance down the path, searching for suitable avenues of escape. "Isaac, don't be so dramatic. I'm not going to do this in public."

"I couldn't call you, could I. Because I'm sure you *did* have better things to do."

His voice was raised, his face was hot. Already he was out of breath, already he was out of arguments. But he couldn't back out now. Maybe this actually was his last and only chance. And with this thought he came the closest he'd ever been to loving her, which did not make it any easier to think or breathe.

"Like we're all gonna hang out together now," he said. "You and me and Guy. And I'll just sit there like I'm the world's biggest sucker."

"There's no need to make a big deal out of it. No reason to make a scene." She was speaking with deliberate quietness, below the usual conversational level, trying to bring the volume of the discussion down. "It's nothing."

"No! That's the whole problem! It *is* nothing! That's the problem!"

He was yelling now, louder than before, and stepped in front of her to block her path. She tried to dodge past him but he wouldn't let her, even though he didn't really have anything more to say.

"You think you're the only one?" he said. "You think it makes you special?"

"No. I don't care."

"But *I* care."

Cordelia, caught off guard by this, ceased her efforts to pirouette past him.

"So what," he said, "you were bored or something? You wanted to feel pretty? You're pretty. There."

"Isaac, don't."

"Don't what? Don't say the truth?"

"Just *don't!*"

Her voice rose to an anguished nasal pitch, and Isaac saw to his relief that the contest was over and decided. She was pleading more on his behalf than on hers. He had no defenses against something that was not an attack. She paused a moment and went on quietly.

"I don't think this is about me and I don't think this is about Guy. I think this is about Hannah."

"What Hannah. I don't know any Hannahs."

"This is not the time to get sarcastic with me. This is the time to tell me what you have to say if you have anything to say."

He thought about it; spent a long moment, actually lost in thought, catching glimpses of the problem and then losing it in the shadows of his mind. But it was only something he could see, not something he could say. Huge like a building, a block-long slab of brutalist concrete, and he hadn't yet managed to map out its dimensions, couldn't yet begin to guess at what it held inside.

"I'm not going to tell you," he whispered.

"What?"

He was staring down at the sidewalk; maybe he hadn't made any noise at all, only moved his lips. Either way, he wasn't going to say it again. Cordelia waited, watching him carefully, giving him every opportunity. And waited longer than she should have, and longer than he deserved, but finally could wait no longer.

"And if you don't want my help," she said, "then

that's something I can't help you with."

She still lingered there a moment longer to see what he was going to say, and moved on when it became clear that he was not going to say anything: stepped easily past him and down the path, and he turned to watch her go the same way he had watched Hannah.

MARTIN HADN'T BEEN SLEEPING. He had expected as much. But he hadn't expected Ellie to stay awake too, keeping silent vigil with him. That was the worst part of it. He stayed as still as possible, feigned deep breathing, but it never fooled her. Their brainwaves mingled through the pillow, and she could sense the disturbance in the minute vibrations. It wasn't like him: he always slept soundly, heavily, without dreaming. He worked himself hard so that he would. But now he was working twice as hard – mining the farthest reaches of his brain for a way to keep his job, devoting all his mental energies to this while he went through the motions of his daily rounds – and it still didn't help. Ellie knew something was wrong. But either she convinced herself she didn't or she had enough tact not to ask.

He still hadn't thought up any course of action cohesive enough to be called a plan. But he had envisioned several approaches he might make. The problem being that each was contingent upon forthcoming circumstances, and there was nothing for him to do now but sit passively as the hypotheticals flooded his mind; nothing to do but wait to see which, if any, would become real. That was why he was relieved to hear the knock on the door. Be it good news or bad, at least fate had arrived, and spared him the pain of waiting. He was aware of Ellie's eyes on him as he pulled his jacket on.

"Maybe you should call the police," she said.

He frowned and shook his head: he didn't want any intermediaries between himself and what was to come. Right now the idea of taking a bullet wasn't entirely distasteful to him. Ellie slipped into a robe and hovered, nervous, at the bedroom door. But Martin was already walking down the hall. Almost bored: whatever it was, he deserved it.

The wind chill had pushed the temperature below zero. Demian stood outside with his lips parted and his clenched teeth showing. He tried to smile when he saw Martin; at least that was Martin's best guess. But it was like he didn't know how.

"What are you doing out here," said Martin.

Demian's lips twitched. His face was swollen with cold and his eyes blinking to guard against the blowing snow. He looked like an android on the brink of malfunction.

"I don't know," he said. "Mind if I come in?"

Under the hallway light Demian's pupils contracted to almost nothing. His skin was pale, his lips and eyelids purple. Martin had plenty of questions. But Demian was shy and squirrelly, sweeping his eyes across the room to avoid meeting Martin's. With nervous hands he straightened a photo on the wall. Something in Martin jumped to stop him. But it was an old photo. George looked how any other child would look at that age. Ellie poked her head out from the bedroom, still unsure if the situation was safe or not. Martin, with a hand on Demian's back, steered him toward her.

"Ellie, this is my friend Demian. You've met once before."

"Yes," she said, "I remember."

She shook his hand and showed her teeth like she always did when she was uncomfortable in a social situation. Her smile remained fixed in place and her worried eyes went to Martin, waiting for a cue. She didn't know whether to be concerned, sympathetic, frightened, all of the above. It was the dread of the uncanny: Demian wasn't projecting emotions like a normal human. Martin took a moment to calculate. He had thought it prudent to reintroduce them, just to put Ellie at ease. But he didn't want her to see what was coming next.

"This might take a while," he said.

She knew what he meant. With a quiet nod she retreated into the bedroom and shut the door behind her.

Martin turned on the lights in the kitchen and thought about returning to the bedroom to get dressed. Under his jacket he was wearing only a T-shirt, sweatpants, slippers. He was exposed. But Demian didn't look much better: fully clothed, mentally shorn. He sat at the table and waited for Demian to join him. But Demian didn't.

"Can I get you anything," said Martin.

Demian swiveled in place, eyes wide open as if staring through the cabinet doors. Martin walked to the sideboard in the next room and returned with a bottle and two glasses.

"Good guess," said Demian.

"If you want to call it that."

Demian had to raise his hand to shield his pinned eyes from the light. "Any chance we could cut it out with these?"

"If that would make you feel better."

Martin killed the lights and sat down. But Demian, instead of taking the seat across from him, began pacing in a tight loop from one wall to the other.

"What is it, Demian. You're making my wife nervous."

The night air, pregnant with morning, sent quasi-light through the window; light that did not illuminate but only revealed with greater clarity the contours of shadow in the room. Martin kept losing sight of Demian. He tracked him by the scuffing of his shoes against the tile. The scuffing stopped, and a voice came from the air, dry and croaking: a corpse's imitation of a human voice.

"I know, Martin."

Martin filled the glasses: one for him and one for fate. And waited a beat for Demian to continue. He didn't.

"I'm not going to guess," said Martin. "I'm not in the mood. What is it you know."

Demian didn't sit down. The scuffing started up again.

"I know why you sent your wife back inside. I know why I make her nervous. She must be smarter than she looks."

Martin let it go. He was too busy thinking. What was it that Demian knew. Which facet of Martin Hightower's disgrace. He made an educated guess: probably the part that mattered least. That was why he was making such a big deal out of it.

"She's just a girl," he said. "We are men. At least I thought we were. Sit down. Have a drink."

"That's what I thought too. That's what I used to think. Just a girl."

The scuffing stopped, but the shadow came no closer. His voice was quieter now, more human; and there was a buried resonance, surfacing against his will, of a certain sober earnestness.

"What's she like when she's with you?"

Martin took a swallow. There was no right answer to the question. He waited.

"I'm just curious. I really want to know. Because I'm still not sure if there was anything *to* her. Maybe she just assumes the characteristics of the host organism. Typical parasite behavior."

The second glass was subsumed in the cloud of

shadow and the footfalls started up again: but slower, more measured now.

"I'll start if you don't want to. She was kittenish with me. Girly. Dumber than she needed to be. And I think it was because of the act I was giving her. Always pushing the dumb jock routine. And she bought it, in spite of her supposed principles."

His voice got hard and mechanical again. It dropped an octave and broke into clicks as it left his robot body.

"But here's the thing. I don't think she really wanted it. She just thought I'd want her to want it. And now I'll never know for sure. So I was just wondering if you could fill me in. If you could tell me what the real Hannah was like. If you could tell me if there ever was a real Hannah."

Martin focused intently on the voice – not on the words but on the sound of it. Ready to cut him off the instant he got too loud. Ellie might have been able to understand if she were leaning her ear against the door and listening with all her concentration. But Martin knew she wouldn't be.

"Because maybe you saw something I didn't. Maybe you saw something that made you want to give all this up. Nice apartment. Nice job. Nice wife." The voice changed again; grew quieter but somehow nearer. "Nice son too. But I've never met him. You never bring him around. Why don't you tell him to come out here a minute. Have him say his ABCs. I can wait."

Martin tried to stare him down. But there was nothing to stare at. Demian's presence was larger, more threatening, because of it. Martin gathered his voice, felt it grow in his throat, and made sure it was strong before speaking.

"I don't care what you think of me. Or my family. But you still shouldn't have done it."

"Done what."

"You shouldn't have told them about Total Mobilization."

There was silence for a moment. Not the silence of guilt – not with Demian. The silence of genuine surprise. So Martin was wrong this time; but at least he had finally gotten Demian's attention.

"Shouldn't have told who about Total Mobilization."

"The school, Demian. They're onto us. Someone tipped them off. It's over."

The chair across from Martin scraped back, and a human-sized shadow dropped into it, slack and lifeless. It remained so through the course of a long silence.

"Up until now I thought you did it," said Martin. "But I guess you didn't."

"No. I didn't."

Martin reached out and tipped the bottle over both their glasses. His nerves were at ease, no longer clashing against the energy of Demian's. They were in a state of de-tente now if not alliance. And so it was with a tinge of re-gret that he came to understand the route that fate had mapped out for him. For the sake of self-preservation; he had no other choice.

"What happened," said Demian.

"They approached me regarding some similarities between the course materials and some old liner notes. Who knows what else. Scraps of paper, notes scribbled on napkins. Whoever did it really knew what they were doing. And now they're looking for names." Martin stopped him-self to let this sink in.

"And what have you told them so far?"

"So far nothing. But they know someone associated with the course is in Total Mobilization. And the more they look into this thing the more of a problem it's going to be. All I can say for sure is they don't know which one of us it is."

"Which means what," said Demian. Hesitant, like

he already knew.

"Which means," said Martin, "only one of us has to take the fall." He paused to gather courage and found that no courage was necessary. He was only telling Demian what he already knew. "Which means you're taking the fall, Demian."

Martin understood then why Demian had spent so much time standing up. He too felt like pacing the room. A show of dominance; a victory lap. But he forced himself to stay where he was. It would be more in character for him to take the moral high ground, or at least pretend to. Demian's laugh was dry and rasping, drawn out like a moan.

"And what makes you think I'll do that."

"Because I have a life here. I have a family. You're just a kid. You could start over. I couldn't."

"Yeah. Start over – sure. What the fuck do you expect me to do, drive a truck?"

"Either one of us goes down or both of us do. It's that simple. And there's no reason both of us have to go down."

"But I didn't have anything to do with any of that. I wasn't even in the band when that stuff was written."

"So what. They don't know that. They don't know anything."

"So wait. Wait. Wait wait wait wait wait." There was another laugh, high and nasal, stuttered out. "You – *you*, Martin Hightower – want me – *me*, Paul Demian – you want me to, correct me if I'm wrong, 'do the right thing.'"

Martin hesitated despite himself. It did sound odd when phrased like that. "Yes. That's right."

Demian put his head on the table and laughed. Musically yet mirthlessly: a series of hollow notes that echoed off the kitchen walls.

"Oh, the irony. The irony, the irony. Me – I'm going

to do the right thing. For no reason. Just because Martin Hightower told me to."

"You're taking the fall or else I call the cops on your girlfriend."

"Which *one*, Hightower."

"The tall one. The one with the phony prescriptions."

Demian's answer was late by a couple milliseconds. Just enough to let Martin know that he'd hit his mark. "She's got nothing to do with this." He pivoted awkwardly, away from sentiment, back to belligerence. "You wouldn't do it anyway."

"You'd be surprised what I could do if I had to. But I hope it doesn't come to that."

Martin's eyes had adjusted to the darkness. In it he could catch the glints of white shining from Demian's pupils, tiny, heatless, starlike. He fixed his eyes on them and beamed his thoughts into Demian's skull: *Let's undo the screws on you, Demian. Let's see how much of a human being you are.* He poured another half-glass for himself and corked the bottle.

"Think about it when you're sober. Maybe it'll make more sense."

"Not likely."

"You'll see."

"I mean it's not likely I'll be sober."

Martin returned the bottle to the sideboard and saw the outline of Demian's shape when he got back to the kitchen: either sleeping or shot through the heart, doubled over, forehead on his fist on the table.

"Maybe we should get you home," said Martin.

Demian didn't reply. Or move or even seem to breathe. Martin lifted him from the chair by his shoulders. His feet dragged like a toddler's – like George's feet when he wasn't cooperating – and it took half a minute and all his strength to get him standing. He leaned him like an inanimate sack against the counter.

"You're fucked up, Demian. How did you get here?"

"Walked."

But his feet could hardly hold him up as Martin pushed him to the door. If a man passed out on a night like tonight he'd be frozen by morning. They wouldn't find him until the spring.

"I'll give you a ride. Hang on."

Martin tried to let go, but Demian wouldn't stay upright. Easing his weight against the wall, Martin let him slide down to the floor.

"Demian's sick," said Martin, getting dressed. "I'm taking him home."

Ellie, curled beneath the covers with her back to the door, rolled over. She searched him up and down with her eyes: without suspicion, without anger, without even much disappointment. Just looking him over to try to understand and empathize with whatever he was hiding from her. And he was relieved to think that this would be the last time, or close to the last time, that he'd ever have to hide anything from her.

The front door was swinging open on its hinges when he left the room, cold air blasting into the hallway. But Demian hadn't finished stumbling past the driveway. Martin caught up and held him by the shoulder.

"I'm taking you home," he said.

Snow had come down in the afternoon, sugared and fluttery, coating the blackened crags of late-winter ice with a veneer of powdered white. Some of it settled on the roads and was scraped away; the rest blew in shifting dunes through the canyons of the city, finely contoured and terraced by the wind, choking the alleys and creeping up to low windows. Puffs of glitter ticked against the windshield and froze into place, grinding against the rubber when

Martin tried to use the wipers. Demian was silent, resting his forehead forward on the dashboard. Not sleeping; just trying to hold it together. Bastard though he was, he deserved Martin's pity. Participation in Total Mobilization had a way of engendering disillusion; encouraging pride and facilitating the fall. As it had happened to Felix, so it was happening to Martin. Demian was next in line.

"And what about Hannah," said Demian.

"What about her," said Martin.

"Are the two of you going to live happily ever after?"

"No."

Martin thought about explaining himself further, but he left it at that. No explanation was necessary. No explanation would suffice.

"And how does Hannah feel about this." Demian, awaiting an asnwer, kept his head on the dash but turned to look at Martin. "Or does she even know?"

"No." Martin shook his head as if preparing to say something else. "No," he said only.

"Mr. Morality. Mr. Do The Right Thing."

"I never touched her, Demian."

"As if that makes it any better. As if that means anything."

Demian tried to hold back a laugh but sputtered it through his lips. It lasted longer than it should have: it was maybe thirty seconds before he could speak again. He sat up, sat back, still laughing slightly, still breathing deeply, and rubbed his closed eyes with the palms of his hands, reluctant to take them away after he had finished.

"That poor girl," he said. "That makes it so much worse."

"THIS IS THE LAST TIME, RIGHT?"

Topher held Isaac's leg steady with one hand and with the other tried to fit his thumbnail between the skin and the sweat-slicked band of tape. "Hold still. I can't get it."

"It fuckin' hurts."

"I'm not the one who told you to tape it to your leg. You could've just put it in your pocket." He found a seam in the tape and worked it slowly up until he could pinch it with his fingers. "Ready?" Isaac shook his head, but he ripped it off anyway.

"Ow. Fuck." Isaac stood and hobbled around the room with his teeth bared, sucking in air. "Son of a bitch." He slumped one shoulder against the wall and took some deep breaths. "This is it, right? We're square after this."

"Sure. If you want it to be."

"What's that supposed to mean?"

Topher shrugged and used his thumbs to count out the little blue pills in their plastic baggies. One had torn open when he removed the tape, and he was able to coax a pill though the hole, popping it into his mouth when Isaac closed his eyes to wince.

"Dan said he could use a guy for things like this. Said he could give me a full time spot. I'm sure I could cut you into it."

"No. I'm not a drug dealer."

"I'm not asking you to make deals. I could use you."

"For what?"

"You make a good mule. No one ever seems to notice you. It's like you don't exist."

Isaac, having passed through the worst of the pain, bent over to roll his pants back down. "Thanks."

"What else are you gonna do? Stay in college?"

Isaac, bent over, picked his head up in surprise. "You're not?"

Topher again weighed the baggies in his hands. They were deceptively light for the weight they carried in his mind. He did some quick figures in his head, calculating the worth of each pill, the worth of each bag, multiplied in bulk through the months and the years, going off the grid of actual numbers and into a space of pure and formless possibility.

"Why should I. My only plan for after graduation is to fuck around. So I figure I might as well get started now."

"So all that shit you went through. Getting that guy fired, getting the class canceled. It was all for nothing."

Topher, still daydreaming, tried to feel again the weight of the pills in his hand. But there was nothing to feel – there was nothing there. That was how they worked, they were magic things, lighter than air.

"Yeah," he said. "I guess you could say that."

Dan Drugs, drying his hair, walked naked from the shower and only wrapped the towel around his waist once he had entered the room. "Everything go okay out there?"

"Yeah." Topher tossed Dan the three baggies, one at a time like one jester helping another to juggle. "Isaac had them taped to his nuts in case he got frisked."

"No one's gonna bother Isaac. Dude's a ghost." Dan watched him pull his arms through his jacket and make for the door. "You're not gonna stick around?"

"No," said Isaac. "I'll be late for astronomy."

Dan shook the baggie of pills. It sounded to Topher like cat food rattling around a dish. "Wanna see some stars?" he said.

Dan wanted Topher to make another run for him – some speed had just come in, and there was a house in the area that had requested some. "Unless you have somewhere else to be."

"No," said Topher.

"It's this spot out in the ghetto where all these crazy hippies live. I forget the name."

"Don't worry. I know the place."

"Here and here." He handed over the bags of yellow pills and wiggled a little blue pill through a tear in the plastic of the other baggie. "One for the road."

"If you insist," said Topher, swallowing it.

He wasn't sure what they were. Either way, there were now two inside of him. He paused on the landing, held the railing, tested the wooden steps. Everything was holding in place, for now at least. He tasted the city air on his tongue, rolled his eyes around his head to test the light. The days were getting longer, and the afternoon sky showed a brilliant blue through the buildings on the horizon line – a blue that had a weight and immediacy about it, convex and not concave, reaching out to him and prodding him ever onward. He couldn't feel his tongue, and the departing bus left lingering trails of light hanging in the air when it flashed in the sun. It must have been ecstasy, he decided, or something close to it. He floated over to the bus stop and waited there for only a moment before floating away again. He stepped to the curb with his finger held out in the middle of the abandoned industrial corridor. Besides some parked tractor trailers and cement trucks there didn't seem to be any vehicles around for miles. But he was a working man now; he could expense it. Twenty seconds later, like magic, a cab arrived.

Topher parted the beads and stepped over the cat. Ravi was sitting in an armchair, facing the door but staring at the wall. Almost like he was waiting for him, except he couldn't have been, because no one knew he was coming. Ravi's eyes found him immediately and wouldn't leave him after that.

"They got the wrong guy," he said.

"What do you mean."

"I mean Hightower. They didn't fire him. They went for the other guy."

Topher shrugged. "I'm looking for a chick named Kim. She around?"

Ravi raised himself slowly from his chair. "That's not fair. I want my money back."

The peace-and-love pills he had just ingested must have also been mixed with something that made him thirst for human blood. He squared his shoulders with the other kid, widened his stance, pointed a finger: "Sit the fuck down. You have no right making demands on me. Where's Kim."

Not even all the way upright yet, Ravi lowered himself back into the chair. He continued the motion even after he was seated, slouching his shoulders, dropping his eyes. "Kim doesn't live here anymore."

"Where does she live?"

"I don't know. No one knows. She left without telling us where she was going."

"Fair enough."

Topher shifted his weight so he could feel the baggies in his pocket against the skin of his thigh. Again he ran numbers in his head, less exact, more amorphous, overestimating decimal places, who cares. He was sure they would not go to waste.

"This isn't over," said Ravi.

"Yeah yeah yeah," said Topher as he left.

Andy was packing his gear into his car when Topher got back home. Light dripped off the streetlamps and stung his eyes like citrus juice, so strong he could almost taste it. It made him feel like he could talk to anyone, say anything.

"What's up," he said.

"I need a break." Andy brought the heavy black cases carefully to rest on top of his trunk.

"A break from what?"

Andy gestured at the Werehouse. "This. What do you think."

"Why?"

"I wouldn't expect you to understand."

Andy continued his work, heaving the cases into the back seat and slamming the door behind them. He glanced once at Topher, getting ready to make a point by departing wordlessly, but couldn't keep himself from glancing again:

"This is all just a game to you. Just a good time. That's what you don't understand. Because you could still turn back any time you wanted. Get any type of life you want. I can't. You ever think of that?"

Topher shook his head, truthfully, and began to smile because it seemed like a funny time to start telling the truth. Andy, seeing this, stormed around to the driver seat, raising his voice, red in the face:

"I don't *have* that option, Topher! I don't have fucking anything!"

And he slammed the door and sped off. Some El Salvadorian kids across the street laughed, thinking they were a couple *maricones* having a breakup. But they could think what they wanted. Topher loved everyone.

They had found a few couches in the trash the week before and hauled them up three flights to their front door. So far they had brought with them no bugs or other harbored vermin. Guy and Blue were sitting on one, Julia and Michael Reality on the other. Guy was busy, but Julia and Michael Reality were just smoking a bowl and talking.

"What's up with him," said Topher, gesturing with his head toward the staircase.

"He's pissed off about Total Mobilization."

"Yeah."

"So you already heard?"

Topher had to think a moment, but instead spent the moment not thinking. "Yeah."

"Who did you hear from?"

Topher shrugged. "I don't know. I just heard."

Julia's eyes were fixed on the embers glowing in the bowl of the pipe. She watched them die out and blew a cloud of smoke in the air, looking at Topher through the haze.

"He said it's over now," said Michael Reality. "He said the album's never gonna come out."

"No," said Topher. He didn't know why, but it sounded true when he said it. "It's not over."

His eyes went to Julia by accident and stuck there like flies in honey. She noticed this and maybe smiled. But everything was starting to blur a little bit. Melt, just a little bit. His heart rate picked up and he had to reassure himself: just a little bit.

"Topher."

It was Guy who said it. He was looking at him, so was Blue. Everyone was looking at him. Topher wondered what they were going to say next. Heart pushing words and blood up into his skull: *Topher, you don't look so good. Topher, are you alright?*

"Have you seen Isaac around?"

"Yeah," said Topher.

"When?"

"I don't know. Around."

"Is he still fucked up about that thing?"

"Yeah."

"You think I should say something?"

"No." Topher thought about it, swayed a bit, caught his balance. "Everyone's fucked up. That's what makes the world go round."

A phone started ringing. His phone started ringing, so his hands started reaching for it. He looked at the thing a while before he could figure out how to use it. But everyone was watching, so he made himself do it, using both slippery hands to pry it open.

"Topher," said Dan Drugs.

"Yeah."

"I'm getting some trippy visuals right now. You?"

"Yeah."

"Man, I'm sorry dude. That shit must've been laced with something. I don't know how it's gonna play out. I might've just given you a bad dose."

"That's okay." He said the words slowly and then listened to them echo around inside his head, fading gradually to nothing. As he waited for them to die out he looked again around the room, at Guy and Blue and Julia and Michael Reality, hating everything about them: hating their happiness and hating their sadness and hating their young living bodies. "No big deal. Life's a dose."


KIM CLEANED. Kim cooked. Kim shared pills. She didn't complain. Demian started staying the night. He ran out of money, but his lease was month-to-month; he moved in. Kim, with uncanny timing, had just gotten a place of her own. He ate her food and drank her beer. She didn't complain. The refrigerator stocked itself. The bed made itself. The rooms cleaned themselves. She never complained. He still couldn't find work. She wasn't complaining.

She was good enough, he told himself. For now, he told himself – just a rebound. They never went out in public. In the dark, at night, he thought of Hannah. Or tried to; but Kim and her were just too different. In body type, in essential temperament, in amorous proficiency. It was funny: when he was with Hannah he derided her, mentally, for her typecast promiscuity; for her careful choreography and practiced gestures, the inner stiffness of her outer voluptuousness. And yet, for all her predictability, he still couldn't find her equal. Like an artist, she had ways of elevating the banal. Her simulation was realer than anyone else's authenticity.

"Listen," he said. "I gotta get out of the house for a second. I'm going crazy in here."

Standing in front of the stove, Kim nodded calmly, her wide eyes studying him. Studying him even though he hadn't changed in any way but the worse since they started dating. Or sleeping together or living together or whatever. She stirred the steaming pan and didn't ask him to stay for dinner. She knew he didn't have much of an appetite these days.

"Okay," she said. She didn't ask questions, didn't complain.

"Paul," she said. He turned around. "Your jaw."

And she took a few steps forward and pressed it shut for him. Again he was swinging it back and forth on its hinges; not grinding his teeth, but wanting to. He wasn't used to taking speed, but it was all they had. He made her knock it off with the forged prescriptions. It was too risky.

It was getting warmer. All the remaining snow had been pushed out of sight, into alleys and parking lots and the farthest corners of Chicago's small lawns. All the tufts of grass that had failed to die were coming to life again in the fissures between sidewalk tiles. The monolith clouds of winter gave way to outsize cotton balls tumbling through the empty blue space above the lake. Demian had been walking a lot more since the snow had started melting. Since losing his job. He had a whole routine worked out: walk to the lake, sit until he got cold, go to the bar to warm up. Kim never asked where he was going, or why. Kim never complained.

He found a bench in the sun and watched the waves lick over the smooth black rocks. He clamped large studio headphones around his ears and started the new Total Mobilization album from the beginning. Unfinished, unmastered, unreleased, for his consumption only – he had promised himself already that he would never leak the tracks to the wider world. Because he was too proud and didn't want anyone to hear them in incomplete form; because he was too ashamed, and didn't want anyone to know how close they had come, how badly they had failed.

It wasn't like their other work. Wasn't just an exercise in brutalism. There was beauty there if you knew where to look; lines of melody threading in feedback squeals through the wall of sound. Blasts of static like treble thunderstorms and quiet moments like pattering rain. It was a whole world in sound: the low frequency gurgling of the earth and sawtooth waves beaming like light through the empyrean. There was purpose this time to the madness. And no one would ever know. He tried to comfort himself: even if it were released, no one outside their little circle of weirdos would care. He had aged enough in the past months to have learned at least that much.

Everything new, everything good was Martin's idea. He could see this clearly now. He wondered sometimes if Martin had the recordings, if he liked them, if he regretted leaving them unfinished. But Martin was a grown man, ready to move on; maybe he didn't care anymore.

It still gnawed him sometimes. A voice inside that came from himself but needled like someone else: You got screwed, Demian. You got suckered; taken in by Hightower and his pity act. Because his wife is boring and his kid is retarded. Because of his own mistakes – that was why you took the fall.

*Do the right thing.* Enough time had passed; the irony

could now bring a smile to his face. Hightower didn't believe in the "right thing." Neither did he. Neither did anyone.

He always brought his notebook out on his walks. At first so Kim would see him take it, so she wouldn't think he was going to the bar. But he came back drunk enough for her to figure it out anyway. Now he took the notebook just so he could see himself take it, and in that moment experience a burst of nostalgia for everything he once thought he'd be at this point in his life.

Once he had tried to write something about Hannah. He didn't know what: a poem, a story, a portrait, a sketch, a single sentence. But he didn't know where to start. He didn't know what she was, to him or to anyone else. He didn't know what she was to herself. He had never known, and never would. He tore the pages from the book and tore them into smaller pieces still and released the cloud of paper into the wind and watched the scraps flutter out over the lake.

Words came too fast for him these days. Too fast to write down, so fast they could only skim along the surface of any given concept. As if thought were an invisible thing, three-dimensional, and his unending wash of words just a coat of paint thrown on top to reveal its shape. He kept his notebook open and fidgeted his pen over the surface. Words fell apart: into circles, into lines. He kept his hand working; the patterns repeated. He drank beer/shot specials to slow the brainwaves down. It didn't work; just made his pen less steady, the patterns more erratic. He burned through pages and pages until he made himself put a stop to it. Then the anger rising up again, bottled and impotent, deep in his chest. It didn't have to be this way, he told himself. That helped a little. But not enough. He turned to a blank page.

*Dear Mrs. Hightower.*

But that was too formal. He wanted to appeal to

her as a friend. He started over.

*Dear Ellie.*

It was the only thing he'd written in weeks. The only thing he'd written with ease in months. Maybe the only thing he'd ever written with any sort of pleasure. He had a few more drinks to celebrate when it was done, and watched as the light outside the window changed from white to gold to purple to black.

He stumbled on his way out the door. The bartender stopped him and asked if he was alright. Demian waved him off, pushed him aside, slurring. One step outside and the world turned diagonal; the lake, flashing black with night, gaped before him like a swallowing mouth. He called Kim so she could call him a cab. He didn't have any money on him. Or on his cards. No credit. He had nothing.

Kim listened. She didn't care how little he had.

She handed a folded bill through the front window and helped him claw his way out of the back seat.

"Paul," she said. "I need you to hold yourself up while I get the door. Can you do that for me?"

He gripped the stoop railing with both hands and felt the follow-through of the world's whirling torque beneath his feet. It never stopped. And imagine if it did. Everyone would go crazy trying to make it start again.

There were certain places in the apartment where the world wasn't spinning. On the couch, lying end to end with his eyes closed, he found such an island. A voice above him, soft and female:

"You should eat something."

There was a knot in his stomach; tied tight, impeding the flow of food. But his head was foggy and big, tottering on his neck, and he could still sense the nonstop motion of the world outside his bubble of calm. Despite the fact that it would please her, he nodded. The smell of food came closer and the voice sounded again.

"Did you get any work done today?"

"No."

"Nothing at all?"

"Nothing good. Only bad things." He tried to open one eye but closed it when the apartment started moving again. "I'm a bad person, baby."

"I know."

He smiled and kept his eyes closed. "I'm bad news. I'm a real bad dude."

"I know."

He opened his eyes. And she was there, filling the frame of his vision, unpretty and companionable, gazing down with unchecked benevolence. Like the spinning of the world; but all inside him now, nothing outside. The same motion, the same principle – it was all the little motions that joined to make the big one. It lived inside everyone. And he saw then, only now and too late, that this was for real and not just for fun, and that she really loved him.

HARRY POURED HIM ANOTHER DRINK. Martin looked at his watch but did not bother reading the numbers. He remembered, after looking at it, that he didn't have a class to teach. He had only come here to hide.

"I don't think you've done anything wrong," said Harry. "And you get to keep your job. So I don't see where the problem comes from."

"From Ellie," said Martin.

Harry turned in his chair and popped his eyes out, astonished, which was his way of telegraphing anger. "My son. You have not *done* anything *wrong!* And I'm not going to sit here and watch you beat yourself up about it."

Martin had tried explaining this to Ellie. Of course he had: he could never lose an opportunity to lecture someone. He explained to her exactly what used to happen when he went to Hannah's apartment; he would explain how only the skin of their hands had ever made contact. But this only made her more upset, so angry that she couldn't even cry: her nose ran and her cheeks grew bright red, her lips parting involuntarily, in a sort of pain. Even if that were true, she said, do you think that would make the slightest difference?

She spent her days in George's room. She spent her nights in George's room. This was her way of telling him he had wounded the boy as well as her. This was her way of telling him she knew exactly why he had felt the need to wound the both of them. Harry knew most of the details, but not all of them. As close as they were, he still didn't know about George. That was why he would never truly understand.

"It's not that easy," said Martin.

"Sure it is."

"Just saying something doesn't make it true."

"Sure it does. I do it all the time."

The office was making him claustrophobic. Heavy drapes drawn, walls lined with books, brass finishings turned dull from wear, old wood moldings showing naked through their layered histories of chipped shellac: he couldn't breathe in this place. The scotch went straight to his stomach and produced there a queasiness that could not be quelled by positive thinking or pithy turns of phrase. The past was as much an illusion here as it was elsewhere. The past was too close now instead of too distant, and had become just as alienating as the present.

"That's just the seminary talking," said Harry. "Just your jesuitical instincts, as it were."

"I was in the diocesan seminary," said Martin. "Not

the Jesuit one."

But Harry wasn't listening anymore. Martin trapped the last of his scotch between his lips and teeth and sucked it through in drips, an IV solution funneled down to a comatose spirit. Harry didn't offer any follow-up questions: how his wife was doing, or his teaching assistant, or the young woman in question. It was just as well, because Martin had no new information about any of them. He thanked him for the scotch and excused himself rather abruptly. Harry watched him go, his eyelids lowered in pity or self-pity or some sort of alcoholic combination of the two. Maybe it made no difference, maybe it was all the same anyway.

The snow had receded and black earth now showed from the gaps, bristling over with yellow stalks of grass. It rained often, and the humidity hung in the air, misting down from the clouds and up from the melting drifts. He got halfway across the campus before he remembered he had nowhere to go. His class had been cancelled for the rest of the semester, and he did not want to go home either. He had been hiding in Harry's office because he no longer felt comfortable hiding in his study. He hadn't even looked at his manuscript in weeks. And he wondered, with a curious mixture of dread and relief, if he would ever look at it again.

It was something worse than silence. He thought he'd known silence before – the silence of the woods, the fields, the mountains, the silence of a suburban study at three in the morning – but it was nothing like this. A silence that lay crushingly in a room, silence that sucked the sound from the world outside. Silence like a glacier, frozen solid and stretching on for miles. For the first few weeks Ellie stared at him with a confused sort of hatred in her eyes. She hated him for making her feel hate. She hated him because there was no way to talk about it, no way for their separate vocabularies to meet. She hated him for making her silent, like him.

He found himself at his car and let himself in. There was a message from Regina on his phone: she would be happy to see him tonight. It would be just like old times, she said — she still lived in the old neighborhood. Which should have been proof enough that he was making a mistake. He fired the ignition and waited a moment for the car to heat up, then pulled into traffic and set out for the north side.

She lived alone on North Clybourne. He drove past twice, double-checked the address: it was a new condo raised up across the street from the demolished projects. The rubble hadn't yet been cleared. The lot was filling with garbage: plastic bags and paper cartons gathering in drifts at the base of the chain link fences, and only a crumbling Baptist church standing sentry against the forces of complete erasure. There was nothing in the surrounding neighborhood but auto shops and union headquarters sitting squat in their blackened brick buildings. The condo looked like it was made of tan plastic. It floated in its own private atmosphere, seamless and born from nowhere, without umbilical cords or roots in reality, as if to mock him and the world around him for the imperfections of age and accident. Martin buzzed in and stepped through a thicket of synthetic plants on the way to the elevator. They snatched at his elbows and batted his face, flooding the air with the rubber fumes of fake photosynthesis.

Regina had dressed up for him. The sleeves of her blouse cut away from the arm and tapered off in long strips that trailed past the tips of her fingers. Some sort of heavy crystals hung in a metal armature from her neck. Her earrings dangled, her hair was artificial red. She had filled out, aged poorly. All this was to be expected – and yet somehow he hadn't expected it. She kissed him on the cheek and ran her palms up and down his arms, fluttery, hardly touching.

"So good to see you, Martin," she said. "I wish I'd known you were still in Chicago. I would've tried to get in touch."

"I've been busy."

"I bet, I bet."

She got him a drink and sat him on the couch, then busied herself lighting candle after candle. The light was dim and the air was thick with the smell of incense and cigarettes. Plants, real ones, black in the shadow-light, hung from the ceiling, dripping tendrils down to his neck. Regina spoke to fill the silence.

She had gone back to school after she fell out of the downtown scene, ended up with a degree in physical therapy. But it wasn't for her – too stiff, too inorganic. She was more into holistic practices. So were lots of aging single women now living out their deferred teenage dreams in gentrified Old Town. She had started a boutique line of beauty products, and she'd made a lot of money. As she talked she leaned in closer, the crystals on her neck swinging in a wider and wider arc. It was almost imperceptible. But Martin was in a mood to be perceiving things.

"And yourself?" she said. "What have you been up to?"

There was plenty to tell her. About his wife, his family, his university post, the brief reunion of Total Mobilization. He could tell her about the scandals and betrayals of the past winter, and she could use crystals and sex and psychobabble to heal or distract him.

"I've been very busy," he said, forgetting that he'd already said it.

She didn't seem to notice. Maybe she noticed and didn't care. She smoothed the hem of her skirt against her thighs and continued.

"You know, I'm almost embarrassed to tell you this. Because we didn't know each other for very long, and we were never that close. But I used to look you up sometimes. Once I got a computer in the house and all that. I found some pieces you'd written. Maybe I didn't understand them perfectly. But I always felt that they spoke to me."

Martin nodded. "Thank you."

"I'm sure it sounds strange to you. But it helped me become who I am today. Helped me to leave old ways of thinking behind. Old inhibitions behind. I'm much more free now. I'm much more happy."

She waited for a response from him, her eyes making miniscule motions left to right, scanning his face for thoughts that weren't there. He had nodded once already in the conversation and wasn't sure how else to respond.

"Certainly," he said.

She smiled with relief. "I think it's very obvious, actually. Not to say that the way you express it is. All I mean is, you know. It's important to really experience every moment. To be really present to every moment. It's important to be happy."

All his life he'd wondered where people like this came from. And now he knew. She believed in all the same things he did. The difference between them was a difference of degree, not kind. Even if he continued with his work, and did it rigorously and successfully, he would only be producing more people like her. She was done talking, and now awaited an answer.

"Regina," he said, "I didn't come here just to chat."

But this was exactly the wrong thing to say. She smiled with her mouth pursed closed, prim and expectant, afraid to show bad teeth. Martin's only option now was to disappoint her. But some people deserved to be disappointed.

"I'm trying to find Felix." He left the couch, ostensibly to pour himself another drink. "It's important. I can't stay much longer."

She hid her disappointment well. She, like Hannah, had most likely gotten used to it. She bothered one hand with the other but maintained the same steadiness of tone.

"Of course. I just figured, you know. You came all this way, and I haven't seen you in so long."

"I understand. Have you kept in touch with him?"

Martin could see already that she had. She was just trying to keep him there longer by delaying the information. Felix had probably made the same promise he did, all those years ago: to remain friends with her, no matter what happened. All young men made that promise at some point in their lives. But only Felix would actually keep it.

"You mean you haven't heard?" she said.

"No one's heard. He fell off the face of the earth."

"Well, there's a reason why."

She waited for him to ask what the reason was. But he wasn't going to beg her. She smiled coyly up at him, watching him go through the motions of mixing a drink he didn't really want. How often he had seen that smile on the face of Hannah when he tried to deliver an academic lecture to her in the privacy of her apartment. The smile of a woman who knows you're being ridiculous. The smile of a woman who knows that she already has everything there is to know inside her but doesn't know what to call it.

"What reason would that be," said Martin finally.

"He joined an order," she said, still smiling sweetly, happy now to have the opportunity to wound him. "He's in a monastery."

And it was a wound. He felt the shock of it first and knew he would feel the depth of it later. He used to be envious of Felix for always seeming to be one step ahead of him in terms of the fashions he wore, the books he read, the music he made, the thoughts he had. And he was still ahead of him – but so far ahead now that he was already back at the very beginning.

"Vow of silence," said Regina. "And everything."

"When," said Martin.

"It must have been five years ago already. Maybe more."

"And why did he feel the need to tell you."

Maybe the question had come out with more venom than he had intended. Or just the right amount. Her smile dimmed and vanished as she considered her answer.

"I don't know. He always saw something in me that wasn't there. He's always been crazy like that."

"And you've talked to him recently."

"Not for a few years. He just sends letters now and then. It's all that he's allowed to do. It's the only mail I ever get anymore." She shook her head and tried to laugh to herself and then became serious again. "The last time I answered him I asked him if he ever regretted it. If he ever got lonely."

"And what did he say."

Her eyes turned red and narrow – real scorn, real anger behind the lenses. Like she was looking at Martin and seeing Felix standing there.

"He said no. He said never."

He made an excuse to leave, and she didn't try to stall him or stop him. All she did was ask, on his way out, if he wanted Felix's information – after all, that was what he'd come there for. But Martin saw now that he'd come for something else entirely. Maybe he didn't know what he was looking for, but he knew he wasn't going to find it there.

The knuckles on his hands grew cold gripping the wheel. Nothing felt right; his body an ill-adjusted suit hanging on a poor excuse for a soul. The world appeared before him for a brief moment as he circled down an off-ramp: nodes of light burning in the blackness of the grid, streets flooded with white flame and neon streaks, everything oiled and purring like the machine dream of a clockwork universe. And it seemed for a moment that the splendor was enough. But this was an optical illusion which lasted only for one swelling heartbeat. The streets up close were dirty and desolate. In the summers the locals would come out to loiter in parking lots and shoot at each other. They lived their whole lives in nothing, and that was what they died for too.

He kept driving south by default. Looking for opportunities to depart from his path, but there were none. The streets all ran in straight lines. The city, for all its boastings of culture, had nothing to offer him. He had betrayed Demian. He had abandoned Hannah. He had forgotten Andy. He wanted nothing anymore to do with Felix. There was no one who could help him; nothing that could wake up the world around him, the world inside him, and he saw now how foolish it was to think that Felix of all people was the person to do it. He had exhausted all his resources. There was nowhere to go but home.

Isaac hesitated before knocking on the door. Of course he did: he was born to hesitate; born hesitating. And he savored the hesitation, or tried to, as the last possible moment he could enjoy the delay of the inevitable. But it didn't work this time; he'd spent his whole life doing it, and couldn't wring enjoyment from it any longer. The knock on the wood made his knuckles sting, but he knew that it would, and that was why he did it.

He waited as the knock resounded down the empty hallway. And a thought occurred to him that made him want to turn and run: maybe she wasn't alone. He wished he could take it back. The knock on the door, the whole of his life beforehand – take it and shove it down a hole where it would never have to happen.

Cordelia opened up in her pajamas and blinked in the light, unsurprised, unoffended. Two, three deep blinks, seconds long each, and she was wide awake after that. She clicked into action: poking her head out the door and checking to see that no one had seen them, then swinging it wide and waving him inside.

"You're that ashamed of me?" said Isaac.

"Who wouldn't be."

She flicked a lamp on and sat up on her bed, tucking her legs beneath the covers. Isaac remained standing near the door.

"I'm just kidding," she said. "This is an all-girls floor. You can't take any chances with them. Maybe you could have told me you were coming."

"I was afraid you'd tell me I couldn't."

"I might have. Would you have come over anyway?"

"Probably not. Would you let me in if I did?"

"Probably." She took a deep breath through her nose, held it, expelled it, like an athlete preparing for a workout. "Why don't you sit down. I have a feeling this is going to take a while."

Isaac cleared a space with his foot in the sea of clothes and took a seat on the cold tile floor.

"Sit on my bed. I'm not going to eat you."

Isaac did as he was told. But sat only half-on, half-off, at the farthest possible corner, separated from Cordelia by several blankets and more than twelve inches of space. She suffered this with patience and mild amusement.

"Well?" she said.

"What."

"What is it?"

"Nothing."

"You don't have anything you want to talk about."

"No."

"You came all the way over here, when we're not even officially speaking, but you don't have anything to say."

Isaac shook his head. Then nodded, then shook it again. It didn't matter; none of it meant anything.

"Tell me."

"No."

"You woke me up for this."

"It sounds stupid now that I think about it."

"I don't care. You don't have a choice anymore."

"I know."

He was delaying again. Just like outside the door, just like the week before, just like his entire life. Which never protected him from harm anyway, never helped him navigate life's difficult passages, only protracted the process to unbearability. He was just making the worst of a bad situation.

"I was chatting with Hannah tonight," he said.

"Ah," said Cordelia, nodding, not without satisfaction. The good doctor taking on another tough case. "But chatting how."

Isaac made a keyboard motion with his hands. "Computer chatting."

"Who started it: you or her?"

"Her."

Cordelia shook her head. "You should have her blocked."

"I know."

"And she shouldn't be leading you on either. I swear to God. One day I'm going to have a talk with that girl."

Isaac let her fume a moment. He knew she'd never do it.

"And I know she was leading you on," she said.

"Otherwise you wouldn't be here."

"No she wasn't."

"If a girl starts chatting with you in the middle of the night, that means she's leading you on."

"She said that human love didn't exist. She said it was all just an interaction of intensities."

"I don't know what that means. Do you?"

"No."

"Maybe it doesn't mean anything."

"Maybe it does though. Maybe she's right."

"She's never right about anything. Especially when it comes to that. Haven't you heard?"

Isaac hesitated, then decided to bluff it:

"Of course I've heard."

Cordelia closed her eyes and laughed softly through her nose. "Isaac, did you hear what *just* happened to her?"

"No. What."

"She was having an affair with a professor. A couple professors, actually."

"How do you know?"

"Everyone knows. Everyone but you."

Isaac saw everything in a flash. Saw the flash first – felt it, deep in some invisible place inside him – and then was able to see all the events unfolding within it. Happening forward and backward, in snippets all out of order. Hannah abandoned, Hannah elated, Hannah embraced, Hannah embracing. After the first second had passed he had already been through the worst of it.

"It doesn't matter," he said. "I still know her better than anyone."

"Isaac, this girl is a *fiction* to you. I don't know how many times I've told you. I don't know how many times I'll have to tell you again."

"I don't care. It's true."

"How?"

"It just is."

Cordelia gave up on arguing, though she probably could have gone on forever if she wanted to. Maybe she was tired, or maybe wanted to spare Isaac his delusions. Besides her, and alcohol, they were all he had.

"You didn't agree to see her," said Cordelia. "Did you?"

"No. She didn't ask."

Cordelia rolled her eyes. "Of course she didn't. Because she's just using you as an emotional crutch. And I can't believe that someone as smart as you can't see that."

It was hard being away from Hannah. Strangers though they were, he missed her. Maybe it was more like a sort of guilt. As far as he could tell she had given him all that was best of her and only held on to the worst. It was like she lived more inside him than she lived for herself. As if she had given up on figuring out her life, and that was why she had recruited people like him and Ravi to do it for her.

"I might drop out of college," said Isaac.

"Why," said Cordelia.

"Because I hate it here."

"So do I. You don't see me complaining."

"Because being here makes me think about killing myself."

"Oh." Cordelia spent a moment trying to figure out if this should concern her. "And you think dropping out is going to help with that?"

"Only one way to find out."

"What are you going to do?"

"I don't know. Work."

"Where are you going to work?"

"I don't know."

"You're not going to spend all your time hanging out with Topher, are you?"

"No. Of course not."

"Because that's what it looks like you've been doing. You haven't been hanging out with me. You haven't been hanging out with anyone else."

They fell silent and both stared at the bedspread between them in order to avoid looking at each other. The silence around them concentrated until it filled every cubic inch of air in Cordelia's room, until Isaac became afraid to disrupt it, as if doing so would send ripples out through the density of the medium and disturb the peace of all the other girls sleeping on Cordelia's floor. But he was losing his audience: Cordelia was resting her chin on her chest, her eyes closed, nodding off.

"Do you want to talk about Guy?" said Isaac.

Her eyes shot open, alert and piercing. "No. Do you?"

"Yes."

She sighed and played with her fingers as if untying a knot. "I don't think this is the right time for it. I'm not sure if there will ever be a right time for it. I don't think it's something you could ever, ever, ever understand."

"Is it really that complicated?"

"No. It's very simple. That's why you'll never understand it."

"But its not still…going on. You and him."

"No."

"It was just that once?"

She closed her eyes and made a wall in front of her with her palms. "Isaac–"

"I need to know."

"I don't think you need to know. I think you just want to torture yourself." She opened her mouth and then closed it again, shaking her head, disappointed. "It was just once. And it wasn't that much fun. I hope that's enough detail for you."

It wasn't a normal type of jealousy. Not a jealousy of Cordelia's body, or her company, which she freely offered to all. He was jealous that Guy, in perceiving Cordelia's willingness, in responding to it and eliciting a response in kind, knew her better than he did.

"And Guy?" said Cordelia.

"What about him."

"Are you going to apologize to him?"

"For what?"

Cordelia made an act of will in order to retain her patience – closing her eyes, taking deep breaths – and then began again. "I'm not asking you to apologize to me, because I know that's beyond you. I'm just asking you to apologize to him."

"Guy doesn't care."

"You don't know that."

"Yes I do. That's why he doesn't have any problems. That's why he doesn't have any worries."

Cordelia covered her face with both hands and slumped over on her side, exhausted. "Isaac, I don't think this is the right time to have that conversation," she said through her fingers. "I think that will have to wait for another night."

There would never be a right time to have that conversation. He knew it already. Not with Cordelia, not with anyone else either. He would have to find another way.

"Sure," he said, and slid off the bed.

"Are you sure you're sure?"

"No."

She opened her hands and revealed to him a small wry smile. "I don't know what we're going to do with you."

"I don't know either."

He was glad to be again standing upright, both feet on solid ground, detached from the scented bedclothes. He took two steps and reached for the door.

"Isaac."

Despite himself, he looked her way. No force in the world – not even spite, not even self-pity – could have made him do otherwise. She was sitting up on the bed with her arms outstretched.

It was like everything else in his life: he wanted it and didn't want it at the same time, was in part compelled but in part coerced. He moved close enough to let her wrap her arms around him and resolved to one day explain himself to her. Surely she deserved more, but this was the best he could do: explain the whole world to her, build a scale model of it just for her, tie it up with a bow when he was finished and hand it over. But all he knew for now was that he couldn't explain anything. All he knew for now was that he was far from the point where he would even be able to begin.

HANNAH WAITED. Hannah was waiting. In the struggling light of early spring, waiting. The time passed too slowly, passed not at all. Still she hated to see it go.

Hannah was perfectly still. The winter still living inside her – the vanished season preserved within her, untouched, without flaw. A whole world inside her, lifetimes upon lifetimes, waiting for someone to take possession of them. How stupid she was to have ever thought this had to be accomplished literally, externally. She could feel the lives being siphoned out of her. From great distances, across the endless span of time. People she knew but mostly people she didn't living within the life inside of her – others living willingly inside that same twilight world, adjacent yet unseen, so that they might be closer to her, so that she might be closer to them. Young men, old men, childhood friends intimately known and then forgotten. Ancestors from centuries ago, corpses melting in their graves. If it had been a space in which feelings could have existed she would have felt very deeply for each and every one of them. She would have loved them so much it would have killed her.

There was a party that night at Neverworld. She knew without fighting against herself this time that she wasn't going to go. The business of life could accomplish itself without her. She was present even in the places that she wasn't: in the classes she skipped, in the parties she missed. Dream-Hannahs, however many millions of them, flitting about from consciousness to consciousness, performing her worldly work for her. And even when she left her room it was their footsteps she was following, it was their commands she obeyed. Her presence was merely incidental.

Her apartment had become the entire world to her, with an entire world's rhythms and an entire world's richness. Now that all her bridges to the outside world had collapsed there was no reason to leave anymore. She kept the blinds closed, and the days ran together in blue infinities. She forgot to eat and was never hungry. She only burned calories from breathing; from being. And could sense, at times, the approach of a state close to ecstasy; felt it crowding down around her skull; and behind her closed eyes, the colorless beginnings of vision. But it never fully arrived, never touched her, whatever it was. It fluttered away, birdlike, and all she could do was wait for it to come down again. She wanted it too badly, and that always managed to scare it off.

Hannah waited. But she wished she could find a better word. Because there wasn't anything in particular she was waiting *for.* Not for Martin; not for anyone else. Martin had left without saying goodbye. But he had never really been there either. They used to sit at opposite ends of the couch, distant like strangers. Sitting there with all the lights off, one of her hands nested within the both of his. Not talking, not even looking at each other. Just breathing, just barely. Until all sensation left her hands, until the silence became a ringing presence in the air around them. Martin's breathing had a subtle rhythm and musicality to it, each exhalation shaped into unformed vowels, pausing in the middle for a barely audible enunciation. It raised the hair on the back of her neck − real bodily fear, close to panic − when she first realized he was saying her name. How many times had she already met this person, how many times had she been through this already − these séances to call into the world the girl she would never be. She would have rather dated an addict, would have rather been one. She had dated men who had threatened her physically, who had vowed to kill themselves because of her. But even that had not scared her as much. She could tell that they didn't mean it when they said it. She could tell that Martin, in his silence, meant whatever he meant by remaining silent.

Silence would settle over them again. Thick like a blanket; so heavy she couldn't move. The numbness crept up her hand to her elbow. Until the two of them had been erased, rendered void, integrated fully into the mute earth and unbreathing silent sky. Not looking for greater intimacy but greater distance; exploring its outermost limits, going farther than anyone had ever gone before. Either that was the point or there was none. She could sleep at one end of the room and he could sleep at the other. She could sleep at one end of the world and he could sleep at the other. They could have been anyone, it could have been anywhere.

He always had to leave early, before sunup. Whenever she hit the lights she half expected the room to be empty, like she had spent all night holding hands with her own shadow. Darkness flowing into darkness flowing into darkness. But he was always there. Martin, he, shrinking from the light, eyes squinted, exposed. Like he was in pain. He always looked like that. That was probably the only thing that had drawn her to him in the first place. Mercy, or something like it. She wanted to put him out of his misery.

The sheets of her bed still held the warmth of the vanished sun; their touch tender, like skin-on-skin. Hannah wrapped herself within them and hung suspended in the warm dark non-place, hungry and not at the same time, thinking but not thinking, feigning complacence, aware only of emptiness. It was ironic: all the boys she'd ever known thought they were the ones receiving life from her, thought that was why they were so drawn to her. But she knew what they didn't. It was osmosis, simple physics: there was nothing in her, nothing to her, nothing there at all. Other bodies moved to fill the empty space, searching for something that didn't exist. In her or anywhere else. So when they found out they were wrong – wrong again, wrong as always – they had to abandon her just to feel a little less stupid.

She lay perfectly still as her thoughts moved within her. Sometimes she wondered if her heart had stopped. She couldn't feel it no matter how hard she tried. She held her breath and searched with inner touch all the hollows of her body. There was no pulse; there was nothing. Only a voice inside her head that was her and some openings in the skull where the light came in.

It was early still, not even ten, and she'd dozed all afternoon. Sleep was like an indifferent lover: she never knew when it was going to show up or how long it would stay, never knew what it was going to do with her, was never sure if she wanted it or not. And just like with a lover she had to wonder sometimes if it wasn't trying to fuck her over just for the fun of it.

There was a sound in the apartment like the buzzing of an insect. It had been so long since she last heard the sound that it took her a while to figure out what it was: her phone, vibrating somewhere against a hard surface. She made herself move slowly. Timing the walk so that the call would have been missed by the time she reached the kitchen table. She sat in a nearby chair and waited a moment longer still before checking to see who had called. Preparing herself, clearing her mind. But her mind was clear enough already.

It was only Demian. She pictured herself shattering the phone against the wall, then thought about it no more. She wished only that she had reason to be more tempted. But she wasn't sure if there was anyone in her life who could tempt her – she ran through names in her head, but they all produced blanks inside her. Like she had never known them, like they had never existed. Something in her itched like a phantom limb, crying out for a sensation that she could never again give it. Maybe it had never been real. She was sick of pretending. She turned the phone off and shut it away in a nearby drawer, hoping that she would forget where it was by morning.

It had been too long since she last showered. She could feel the grime crawling over her skin and leaking from her pores, all the excess life in her turning parasitic and putrescent. She imagined, in an unreal flash, men gathering outside her apartment; faceless men from the alleys and underworld, clawing at the walls, drawn by the scent. They all wanted to save her from herself. But even if they truly believed it, or truly tried to, it wasn't true. They were men: they weren't wired for it. That was why the ones who wanted to help you always left you worse off in the end, and the ones who didn't pretend to care vanished more or less without harm.

She stepped into the shower and let the water blur her sight and blast away her scattered thoughts. And then there was nothing. For a hushed moment, one consuming moment. She took down lungfuls of sweet steam and let it puff shape back into her empty envelope of skin. For a moment she forgot where her legs were. And the rest of her body too; forgot also where her breath was going, couldn't feel it coming in. Like it was just emptying into a hole, except the hole took up all the space where her body once was. She closed her eyes and watched her blood draw red and purple blossoms and fractals on her eyelids. It was better than drugs, this feeling: a starry disembodied warmth, a whole new life in her, ready to spill out; a buzzing all over that turned into numbness, and the quiet thrill of feeling like you might fly apart and never come all the way back together. She swooned for a moment – let herself swoon, except staying in control, always in control – until the cold touch of porcelain on her shoulder shocked the life back into her.

Her hair coiled around her neck and shoulders in heavy vines, each terminus producing a single drop of water that kissed against her skin when it fell. She kept her towel wrapped as tight as she could, afraid that her body might spill onto the floor if not properly contained. But she stopped herself at the door to her bedroom, at the sight of her bed, cold and swallowing in the unadorned moonlight. She didn't care how many times she washed them; those sheets still held the residue of all the men she'd ever brought home with her. Hair follicles, skin cells; a sea of flesh like the molecules of her nightmares. Maybe once she was back in the tumult of life, harried and begrimed, too tired to care, she would throw herself once more on those sheets. But not like this; not right now; not tonight.

She sat at her desk instead. Her empty desk, from which she kept all trace of schoolwork and reality. That was its purpose: it was the place where she did nothing. As long as she showed up to her finals she would probably pass most of her classes. And she didn't have to write Martin's paper anymore. No one did: after the scandal all the students were promised A's as compensation for any "emotional distress" they may have experienced under the tutelage of Paul Demian. Demian was run out of town, Martin's class suspended. She hadn't seen or heard from either of them since.

She leaned forward and rested her head on her crossed arms. But the angle was too severe for comfort: she grabbed a nearby book, the thickest one at hand, to even it out, and rested her skull against its cardboard binding. It was all there, inside her; it would be a waste of time to write any of it down. She might as well spill her blood. The thought made itself present in her mind, instant and total like sunlight: I am the paper. I am the book.

She shut her eyes and opened them again at three AM. And came to consciousness with the dirty mouth and gut-punched feeling she always got after taking a nap. Everything was mixed up now: there were only naps, and she never felt good. She knew she wouldn't be sleeping again until sunrise.

She moved to the living room and lay down on the floor. The couch, tonight, was too sumptuous, too sensuous for her. But the floor was perfect: austere as early morning sunlight. She savored the pressure and the certitude of the hardwood digging into her shoulder blades. Things only became real when they passed through her body. She was almost used to it: used to being treated as an accessory, an appendage, a stomach through which the consciousness of others was digested. Because the others always left so very much behind after they had fled her; because she had collected all of it, and now possessed a store of knowledge, vast but unarticulable, living inside her like the drawers full of boys' clothing she kept in her bedroom.

She could feel all the lives racing around inside her, some towards birth, some towards death, most towards a confused combination of the two. Martin and Demian – they were human too, and beautiful if only for that. She forgot sometimes. About herself also, and everyone else. Kim, Ravi, Isaac. And the dead trees and black sky and the ugly concrete campus where she was throwing away the best years of her life – everything was human in a way, everything was beautiful. She was void of everything and filled with everything, barren like a nun, happy like a nun. Her body was a lost cause; just a wasted and vampirically-sucked thing sprawled inert on the hard surface beneath her. But her mind, pricked to attention by the hunger, was suspended, just a millimeter, just a fraction thereof, above her body, thinking one long unspooling thought like a million thoughts thought all at once and cut up and pasted in fragments back inside the linear order of time. Floating – it was like floating. A gentle perfect agony of perfect floating. The understanding poured into her where the emptiness was, and she wondered why she had ever fought against it. Understanding and emptiness both: the one was required for the other. She thought about all the people she had promised herself, minutes before, never to think about again. All of their lives were hers also, and there was nothing she could ever do to get rid of them. But there was no anger in her, no envy, no self-recrimination. It was over; it was hardly worth thinking about. And that was all it would ever be.

It was spring now for everyone but George and Martin. Dense clear light filled the air and the grass sucked deep green from the earth below. A sweet breeze, charged with pollen, quick with life, pushed itself through the cracked windows of Martin's duplex. The days were long and warm in the sun when the wind didn't blow. But George wouldn't leave his room anymore; he hid behind his bed, in the smallest and darkest corner. It was like he'd never seen the spring before, and never knew that it hurt him. It was like he was finally figuring out that he'd never be a part of the blooming world around him.

Ellie retreated to the kitchen with the coolers and blankets: unpacked the picnic lunches, repacked them again. She turned on the faucet and watched the water ripple gold in the sunlight. She wiped her hands and fussed and didn't know where to turn next. The kitchen was where she went to worry, drawn by some deep racial instinct to this past site of warmth and community. Now it was mostly fake, mostly plastic. Microwaves and electrical currents; the whole world just a scrim of moving particles, an insignificant sliver of an infinitely large spectrum. That was the hardest part of it for Martin. Simple, honest Ellie: she wanted so badly to believe it was real.

He stood in the doorway, watching her watch the water. Do something, said a voice inside him. But he didn't know what to do.

She shut the water off and turned to face him. Her eyes, magnified behind her big glasses, had been reddened by the inflamed veins which spiderwebbed across them. Every time she looked at him now, even in moments of detente or fleeting affection, these veins seemed to challenge him, reminding him of the day he had first noticed them, reminding him of the weeks that followed.

"Well," she said, her voice quiet but her eyes still

trained steadily upon him. She never seemed to blink anymore. And when she transfixed him like this Martin was unable to reply back, unable even to think. He was reduced to silence, reduced to sullenness, slouching in her sight, all of his tools and weapons stripped from him. "Are you going to talk to him?"

It wasn't exactly a question. There was only one possible answer. Still it hurt to give it. Like it was a lie, even if he didn't want it to be.

He still had never said he was sorry. That would have been too much for him. And he knew better than to give her some of his lecture-hall circumlocution as to why he couldn't. Slowly they were working through it. Every day was work.

He halted in front of George's door. He didn't know how he would proceed; was hoping simple proximity would solve the problem for him. He was finding out now that he didn't know much, really. He could fool everyone else – his wife, his lovers, his students, his colleagues – but he could never fool himself. Anyone acquainted with the history of thought knew that there were not terribly many things to believe. And even fewer worth believing. He was smart enough, at least, to have admitted this much. His career, in retrospect, had never been anything but an adolescent sort of daydreaming. All the books he'd never write, all the speeches he'd never give, all the accolades he'd never receive: just more of those little megalomanias with which we keep ourselves company.

George was getting strong and smart enough to start shutting the door behind him when he fled to his room. Not smart enough to barricade it yet. But Martin imagined the time would come. It was only going to get more difficult from here.

George's plastic bed sat flush with the ground so he

wouldn't hurt himself if he fell. Instead of hiding under it he wedged himself in the space between the bed and the wall with his hands clasped tight over his neck. It was like an air raid drill: maybe in his mind the sirens were always going. Near the start of the fit he trembled with emotion, sometimes growling with deep inner hatred. But he always calmed down after that, closed off from the world, alone with whatever kind of thoughts were had by a boy who couldn't speak. Martin could remember similar scenes from his own childhood. It wasn't so bad being small. Powerless as you were, there were always plenty of places to hide.

Martin shut the blinds. Spring had never been his favorite season either. Too many allergens, too many fluctuations in weather and air pressure. But how to tell this to his son. He, who couldn't manage to explain his ideas to anyone, even to himself – somehow he was supposed to explain all of life to George. He ventured phrases in his mind. But in his inner ear they rang false and forced. Kids could tell when you said something you didn't mean. Even his.

It was quiet in the apartment; so quiet Ellie would be waiting to hear his voice. Maybe not the words but the sound of it, rumbling low and fatherly through the closed door. He sat on the bed and hovered his hand over his son's sand-blonde hair. He dropped it; his son didn't flinch, didn't twitch, didn't yelp. Maybe he was expecting it.

"George," he said.

George dropped his hands from his neck and picked his head up. And stared and sniffed and with clumsy hands tried to wipe away the issue from his nose and eyes. But he just made it worse. Tears and mucus mixed together and stuck in a tacky white mixture to his cheeks. Martin cleaned him up with a corner of the bedsheets; held him under the chin with one hand and wiped with the other. George watched him do it. He was waiting for something.

Martin knew that it didn't really matter what he said. But his vanity was such that he couldn't get any words out. Imperfect though he was, he still couldn't reconcile himself to imperfection. He couldn't make the leap.

He thought of Felix then; as if Felix would know what to say; as if he would be able to heal George with a word or a touch. But that would be going about it all wrong. George wasn't the problem. The problem was himself, and had always been. Heal *me*.

Looking into George's eyes, searching those tiny marble galaxies for signs of intelligence, he remembered walking with Felix through the ruined church across the street from their apartment. It was quiet like churches always were; humming with the pregnant silence of a hundred people all holding their breath. The door of the tabernacle had swung open, and there was nothing inside. When Martin saw it he remembered the Good Friday liturgies his grandmother had taken him to when he was very young: at the end of the service the tabernacle was left open and empty in just the same way. He could articulate now what he had only intuited then. There was no escape from the metaphor. There was no such thing as a symbol.

They made it to the park just as the sun was stretching the shadows of the trees over the entire length of the lawn. The air was still and the heat had been baked in; even the shadows contained intimations of warmth. They spread the blanket on the last sliver of sun and waited for the day to end.

George stained green the knees of his jeans as he tumbled through the grass. Wide-mouth, wide-eyed: experiencing only, not indexing, not recording. Martin and Ellie had white wine and light sandwiches. Sunset turned the sky a caramel color and brought black wind down from above. Ellie slipped on a cardigan and touched her shoulder to his.

Maybe by accident, maybe not.

"You know who I was just thinking about," she said.

"Who," said Martin, though he was pretty sure he already knew.

"Felix. I don't know why."

"That's funny. I was thinking of him too."

She cocked her head at him. Real concern, real perplexity: the same look Regina had given him, the same look Hannah sometimes gave him. His mother used to look at him this way when he was doing something heartless, or when in doing something selfless he had opened himself up to too great a degree of vulnerability.

"Why?" she said.

Cool invisible liquid surged up from beneath the loamy earth and coated his palms where they rested against the grass. He raised one hand and gestured as if the answer could be found in the open lawn before them, in the blinking of fireflies and in George stumbling behind in fruitless pursuit. Ellie, still concerned, once more rocked her body gently against his.

"Tell me why."

"I wouldn't really know how to explain it."

"I thought you knew everything."

"No."

Turquoise haze floated in from the streets and scattered electrical energy into the sundown color hanging in the air of the park. All blended together: the trees in their rows and the streetlights beyond, the weight of the lower atmosphere and the swelling of the earth. George was leaping up, spinning in place, arm outstretched, small hands grasping, trying to pull the one down to the other.

"And nobody knows what happened to him?" said Ellie.

"No," said Martin. For a moment he thought he

was going to say something more. But the moment passed, and he had already said what he had said.

"That's a shame. Sometimes I miss him."

Martin shut his eyes. Within him purple twilight, lilac scented and endless. He breathed it in and then out again.

"Sometimes I miss him too," he said.

# III.

# Coda: The Survival Of The Organism (Reprise): Isaac & Cordelia

"ONE DAY I'M NOT GOING TO FORGIVE YOU, ISAAC," said Cordelia. "And what are you going to do then?"

It was a short walk on Chicago Avenue under yellow sunlight and tree shadow. Economy cars on luxury rims rattled over the potholes and bicycles outfitted with third party motors buzzed along the curb. It was spring but still cold: the type of weather that made you feel for the naked flowers when their stems were snapped flat in a sudden gust of wind. Clouds moved fast and low through the sky, blocking out the sun and then revealing it again, turning the ambient light from gold to blue and back. Cordelia wore a denim jacket over a premature summer dress. We walked – canvas shoes dampening rapidly as they pirouetted around shallow brown sidewalk puddles.

"I don't know," I said.

Cordelia said nothing in reply. Exasperated in a calm and practiced way, having had plenty of practice. It was more like disappointment than any sort of personal offense: like she was forever auditioning me for the role of myself, but I could never manage to land the part.

Flowerless potted plants unfurled in green ribbons on shelves and alcoves, growing fat off the humid indoor heat. The coffee was the same color as the black soil specked across the table. It was so fresh it tasted almost fruity, almost like a living thing, which of course it was, or used to be.

"So," she said, trying to make her voice come out normal. "What have you been up to."

"Just thinking."

"For the last three months you've been just thinking?"

"I've had a lot to think about, Cordelia."

She picked up her napkin and began worrying it with her fingers. "You're not still getting work from Topher?"

"No."

"What happened?"

"Dan Drugs is on probation. Topher's parents flew out and made him to go rehab. Michael Reality thought the TV was talking to him for a little while and had to go on lithium. Things are pretty quiet right now."

"And that girl?"

"What girl?"

Cordelia, staring intently at the napkin, repeated herself without any change in inflection: "That girl."

"Julia?"

Cordelia didn't react at all to the guess. But this was a clear enough signal in itself.

"No," I said. "I never see her anymore."

She put the napkin down and began to pinch it like a cat kneading a rug. "Did you really sleep with her though?"

"No. I was just trying to make you upset."

"It worked." She spun the napkin, more or less intact, back to the center of the table. "And Hannah?"

"What about her?"

"You haven't tried to get in touch with her?"

"No." The thought hadn't even crossed my mind. "Why would I do a thing like that."

"I don't know. Because you think she's pretty."

"No." I shook my head. "Nobody's prettier than you, Cordelia."

She smiled despite herself. "You shouldn't say that if you don't mean it."

"I do mean it."

"Let's talk about something else."

"Okay."

We were silent for about a minute after. I finished my coffee first and then decided to speak.

"How's Paolo doing."

She reached for the napkin, reached back again, and placed her hands deliberately in her lap. "Fine."

"Just fine?"

She pursed her lips as if to keep herself from talking, and went on with forced patience: "We're doing well, Isaac."

"Well." I had to clear my throat. "I hope it works out for you."

"I hope so too," she said quietly.

We walked. The weather turned quick and uncertain, swapping fits of rain with splashes of sun. Walked in a window of time between cloudbursts, walked through curtains of dampness hanging in the air, walked in the changing light, in the changing season, blood humming hot like coffee in our veins. Cordelia asked what I was doing for work and I told her: filling some shifts doing loading dock and mailroom duty at the tech company Guy was working at. I told her I missed the east coast; was thinking of moving to New York. She received this news without any follow up questions, without a reaction of any kind. She kept her head pointed forward, lips parted slightly as if slowly releasing held breath.

We walked. Walked in winter when the wind blew and walked in spring when it stopped. Icy gales that contained in them the scent of new grown grass; rays of sun that stung with a fresh dewy cold; through these we walked. Through blocks of houses with paint peeling from their façades and dingy floral curtains drawn over basement windows – homey, lived-in houses huddling low to the ground, cowering from the glassine skyscrapers rising up on the horizon like alien invaders. After half a dozen blocks the houses gave way to brownstone-bordered parkland: fields of grass that plumped with growth and sank underfoot, lines of trees that fooled the eye into thinking they stretched back to infinity. The city beyond diminished to a thin and distant roar as we strolled around muddy ponds on cracked blacktop footpaths. Waterbugs traced delicate wakes across the stagnant water and squirrels gorged with trash stumbled in diagonals through the lawns. A large flat cloud covered the sun and dampened the sound and motion of the afternoon. The wind was so loud that it became difficult to talk. We walked: eyes squinted against the pressure, shoulders hunched forward, walking nowhere.

A threadbare hill led down to the park's edge: the noise of cars and the smell of exhaust reached us, and just beyond the haze of fog we could see the streets and storefronts of the city. Somewhere people were shouting. Elsewhere, spending money; lying, starting families. Whatever it was people did. Our feet, dragged by gravity, fell thudding on the slope. Halfway down I stopped walking so that Cordelia would notice and stop too. She turned around.

"I don't want to go," I said.

"No?"

Rain started falling: sparse but heavy, white like cosmic spume, weighted with ice and cracking hard on the mud.

"No. I want to stay here."

"And what about New York?"

"I don't know. Eventually."

Cordelia laughed, and in the unguarded moment let the wind snatch her hair from behind her ear. She needed to use both her hands to pry it away from her eyes and mouth.

"Isaac."

"We don't need anyone else. Just this."

I spread my arms and pivoted to show her: the stricken trees and collapsed pagodas, rusting fences and dying tulips, the airborne litter and steadily falling rain.

"Isaac," she said. "This place is a nightmare."

And she reached forward and tugged on my arm to make me follow.

# Acknowledgements

Special thanks to: the D.F.L. boyz, Manuel Marrero for his technical advice, James Nulick for his encouragement, Ted Sweeney for the splash page photo (and for the memories), and all the friends who were forced to read far inferior versions of this manuscript throughout the years.

NICHOLAS CLEMENTE is a writer living in New York City. His work has appeared in *Glimmer Train*, *Hobart*, *New World Writing*, and elsewhere. This is his first novel.

Author portrait by CASH4